THE PALMS

The Palms

A novel
by

CLAY ANDERSON

BOOKS

Adelaide Books
New York/Lisbon
2019

THE PALMS

A novel

By Clay Anderson

Published by Adelaide Books, New York / Lisbon
adelaidebooks.org

Editor-in-Chief
Stevan V. Nikolic

For any information, please address Adelaide Books
at info@adelaidebooks.org

or write to:

Adelaide Books
244 Fifth Ave. Suite D27
New York, NY, 10001

ISBN-10: 1-951214-42-0

ISBN-13: 978-1-951214-42-5

Printed in the United States of America

Dedicated to CB.
Without your friendship and guidance
none of this would be possible.

Chapter 1 – Prologue

Pensacola, Florida—1979

In the darker provinces of his heart, Ronnie Wells knew something terrible was amiss. Through the windshield, the woodlands looked menacing in the morning light. The birds, the insects, and the breeze in the trees created a cacophony that ached his thundering head. It was hot, and he'd sweated through his vomit- and blood-stained shirt. Ronnie was confused but not surprised. In truth, he'd come to in places far stranger than this.

Ronnie climbed out of his car and faced the oppressive sun. He clenched and released his fists. They stung with pain and were swollen. Still a little drunk, he squatted in the sand and tried to piece together the events from the previous night. A few parts returned from the depths of his memory—the fight with his wife Sandra, tying one on at the bar, the barman kicking him out.

Ronnie turned to spit onto the sand, when he noticed a busted yellow Honda parked at the foot of the swampy inlet before him.

Then he saw the body.

For a brief moment, his past engulfed him. All his misdeeds in their multitude seemed weightless compared to this.

He moved like a mawkish madman through the sand, eyes enormous with childish fear. A snapping turtle scuttled away from the body and dove into the swamp at Ronnie's approach. Blood mixed with the boggy water, turning it into a strange and unnatural color. Animals in the night had tested the corpse. The skin looked taut.

The horror Ronnie had created flashed through his mind. Events and things he couldn't make right. He nudged the floating body with his foot and it was stiff and rocked woodenly. Ronnie knelt in the water. With trembling hands, he took hold of the man's shoulder and turned him over.

The sight was the stuff of nightmares. A vision that would haunt him through the years. The barman's face was purple. His tongue was swollen and sticking out of his mouth. A leech attached to his eyeball undulated as it drank the congealing blood. Ronnie tasted bile. He pried away the leech and retched several times. The cries of birds reverberated across the expanse. For whom did they sing?

After a long time, Ronnie decided what to do. He picked up the barman's legs and dragged him toward the Honda. While he tugged the body, it belched loudly. For a moment, Ronnie felt relief that the man was alive. But the sound seized him with the knowledge of the terrible certainty of death. The expelling gas evoked a horrible death rattle.

With a great deal of maneuvering, Ronnie got the barman into the driver's seat, put the car in neutral, and shut the door. He stood back and looked the scene over. Everything was odd. The wetlands were beautiful and animate but for the dead man whose life Ronnie had stolen. He felt a doomed austerity. Regret mixed with sorrow. His whole existence leading to this moment. Ronnie cast his eyes down upon the dead man with the frozen grin. The ballooned face smiling at the world about.

Nothing in the eyes but glazed reflection of the blistering sun and the known world. Eyes are the windows to the soul, and these were hollow and empty.

Unmistakably dead.

Ronnie tried to push the car into the swamp, but he slipped on the loose sand, and the car wouldn't budge. He paused for a moment to think through his next move. His head was in agony and he needed a drink. But the panic kept him going. He'd drink his fill once he got rid of the barman's car. He contemplated leaving the vehicle as it was and fleeing, but that wouldn't do.

Going back to his car, Ronnie put it in reverse and tried to back up. The car was stuck in the sandy mud and he swore loudly. Ronnie got out of his car and searched for a good-sized stick. He then set to digging out his car from the sand. He made two long trenches and returned to the wheel. Ronnie backed his car up slowly and kissed the rear of the barman's car. There was a concussion sound of metal on metal. The barman's car loosed from the sand and rolled into the swamp. It kept on until the water entered the open window and started to fill.

Ronnie watched the rearview mirror as bubbles kicked and surged the filthy water. A host of fowl sprang from the wetlands, cried out, and flew away. Ronnie pulled his car forward and stepped out. The Honda's rear was visible under the water, but there was nothing Ronnie could do about that. He walked over to the sand where the body had been. He kicked away the blood and vomit and smoothed out the drag marks in the sand. He backtracked cautiously to his car and erased his own footsteps. Pausing at his car, he surveyed the scene. It wasn't perfect, but it would have to do.

In the driver's seat, Ronnie stared at his reflection in the rearview mirror. He looked haggard and sweat beaded on his forehead. This wasn't supposed to happen. He never meant to kill that boy. Beat him within an inch of his life, yes, but never more. Ronnie thought about his wife and unborn child. He swore and placed his head on the steering wheel. Despite his total lack of religious faith, he looked back and said a prayer. Words for the young man whose death he wrought. God bless him and keep him, he prayed. Accept him into heaven and your warm embrace. Watch over his loved ones and help them find peace.

At the end, he prayed for himself. God, please protect me.

Ronnie finished his perverse entreaty to the almighty, put his car in drive, and fled the scene. He'd not noticed the quiet figures observing him from the wood. Watching closely with wild eyes. Three thin and spiderlike young boys who'd come to fish but found more than they'd bargained for.

Chapter 2

Pensacola, Florida—2015

The Paradise Palm Villas was neither paradise nor villas. The few palm trees were sickly looking and seemingly placed at random throughout the property, many having died or been carried away in storms. The Palms, as the trailer park was commonly called, was built with lofty ideals. New residents were screened and forced to follow strict protocols of maintenance and care. Yet, when the original owner died, the park began its steep decline. All pretense was dropped, and the Palms morphed into housing for the lowest common denominator. The park was home to migratory degenerates, vice, poverty, and hints of violence. Care for the trailers was nonexistent and the homes were marked with decay. Burning refuse, wild onions, drugs, and cigarette smoke were ever present. Not even the Gulf winds carried it away. Hot air redolent of rancid breath seeped into your clothes and followed residents like a rider. You tasted the stink and saw visions of spoiling waste. Nightmares of a deluge of fat and hairy flies. A world of putrefaction. God's own creation of wicked earth. A baleful maelstrom eternally consigned to execrable empiricism. Like a community beset by the plague. One whiff and outsiders knew where you called home.

The Palms was two miles from the beach as the crow flies. The park full of ruminations and voices sounding like lost souls. Wild dogs rambled about, stopping occasionally to scratch their beggar lice. A short walk around the park highlighted the neglect: cast-off debris everywhere, the roads pockmarked and decaying, weeds and wildflowers growing through the cracked concrete, trailers of varying sunny hues caked and brown with dirt, their walls grim with crud and green growth. The trailers had been painted sky blue, light pink, and pale yellow. Yet the single layer of lacquer from 1973 was all but a memory. The dirt and soot that filmed over the trailers created a uniformity of filth. Paint-flakes scattered in the breeze. The hues morphed into a gray with rust colored teardrops from the metal joists and ruined tin roofs. Broken or cracked windows were left unrepaired or healed with duct tape. Some missing entirely were replaced by cardboard boxes or rotting secondhand plywood. Loose gutters rattled in the Gulf breeze and others swung like giant pendulums from the gables. The latticework around the trailers was broken and chipped from wear and wild animals. There were leaning porches and broken steps, each with a precarious declination.

From above, the park looked like an enormous old outdoor television antenna. One long thoroughfare ran the length of the property with parallel, intersecting streets that were numbered one through nine. On the seventh street, one trailer at the end stood out from the rest. The grime and rust was power-washed away each year and the pale-pink trailer lacked the common aura of benign neglect. One might even consider it new. The stairs and porch stood true and the latticework was patched soon after the opossums, raccoons, or other wild animals passed through. The yard was well manicured with a weed-whacker once a week and any trash was picked up from the environs and placed in the bin. Potted plants on the porch grew chubby red tomatoes and little green jalapeños. All along the base of the trailer, dwarf juniper bushes grew that were pruned delicately by the householder. An American flag flew proudly outside the door. On the opposite side the shiny bronze house-number thirteen reflected the sun. A black metal swing with a small canopy sat on the porch. The trailer was as unique as the man who rented it. Meant to be there, but totally out of place.

Sixty-eight-year-old Ronnie looked aged well beyond those years. His hands were battered and mangled. He was scarred both inside and out. He had a daughter somewhere in this world who carried his last name, but had never met. An ex-wife who made sure of that. The girl was brought into the world while he sat in prison. All he knew of her was a worn baby picture with a name scrawled on the back. She'd be thirty-six on March 15. He often sat on his porch swing and imagined her life. Perhaps married with a child of her own. He wondered if she thought about him. Often at the grocery store or around town when he passed young mothers with squealing children, he imagined they were her. With her own little life and her own little world. It ached his heart to think about her. Yet, she was always on his mind. He wouldn't wish the thought of her away.

Ronnie kept his trailer and grounds immaculate because that was how he was trained. He'd spent six years in the army after high school and thirty-three years in prison. Oddly, both places had similar opinions on personal space, cleanliness, and hygiene. Yet, upkeep on his trailer wasn't a chore. He enjoyed it. Ronnie took pride in his property and relished his freedom. All those years sharing an eight-by-ten-foot cell with another person taught him to savor the small things. His neighbors in the Palms didn't respect the trailer park, but he did. It was his own personal slice of heaven. He owned his own flat screen television and a faux leather couch. In his bedroom a queen size bed swallowed up most of the room. He didn't care. It was bliss to stretch out or roll over and not hit a concrete wall. To top it all off, Ronnie was saving up for a used car. He set aside a little out of his check each month and hoped to buy a used pickup truck. He checked the newspapers every day on his way to work down at Donahue's Hardware. No more waiting in the rain. Just the thought of it made him smile.

Ronnie had moved into the Palms, after getting parole. The trailer was a mess and he spent a lot of time fixing it up. He learned after the first week that the landlord wasn't concerned with anything besides collecting checks. The Palms had a high turnover rate and he watched many renters come and go. About once a month, someone's possessions were chucked into the street to be picked over because of nonpayment. He hardly knew anyone from the community and Ronnie mostly kept to himself. For all the good prison did towards rehabilitation, he still wasn't fully acclimated to life on the outside. Still often ill at ease. Considering all the worldly changes in thirty-three years, he was still playing catch-up. He'd never worked a computer, but he did have a flip cell phone. No one to call, but it made him feel connected. Maybe his sister, but she was as much as stranger as anyone on the street. He watched a lot of documentaries and was shocked at the ways of the world. Never the news though. Ronnie had dealt with enough evil to last a lifetime. Some of it his own making. He didn't need to be reminded that it still existed.

Ronnie stood on his porch as the sun broke over the horizon. He allowed the warmth to sink into his skin and loosen his old and weary bones. He lit a cigarette and inhaled deeply. He felt wonderful and in sync with the world. Almost felt the earth slowly turning and pulsing under his feet.

Something across the street caught his eye. His neighbor Victor was passed out along the side of a broken-down truck. The vehicle was on blocks, and he was using one as a pillow. An empty bottle of whiskey sat cradled in his arms.

Ronnie laughed and shook his head. He finished his cigarette and tossed it in the ashtray. He walked down the steps and across the street. Victor was snoring loudly, and his mouth hung open. Ronnie stood over him and gently shook him awake.

Victor opened and closed his eyes slowly. Then, he jumped in recognition that someone was standing over him. He shot his arms up to fend against the outlander. He stared wild eyed and let out a high shrill. "Who the fuck is you? Don't hurt me," he screamed.

"Calm down. It's just me, your neighbor," Ronnie said, chuckling a little. He scratched his jaw and looked around. A dog barked in the distance that sounded muted against the wind. The sun in the east cleared the trees. Already it was muggy at seven in the morning. Ronnie clicked his tongue. "You were passed out."

Victor blinked several times, then looked down at his bottle in his arms and back at Ronnie. Something connected in his mind and he gave Ronnie a toothy grin. "Oh, grandpa," he said. "Shit, I was drunk." He started to laugh loudly. Then he turned a half-cocked bloodshot eye towards Ronnie and whispered, "I might still be a little drunk."

Ronnie shook his head. "I'd say, partner. Need some help?" He put out his hand and Victor took it. Ronnie lifted with all his might and Victor got to his feet then slipped back to the ground. Victor started laughing like a madman. He rolled on the ground and seemed to be having a fit.

"Hush, you're gonna wake up the whole neighborhood," Ronnie said.

"You right, grandpa." Victor cackled. "I just need to get my sea legs."

Ronnie stepped around Victor and collected him under the arms. "Let's get you home, friend."

Victor got back to his feet and stood uncertainly. He was stooped over and seemed to slowly melt back into the ground. He tried to take a step but stumbled. He'd have fallen on his face if Ronnie wasn't holding him. The man was swinging the empty bottle around and humming some nameless tune. Ronnie worried he'd break out in song.

"Come on, buddy. Let's get you to your house."

"Aye, aye, captain," Victor said with a pirate accent. He brought the bottle up to his forehead in salute.

Ronnie practically carried Victor the rest of the way. Victor opened the door to his trailer and tumbled inside. Ronnie nearly toppled over top of him. The bottle went tumbling across the room and shattered against the wall. Victor was laughing uncontrollably now. Ronnie shook his head and looked around. He'd never been inside Victor's trailer and saw that it was covered with a collection of empty liquor bottles. They were on every available surface.

"Great God," Ronnie muffled under his breath.

Victor was singing loudly now and crawling towards the dingy sofa. A door opened, and a huge woman entered the room. She was wearing a robe and had her hair done up in curlers. She looked pissed.

"No, no. That crusty nigga ain't comin' in here. He pissed the bed again." She was yelling and Ronnie took a step back. Her eyes were on fire and she was clenching her fists. He'd fought men in the penitentiary with homemade knives, but this frightened him. Victor, still on the floor, was howling with laughter. "That son-of-a-bitch knows that when he piss the bed he sleeps outside with the dogs."

Ronnie hesitated. He didn't know what to say. He contemplated fleeing the trailer, but instead he said, "I was just trying to help."

"Well, help works both ways," she said. She pursed her lips in a sign of disapproval. "You can take him out the same way you brought him him."

Ronnie studied the scene and sighed. There was movement from the darkness of the trailer. He noticed a tiny figure—a little boy who was naked but for a dirty pair of drawers. The child looked scared, and a strange air of resigned desperation tore at Ronnie's heart. Victor was still crawling towards the sofa like an enormous gibbering infant.

"Yes, ma'am," Ronnie said. He approached the delirious drunk, grabbed him under the arms, and lifted him for a second time. He walked with him as before out the door. Victor's legs gave out and the two nearly toppled again. Ronnie was straining under the man's whole weight. Despite his age, Ronnie was strong and hauled the drunk forth into the outer light. The new day acted like a blinding spotlight and he clinched his eyes for a moment against the white-hot rays.

The sun gleaned and Ronnie saw a seagull flair and glide against the breeze. It flapped its wings, but was stationary against the crystal blue sky. The door to the trailer slammed shut and Ronnie set Victor down. The drunk man clutched a new full whiskey bottle and put it under his head for a pillow. Ronnie laughed and stood to go. As he did so, the drunk man started to sing some made-up tune. "My ole witch done let me piss no mo, piss no mo, piss no mo. Witch done let me piss no mo in my own damn bed." He repeated the song several times and howled with laughter. As Ronnie walked down the steps, he heard snoring.

"Sleep well," Ronnie said.

Ronnie crossed the street and briskly walked to his trailer. He stepped through Victor's unkempt grass and heard the faint whispers of the blades against his shins. He needed to hurry and get ready for work. His watch read seven-thirty and he was behind schedule. As Ronnie strode up his driveway, a car was driving erratically down the street. A chorus of outraged dogs trumpeted its approach. It stopped out front of his next-door neighbor's house. The brakes screeched deafeningly. It was a badly used Toyota Corolla. The whole vehicle was pockmarked and dented. Chipped paint from the hood and part of the bumper torn away. One of the doors was a different color from the rest. The back-passenger window rustled from the sound of white garbage bags taped around the sides. There was loud music playing from within that echoed in the silent dawn.

A stunningly beautiful young woman exited the car. Ronnie knew her as his next-door neighbor, but they'd never met. She was dressed gaudy and her face was painted in thick layers of makeup. The young woman wore a skin-tight top that showed her cleavage and midriff. Her mini-skirt was so tight that her butt-cheeks hung out from the bottom. It didn't look like she was wearing any underwear. Ronnie averted his eyes quickly. He watched the driver exit the vehicle. A tall, lanky man, trouble radiated off him. His bloodshot eyes ticked at the surroundings. Ronnie sensed this man watched but saw little.

As the woman opened the rear door, the trash bag window billowed in the breeze. She hauled forth a young girl in pajamas who resumed sleeping on her shoulder. The gangly man spoke harshly to the mother, and she hurried along. She must have sensed Ronnie's gaze, because she paused briefly and looked at

Ronnie. He stood facing his neighbors. The mother's brunette hair came undone and fell across her face. She smiled sweetly at Ronnie and blew the loose strands out of her piercing blue eyes. He waved at her and smiled. Ronnie watched as she carried the sleeping little girl towards the trailer. The man stood impatiently by the front door and shouted for her to hurry. The young mother strained under the child's weight and walked up the stairs, gingerly taking one at a time.

The man barked an order that Ronnie couldn't hear. Recriminations rose and fell in the sultry air. Indecipherable words sounding so harsh that they might've seeped from the very depths of hell. When his neighbors disappeared into their trailer, Ronnie put out his cigarette. The sun was well up and the day was warming. Its burning rays demarcated the shadows like a floodlight. Ronnie went inside and got ready for work.

Chapter 3

Since getting out of the penitentiary, Ronnie had worked at Donahue's Hardware and Repair. His boss, Timothy Donahue, was the original owner's second son. The elder son had been killed in Vietnam. A portrait of him in uniform hung behind the register under an American flag. Ronnie had known the family since before his time in prison, and he was grateful the Donahues decided to take a chance on him. Ronnie worked hard and was never late. He never called in sick or complained. He knew Tim had been weary of him at first and he was watched like a hawk. But Ronnie slowly gained his trust and now even had a key to the shop.

Ronnie was always the first one to arrive and the last to leave. After a year, Tim gave him the code for the safe and let him handle the money at the start and end of each workday. It was a lot of responsibility that Ronnie took seriously. He was filled with pride knowing that others found him reliable.

Ronnie had his own area in the shop. It was a little cubicle and a desk. There was nothing on it but shipment forms and dull pencils. Yet, Ronnie was thrilled with it. He oversaw the loading and unloading shipments in the back. He restocked the shelves and helped carry goods in and out for customers. He'd haul broken televisions, vacuum cleaners, and lawnmowers through the storefront to the rear. Tim was a master at fixing things. Ronnie never saw Tim get stumped over a repair job. You name it and he could fix it.

Overall, Ronnie was a dogsbody and a gofer but didn't mind. It was a job that paid the bills. His life had a purpose. There was pride in his heart for an honest day's work. He felt like a man again. All those years inside had taken away part of his self-worth. Endless nights staring at concrete walls made him feel less than useless. It was impossible to be a man when you were stripped of your freedom. He didn't blame the courts or prison system. Many convicts marinated in rage over their incarceration. He did so at first, but he later came to accept his punishment. No one was to blame but himself. Working at Donahue's was his second chance.

On the bus to work, Ronnie sat up and watched saw a white truck as they slowly passed. It was still for sale at twenty-five hundred dollars. He quickly wrote down the number to call on a small piece of paper and put it in his pocket. Ronnie figured he might talk the seller down to two thousand.

Ronnie stared out the window with a smile on his face and daydreamed of the wind in his hair. Driving with sunshades on and the beach in the distance. Watching the waves break along the surf and sand. Seeing the gulls flying above the ocean and diving to catch their prey. He'd stick one hand out the truck window and roll it with the current. He closed his eyes and saw this clear as day, as if it had already come to fruition and he was only recounting the past.

The bus stopped beside a rundown shopping center. Donahue's and a Mexican restaurant were the only places of business in the strip mall. There were open spaces between that hadn't been rented since Ronnie was hired. He thanked the bus driver and exited onto the hot pavement.

Ronnie double-timed over to the front door and got out his keys. He walked in and punched in the alarm code and turned on the lights. He went into Tim's office and opened the safe. He took out the cash drawer from the day before and set it in the register. Then he went into the back and unlocked the delivery gate. It creaked loudly on its hinges. There was WD-40 in the shop and he'd grease the wheels later.

As Ronnie was sweeping the shop, Tim's car pulled into the parking lot at eight thirty like clockwork.

"How you, Ronnie?" Tim smiled at his employee as he entered the shop.

"Just fine, Tim. How about yourself?"

"Above ground."

"I hear ye." Ronnie extended his hand and his boss shook it. Tim walked around the dust pile Ronnie had swept up and headed towards his office.

At eight-forty-five, Sue Ellen arrived and placed herself behind the cash register. She was an old woman who was related to Tim in some way. Ronnie never figured out how. She often brought in baked goods for the customers. She set an enormous tray of cookies by the register and sat flipping through a magazine. Ronnie walked up and selected a large oatmeal cookie.

"How are you, Ms. Sue Ellen?"

"My feet are dealing me misery, but I can't complain. Not a soul in this world would care. Certainly not my children." She sighed. "Cometh from mine own bosom." She clutched her heart. "None of them care about me at'all."

Ronnie chewed the cookie and didn't respond. He wasn't used to this type of conversation. Tim approached and selected the largest cookie from the tray. He took a bite, moaned, and shut his eyes.

"Ms. Sue Ellen," Tim said, "you have certainly outdone yourself."

"I thank you, Timothy. It warms my heart knowing that some people appreciate me."

"That we do," Tim said with a smile. He cut his eyes over to Ronnie, who grinned back. Tim turned to go, and Ronnie followed him.

"Hey, Tim, can I talk to you for a minute?" Ronnie asked.

"Sure thing."

"I was wondering if you might do me a favor. I'm looking at buying a truck and I was hoping you might come along with me and check it out. Make sure it won't fail on me soon as I leave the lot. You can fix about anything and it would mean a lot if you could give it a once over before I hand over the cash."

"Absolutely. That's not a problem. After work?"

"If that's all right with you."

"Sure. I'll drive us over and we'll look."

"All right, it's just down the street."

"That white truck in front of the cash for gold and title loan?"

"The very."

"Sounds good."

Tim went back to his office and Ronnie walked over to the telephone. He took out the piece of paper with the truck owner's number and dialed. On the second ring, the seller picked up. It was the owner of the cash for gold and title loan who'd recently acquired it from a patron. "I tell you good sir, I drove it and it is worth every penny," the man said.

"Will you hold it for me?" Ronnie asked.

There was a moment of feigned trepidation. As if there were a line of people baying at the door or others milling about waiting for an auction.

"I'll see what I can do, but I can't promise anything."

"Thank you," Ronnie said with a sigh. "I'll be there around five-thirty." He hung up the phone and got to work.

Throughout the day, Ronnie kept thinking about the truck. The money burned in his pocket. He busied himself restocking the paintbrushes then carried in a shipment of wrenches. Just after lunchtime, an old woman brought in a leaf blower that needed repairs. By the time Tim finished fixing it, the clock read five on the dot. Tim turned to Ronnie with a smile.

"Let's go get you a truck."

"Yes, sir."

Tim waited outside as Ronnie locked up the shop. He turned off the lights, set the alarm, and locked the front door. Ronnie was sweating through his shirt and he checked his pocket one last time. All the money was there. He entered Tim's car and off they went. Tim pulled onto the coastal highway and rolled down the windows. The radio played a country station that sounded nothing like the genre. Ronnie tapped his legs to the music to keep from fidgeting. Off in the Gulf, bleak clouds hung in the sky. Thin blades of light shone through like stripes against the dark. The storm was moving away from land and the beach road burned brightly in the sun. Ahead was the white truck.

As they pulled into the parking lot, Ronnie noticed that the proprietor had changed the price to four thousand dollars. The white polish was still wet from where he rewrote the amount. Tim guffawed. He noticed the trick as well.

Tim turned to Ronnie. "You just watch how I play this thing out. I'll talk him down to fifteen hundred."

Tim got out and wandered around the truck, inspecting the body work. Ronnie was anxious, but Tim's coolness calmed him. A fat squat man exited the pawnshop. He waddled over and extended his hand to Ronnie and shook it loosely. Ronnie thought the seller seemed out of breath. His face was blotchy, and he wore a tiny spyglass attached to a chain around his neck.

"You called about this fine automobile."

"Yes, sir, I did."

"You won't find another'n like this for the price."

Ronnie didn't know where to begin. He wasn't sure if he should immediately broach how the price jumped in eight hours by fifteen-hundred. Just then, Tim rose from around the side of the truck. He'd been inspecting the undercarriage. When the seller saw him, his eyes went wide with surprise and dread.

"Charles!" Tim yelled. "Chucky, Chucky, Chucky. How the hell are you?" Tim walked around the side of the truck and shook the seller's hand vigorously. Charles looked like he was in pain. "Chucky, this is Ronnie. Ronnie, this is Chucky." Tim looked like a cat that ate the canary. He turned to Ronnie. "Ronnie, me and Chucky go way back. We went to high school together." Charles's face turned crimson. "What was it that we used to call you? You had the funniest nickname, but I can't place it."

Charles cast his eyes downward. He stuttered as he said, "Chucky the fat F word."

Tim threw his head back and roared with laughter. "Oh yeah!" He doubled over. Ronnie looked away. "Chucky the Fat Fucky! Who could forget?" Tim hooted and patted Charles on the shoulder. The seller looked like he was about to cry. "Good times."

Charles turned to Ronnie. "So, the truck is four thousand dollars and worth every penny." He had an earnestness about him. The seller brought out a set of keys from the folds of his pockets. Tim continued to laugh and was wiping his eyes.

"I was meaning to ask you," said Ronnie, "when I passed by earlier, the sign said twenty-five hundred."

No change in the temperament of Charles. As if he was prepared to respond to this. "Yes, well, I had a dealer come by after you called. He said the car was worth six thousand. I couldn't in good conscience sell it for such a low price. You understand." There was an annoying smirk plastered across his face.

"What was his name, Chucky?" Tim asked.

A flash of apprehension. "It was Agee. David Agee. The owner of the Ford dealership. He'd most certainly know these things. He even wanted to buy it, but I said no. I had someone call and I wouldn't do that."

"Well, hells bells, Chucky, that sure was nice of you." Tim quit laughing and looked very serious. "You know me and old Dave are related through marriage. I fuck his sister nearly every night. Can you believe it? Small world." He reached into his pocket and brought out his cell phone. "I'm gonna have to give him a call and chew him out. I see a lot of problems with this truck. It sure as shit ain't worth no four thousand."

Sweat dripped down Charles's face. "Don't worry about that right now. Take it for a drive and see what you think." Ronnie and Tim got into the truck, Tim behind the wheel. He winked at Ronnie.

Ronnie watched as Tim slid the car into neutral and put his right foot on both the gas and brake pedals. Tim cranked the engine and pumped both pedals at the same time. The truck hiccupped badly, and Ronnie saw Tim smiling. He looked in the rearview mirror and saw Charles biting his fingernails.

Tim pulled the truck out of the parking lot and drove it down the highway. They switched places and Ronnie drove back. It rode and drove like a dream. When they pulled back into the parking lot, Charles approached the truck. Tim got out, shaking his head.

"Ronnie, this car has so many damn problems, I can't let you pay no four thousand."

"What's wrong with it?" Charles asked.

"Shoot, where to begin. The starter's messed up—that's a few hundred to fix. The truck pulls when you drive it. It's not the tires, so the frame is wonky. That's another couple hundred, if not more. The bodywork is rusting underneath. The belt is about to go. The brake pads are practically nonexistent…"

"Well," Ronnie said. "What do you think is fair?"

"I wouldn't pay a cent over fifteen hundred."

"I can't do that," Charles blurted.

Tim took Ronnie by the arm. "Let's go. He'll be in a load of shit when the person who buys it shows back up madder than hell. I wager it's a sweet old lady who buys it. Or better still, a poor single mother who works two jobs. Her hard-earned money gone to hell. Betcha anything this scam will make the news. They'll take him to court."

As they walked away, Charles called out, "I'll go eighteen-hundred."

Tim gave Ronnie another wink and they turned around.

"I'll go eighteen," said Ronnie. He took out his wad of cash and counted out the bills. Charles watched him intently.

"Okay," said Charles. "Let me go inside and get the title."

When Charles was out of range, Tim clapped Ronnie on the back. "Yes, sir," he said, laughing.

Ronnie wore a look of concern. "Is it really that bad?"

"Hell no," Tim said. "The damn thing just needs a tire rotation. There ain't nothing wrong with that truck."

"I feel bad though."

"Don't. He'd gladly have ripped off someone who didn't know any better. He makes his money by preying on the misfortune of others. Think of this as one for the good guys."

Ronnie smiled and shook Tim's hand. "Thanks, Tim."

Tim told Ronnie that he'd see him at work in the morning, then got in his car and drove away. A few minutes later, Charles came outside with the title signed and handed it over with an additional set of keys. Ronnie thanked him and got inside his new truck. He put the title in the glove box and sat in the driver's seat for a long time. He ran his hands over the steering wheel and dashboard and couldn't stop smiling. Ronnie folded his arms and sniffed the air. Despite being used, there was the faint odor of new-car smell. Perhaps it was in his mind.

A bus passed on the highway and Ronnie smiled. Yet, that faded as he remembered the last time he drove a car. All those years ago, and the wreckage it wrought. He thought he heard his name called from someplace in a voiceless dream.

Chapter 4

Clara's boss grunted, gyrated spasmodically, and rolled over. He was a huge fat man and had sweated all over her naked body. It had dripped off his forehead, into her eyes and mouth. He reeked of ruin and was wheezing heavily. She'd not moved and felt dirty. Her legs were spread, and she was slick with his cooling filth. Neither spoke. Her boss calmed his breathing, but the slight whistle in his nostrils remained. He sat up in the bed and slid his legs over the side. He used the pillow to wipe his member and stood. His fat body glistened in the light. Clara looked over and then turned away.

She thought of the ocean and little Mary playing in the surf. Little eyes full of wonderment as she splashed in the water. Mother and daughter sitting on a blanket sharing saltine crackers and Kool-Aid. The two sticking their deep red stained tongues out at each other. Mary laughing so hard that she toppled over onto the beach towel.

Something landed on Clara's stomach and she returned to the stinking hotel room with its gaudy wallpaper and faint smell of bleach. A wet washcloth lay across her exposed breasts.

"Clean yourself," her boss said.

Clara wiped her thighs with the towel and between her legs. She sat up, facing away from her boss, and ran the wet cloth over her stomach, breasts, and neck. It was cold and gave her goosebumps. She hugged herself and stood. Her boss walked around the bed and stood facing her. He was fully clothed and wore a shit-eating grin. He'd covered himself in cheap cologne that nauseatingly mingled with the odor of sex. She crossed her arms to cover her chest.

"You can use this room today. Just make sure you clean it."

Clara nodded and gave him a faint and forced smile. He reached up and forcefully separated her arms. They hung by her sides and he cupped her breasts. He licked his lips with a wet sucking sound and Clara turned her head away. He pinched and twisted her nipple and made a guttural noise. Clara winced in pain.

"You've got a nice set. I'd give it to you again if I had the time." He made a bizarre noise and let go. "You'd like that, wouldn't ye?"

Clara nodded her head slowly.

"I knew it," he said and laughed. "Mind what I said about the room."

After Clara's boss left, she walked over to her pile of clothes and picked out her black thong and matching lace bra. She put them on and walked into the bathroom. The lights were bright, and the dirty washcloth lay on the floor. She shuddered and leaned close to the mirror. Clara's mascara ran, and she didn't know if it was from his sweat or her tears. Probably a mixture of both. She turned on the faucet and let it run. After a few minutes, steam wafted up onto the mirror. Clara wet a fresh towel and carefully washed her face. She cleaned off her makeup and went back into the room for her purse. Clara carried it back into the bathroom and took out a small baggie filled with clear crystals. She wiped a space clear on the counter and tipped out some of the meth. With a hotel room keycard, she smashed the crystals and chopped them into two fine lines. She rolled a dollar bill into a straw and snorted the powder. She threw her head back and used her finger to cover her nostril. She sniffed and tasted the bitter mixture drip down the back of her throat. Clara then bent over the other line and repeated the exercise.

The drug took hold and her pupils dilated. They grew enormous. Clara's blue irises disappeared, and her eyes looked black. Her pulse raced, and she felt euphoric. Clara quickly re-applied her makeup. She seemed like an amateur clown, so heavy was her foundation. Stepping away from the mirror, she arched her back and posed. She mimicked the moves of a model, laughing and blowing kisses to her reflection. She was lost in the moment.

In her mind's eye, Clara stood on a red carpet before cameras. The bulbs flashed, and a row of microphones were lined in front of her. She mouthed the words thank you and posed from side to side. She stuck out her rear and looked over her shoulder. A crowd cheered her name. She clutched both hands over her heart. Clara's dreamscape carried her away. It took her to another world. No drugs and no johns. A land without wickedness or hurt. A place where she didn't feel ashamed. Another and better world. Solely, a landscape of escape in her mind.

Clara's cellphone chimed from within her purse. She blinked and stared at herself in the mirror. She took out her phone. It was a text message from Joe, her boyfriend, with a question mark. She responded with the number of the hotel room. He didn't text back. Joe would post her phone number, a fake name, and pictures online. Soon her phone would start ringing. Men asking for a location and the price. She'd make sure to reiterate that the money was a donation for time spent. That way she might try to skate around the illegality of prostitution. Clara's rates were $80 for fifteen minutes, $150 for thirty, and $200 for an hour. There was no haggling with the cost. Most of the time, the men opted for fifteen minutes.

Joe and Clara had a system. She paid for their trailer and all other expenses in exchange for an unlimited supply of drugs. It worked as far as she was concerned. She'd known no other life. From a young age, Clara was abused by the various men in her mother's life. Of all the stepfathers and live-in boyfriends, only one hadn't molested her. In fact, the abuse was so commonplace that Clara remembered resenting the one who didn't rape her. She thought he hated her. So twisted were her formative years that it took her a long time to realize the abuse wasn't normal. By that time, it was too late. The damage was done. Abuse, violence, sex, love, and self-worth were knitted together so tightly that nothing in her power could divorce them.

She serviced all races and anyone over eighteen. Old men to fraternity boys. As long as they had the money, it didn't matter. Sometimes more than one at a time if the price was right. Clara had several regular clients. One was a married banker who was nervous and polite. He always left Clara a ten-dollar tip. Another regular was a school teacher who paid her extra to wear her hair in ponytails. And there was the aged man with grandchildren a decade older than Clara. There was a youth minister who brought along drugs he purchased from Joe. He'd do meth and Clara at the same time. He'd snort a line off her chest and sing gospel hymns. Quote scripture while inside her. It frightened her at first, as if the preacher's deity would come down and smite her for sinfulness. But, she'd long quit believing in God. No almighty being would allow such tragedy in the world.

When Clara had been a fourteen-year-old high school dropout living in a tent behind a liquor store, she'd met

Nathan Bickett. He was fifteen years her senior, and she was in love. Her mother didn't care when she ran off and shacked up with Nate. Not long after moving in with him, she became pregnant. A tiny bit of life forming slowly from within. He promised her the world and she was overjoyed. When she miscarried, and went to the hospital, she thought nothing of their age difference and the illegality of their union. Clara's short period of happiness came to an end when the police showed up at the apartment to arrest her boyfriend on statutory rape charges. Clara watched in horror as the love of her life ran into the bedroom and returned with a pistol. With the police pounding on the door, he put the gun in his mouth and pulled the trigger. Clara remembered vividly the back of his head separating from the rest of his skull and flying across the room. No amount of meth would erase the memory.

Clara dressed in her room service uniform. Her nametag wasn't lined up properly. In her drugged state, this was very distressing. She rearranged and attached it half a dozen times. Finally, she gave up and threw it in the waste basket. She'd pricked herself and was bleeding from her thumb. Clara held her hand close to her face and studied the red smear. She felt her heart beat rapidly through the pain. She turned on the water and washed the prick. Clara picked up the bag of meth and poured out more onto the counter. She crushed and snorted it quickly. The drug took effect. Her mouth was dry, her vision blurred, and Clara felt hot and restless. She unbuttoned her shirt. Clara was sweating. Her mind raced, and she remembered her job. Clara had to clean the room and the others on the floor. Two Mexican women cleaned the even-numbered rooms and she worked the odds.

Outside, the sun hammered down onto the pavement of the parking lot and radiated heat upwards. Wavy lines hovered over the cooking asphalt. The motel's pool was green and hadn't been cleaned for as long as she'd worked there. A yellow used condom bobbed like a buoy.

Clara walked towards the laundry room to retrieve her housekeeping trolley. Even if they hadn't been slept in, the rooms were cleaned daily. Being so close to the ocean meant that dampness and mildew proved a constant problem. Management couldn't let it get a foothold in the rooms.

She passed under a menacing-looking wasp nest that was animate with activity. She heard the angry hum of their terrible wings. Clara gave the nest a wide berth. She'd tell the maintenance man later, though he was probably laid up in a room drunk. The flower bed near the front office was covered in poison ivy, but no one noticed or cared. Clara paused and looked out over the parking lot again. There weren't any cars in the lot but for her Toyota and the boss's SUV. Cars passed on the road and a truck honked several times in quick succession. Clara waved absently and continued walking towards the laundry room.

She passed an open room and looked in. The other two cleaning ladies were fixing the room and chatting in Spanish. They had a small portable radio that played Latin music from a staticky AM station. They worked diligently and spoke rapidly to each other in hushed tones. Clara popped her head in the door.

"Good morning," she said.

Both women jumped and turned to face the door. They looked frightened, and one grabbed at a rosary she wore. Clara stepped into the room and waved.

One of the women smiled broadly and waved back. "Hallo," she said brokenly. Neither moved from where they stood. The woman who responded was holding a pillow mid-fluff. The other still cradled the rosary above her heart.

"I just wanted to say good morning," Clara said, then turned to leave.

The women began speaking loudly in Spanish. One seemed to argue with the other. As she walked back to the landing, Clara heard one say, "Ella es una puta." She heard the other audibly suck in her breath. Clara didn't speak the language but knew what that meant.

She hurried down the walkway to the laundry room and got her cleaning trolley. Tears were in her eyes. Clara was struck with the wanton feeling of moroseness and regret. She closed the door and hurried back towards her room, pushing the large cart. A huge green squirt bottle sloshed on the side of the trolley overcrowded with fresh linens and trash bags. A cheap vacuum cleaner rested on the bottom. Clara looked back at the road and it was making a mirage of standing water in the distance. She shook her head and pushed on.

Back at the open door, she glanced inside. The radio was turned off and the women were kneeling at the foot of the bed with their hands up in prayer. They both moved their lips without saying a word, as if chanting silently in tandem.

Over the next hour, she cleaned three rooms and they looked pristine. The meth made her hands quiver, and she had a laser-like focus on the job at hand.

Clara returned to room 211, where she'd been with her boss earlier. She remade the bed with a clean set of threadbare sheets and pulled them tight. With the bed made, she stood back and looked it over, feeling a strange sense of accomplishment that was purely drug induced. Then, Clara gathered up the spray bottle of bleach cleaner and her baggie of meth and went into the bathroom.

She tipped more of the drug onto the counter and smashed it into a fine powder. She snorted the line and then sprayed the counter down with the bleach. The smell mingled with the meth and she felt light-headed. Her mind wandered to a safe place. She and Mary were at Disney World. Her daughter posed with the princesses and dreamed of something better. Then Clara was back at the motel. She sprayed down every available surface in the small room and began scrubbing. She started in the shower and rubbed away the grime and rings around the tub.

Then she started on the toilet, which had dried and caked shit around the bowl. It didn't matter, she sprayed it again and continued to scrub until the feces were wiped away. She got down on all fours and scrubbed between the tiles with care, the meth pinpointing her concentration. After that, she scrubbed the sink and counter and cleaned the mirror. With the bathroom complete, she went back into the room, dusted, and vacuumed. Clara repeated this exercise and headed for the next room when her cellphone rang.

She told the caller her location and the motel room number. She backtracked to room 211 and pulled out the little day bag she kept in the closet. Inside the bag was a short black dress that she laid on the bed. She took off her cleaning uniform, unclasped her bra, and put them in the little bag. Then, she stood in front of the mirror and regarded her body, making sure everything looked right. Clara undid her hair and spread it out with her fingers. She then put on the short black dress and waited on the bed.

After sitting for some time, she got up and went to the window and looked out. As she did, a car pulled into the parking lot. A man got out and looked the motel over. He seemed to hesitate. After a moment, he started walking towards the stairwell. Clara stood back behind the door and waited for the knock.

It followed and she opened the door.

A tall white man stood in the doorway. The bright sunlight shone around him like some saint in a painting. After Clara's eyes adjusted, she saw he wore a tan suit and seemed nervous. A sight that set her at ease. Cops don't get nervous.

"Hey, come in," Clara said as she stepped back.

"Okay."

Clara shut the door behind him and flipped off the light. She was smiling. The man turned to face her. Clara slipped the dress from her shoulders and stood before him naked but for her thong.

"Touch my tits, please," she said, pointing. He looked confused for a second but did as he was told. "Okay, thanks. That was to make sure you weren't the cops. How long are you wanting?"

"Half an hour," he said with skittering eyes.

"That'll be one hundred fifty," Clara said with her hand out. The man reached for his wallet. This motion gave her pause. She had to be careful always. You never knew who was on the other side of the door. He might pull out a knife, a gun, or a badge. Her heart thundered until she saw the little brown billfold.

"I don't suppose you have change for a ten?"

"No, sorry. Next time you can pay one-forty."

The man nodded and counted out eight twenty-dollar bills. He handed them over and Clara recounted them. Satisfied, she went over to her purse and placed the folded money inside. She walked back towards the man with a slow gait, trying to look sexy for this new client. But, she ended up looking crazed and awkward. Clara stood before him and looked him in the eyes. Hers were dilated and glazed. His full of lust and fear. She undid the belt he wore. Then, she took hold of his zipper and dropped to her knees.

When he left, Clara did another line and washed between her legs. Shortly later, another arrived. This time it was a cop, but one Clara didn't have to worry about. Officer Brooks was a crooked cop who worked closely with Joe. They were related somehow, and badge only separated their criminality. He was grinding painfully now and making sickening noises. There was something ghastly and horrific about the man. His nose was whistling as he grunted and she fought the urge to vomit.

She escaped from the disgust by dreaming of another world. Her mind floated from the seedy motel room and thought of little Mary in a happier place. Anywhere but Pensacola. A place like California. Away from the Palms, the drugs, and this pitiful life. Clara knew all about the latter. It was part and parcel of what drove her to prostitution. Her greatest fear was that Mary would experience the same tribulations as herself. It was a persistent dark cloud that hung over their lives.

Clara opened her eyes and watched the spectral shapes of the crooked cop's movements dance on the ceiling. The light played his shadow like a terrible marionette. What devil pulled the strings? It reminded Clara of a dumpy troll or some other demon beast attacking her repeatedly. She didn't dare look away. His nasty grunts and snorts crescendoed with the squeak of the cheap bedframe. The cacophony peaked and he was done. He got up and dressed quickly, fixing his gun belt with a devilish grin. She didn't move. He whispered menacing threats and left.

His sweat glazed her chest and smelled rancid. She threw up in the bathroom sink. As she turned on the shower, a miserable sucking sound came from deep in the pipes. Brown-looking water slushed out from the faucet and pooled in the tub. She pulled the knob and turned on the shower head. The water looked a little better. She let the hot water run until it steamed the small room. While waiting, she stepped out of the bathroom and snorted two lines of meth. The drugs electrified her brain, and for a little while, all was right in the world.

After a hot shower, her tiny hands fumbled with the buttons of her work shirt. She scrubbed the room with so much cleaner that it looked coated in grease. Her bra looked loose from the amount of times she had taken it off. Clara's movements created a phantasmagoria of silhouettes against the back wall. Her baggie of meth and phone rested on the little table stand. She slipped out of her black pants and turned to look at her rear. Red hand prints were visible of different sizes. She admired her firm buttocks in the faint light. Clara picked up and slid on the short and thin black dress. She stood back and admired her figure. An easy peace settled over her.

Clara walked into the bathroom and filled a little paper cup with water and drank. Her mouth felt like sandpaper and tasted like men. She'd not eaten in two days. The water felt heavy in her gut, but she wasn't hungry. Clara stuck out her tongue for the mirror and saw the white, cracked, and calloused-looking thing staring back. She refilled the cup and drank again, then went back into the room and got on the bed. She turned the television on but didn't watch the screen. Instead, she stared up at the ceiling and studied the shapes and flicker of light. They were rapid and sure and seemed preordained in her drug-addled mind. The water in her stomach bobbed back and forth against her diaphragm. A wave of nausea passed over her and then was gone.

Clara stretched her legs on the bed and closed her eyes. She listened intently for the phone. It was nearing seven o'clock and her daylight hours of hooking were coming to an end. It was slowing down. She felt her pulse rapidly in her neck. Soon she entered a drugged daydream. She saw herself watching something—she was distressed and crying out mutely, trying to break the grip of some shadowed other. She kicked and thrashed but to no avail. Then she heard her daughter cry out for help.

Clara practically jumped out of the bed. Her heart was racing and she was in panic. She snatched her cell phone off the table. The baggie of meth flew across the room and bounced off the wall onto the floor. She fumbled to unlock the phone and tapped in the wrong password twice. Finally, she inputted the right code and called Joe. It rang for a long time then went to his generic voicemail. Clara hung up and tried the number again. On the fourth ring, Joe answered. He sounded annoyed and high. There was a distractedness to his voice.

"What," he barked.

"Have you seen Mary?"

"Have I what?"

"Did Mary come home from school today? Is she there?"

"Um...I don't remember," he said. "She might have."

"Can you find her for me, please?"

"What the fuck, Clara. She's your daughter. I'm not a goddamn babysitter."

"Joe, please." Her voice cracked, and she was on the verge of tears. "Just look for her."

"This is the fucking drugs. They've got you paranoid. She's around."

"Joe!" she yelled. "Just check!"

"Fine," he said. "Hold on." She heard Joe exhale loudly like a petulant teenager and set the phone down. There were steps amid the background noise. A door opened that she presumed was to Mary's cubby. It creaked loudly and dragged on the cheap carpet. Clara heard him call out then shut the door. She heard more steps and he said Mary's name again. A second later the phone rattled. "She's not here."

"Where is she?" Clara was crying now. "Check outside, please."

"All right, but that's it. Leave me the fuck alone after. I'm busy.""Okay." Clara was gnawing on her fingernails. One cracked loudly and started to bleed. The pain felt good. She heard the trailer door open and then close after a few moments. Joe picked the phone back up.

"She ain't here," he said with annoyance. "And I ain't lookin' for her."

Clara hung up and rushed to the closet. She gathered her things and picked up her purse. She opened the door and glanced back over the room. Something was missing. On the floor was her little baggie. She rushed over to it and shoved it in her bra. She lit out of the room and ran down the walkway.

Her bare feet slapped on the concrete. Clara fished out her keys and had them out and ready when she hit the door. She jumped into the seat and cranked the engine. It sputtered and kicked and fell silent. She bashed the steering wheel with her fist and tried again. This time, she pushed the accelerator as she turned the key, and the car bounced into life. Without looking, Clara backed up from her space and burned rubber out of the motel's parking lot. Bits of tire flew and smoke followed her out. She cut off a passing driver who honked and waved his arms. Clara wasn't paying any attention. There was only one thought in her mind. She had to get home and find Mary. Scenarios raced through her mind, each more horrible and ghastly than the one before. Tears were in her eyes. She put her foot down and drove as fast as the car would go.

Chapter 5

Mary sat on the grass outside their dingy trailer playing with her mismatched dolls. The sun hung low in the sky, but it was still hot. Her little cheeks were rosy from the heat and she wished she owned a hat. Her curly dark hair danced in the breeze and blew across her face. She looked across the street to a path by the gutter where flowers once grew. The flowers were gone, and this made her sad. A coal-colored cat trotted down the street and disappeared. Something rotten danced in her nostrils and she squinted her dark face and exhaled.

Her mother still wasn't home from the motel and it was getting late. Something always felt looming until Mom came home. Joe was inside, but Mary didn't like him. She never had. He was mean-looking, with bloodred hair and a face covered with freckles. Joe spent most of his time on his cellphone, but there were times he used bad things and acted like a crazy person. Like the time he put something in his nose, got down on all fours, and growled like a dog. Mary remembered the wild look in his eyes. She had run from the trailer and hid in the tall grass, where her mother later found her shivering with fright.

Mary danced the dolls together and chatted softly with them. Her imagination took her far from this place. She'd left the trailer because Joe was cooking something on the stove that made her feel sick. The fumes stunk up the trailer and seeped into her little cubby room. So she fled, coughing and teary eyed, into the outer world. Several cars came and went as she sat outside playing. The people never stayed at their trailer for too long and paid her no mind. It was better that way. She didn't like Joe's friends or the strangers who knocked on the door at all hours.

Mary missed her mommy and wanted to talk to her. She'd had a bad day at school. This wasn't entirely new, but today was altogether worse. The teasing began first thing in the morning on the bus and she'd heard the mocking laughter as she stepped off the bus at the end of the day.

Most days the other kids teased her about her clothes and ratty shoes. They laughed about her book bag and how she smelled. The school kids giggled about where she lived and her free school lunch. She had no friends in the world and it was a lonely existence. Today, the other students called her a new name. She didn't know what it meant. No one would tell her. The kids just screamed it, pointed, and laughed. Mary hoped her mother would hurry home so she could explain what it meant.

Mary watched the road as a new truck slowly approached. She'd never seen it before. Usually strange cars parked at her house, but this one kept on and pulled into her neighbor's driveway. She clutched the dolls in her lap and watched attentively. Perhaps the person was lost. She sat up on her knees to get a better look and realized the man behind the wheel was her neighbor. He was an old man who seemed nice. She would watch him as he worked in his yard, but had been too shy to say hello.

Mary got up on her feet with both dolls hanging by her side. She took several steps towards the running vehicle and saw that the man held his head in his hands. He was shaking. Mary walked gingerly over the partition between her yard and his. She clambered atop the rocks and dead grass. There was a clear demarcation between the two. Her yard was overgrown with weeds and littered with trash. Whole patches were bald and nothing grew. Yet, his yard was groomed and litter-free. Mary hesitated to step on it. The truck was idling and didn't make the coughing sounds like her mother's car. Everything seemed silent but for the soft rumble of the engine.

Mary stepped lightly and crept up to the truck. The man hadn't moved except for the slight tremors of his cupped head. A shadow crossed her feet and she jumped with fright. Mary looked up and saw a gull pass overhead. She tiptoed up to the driver's door and knocked. Nothing. Mary knocked again. The man's red eyed and wet face came into view and he smiled. Her neighbor rolled down the window.

"Hello, little girl," he said.

"Hi." Mary was a little embarrassed. The man had been crying. She took a step back and he opened the truck door.

"Can I help you?" he said, smiling.

"No, sir," she said. "I just wanted to say hello. I live next door."

"I know, I've seen you." He pushed a button and rolled up the window, then shut off the engine. He used his sleeve to wipe his eyes. "My name's Ronnie. What's yours?"

"My name is Mary."

"That's a beautiful name, Mary."

"Mr. Ronnie, why were you crying?" His face twitched and she became afraid. She felt she'd breached the bounds of proper conduct. She backed away and prepared to run. But instead of yelling, he smiled at her.

"I'm just happy, Mary. Sometimes I cry when I'm happy."

"I cry when I'm happy also," Mary said. She was relieved. "But I mostly cry when I'm sad or scared."

"Me too."

Mary noticed that something about Mr. Ronnie wasn't happy. He looked sad, but she didn't want to say anything to upset her new friend. So instead she asked, "Why are you happy, Mr. Ronnie?"

"I bought a new car," he said, pointing at the truck. "Do you like it?"

"It's cool. It sounds good. My mom's car makes the worst noises. I'm surprised it doesn't wake the whole neighborhood." Ronnie laughed and Mary joined in.

"I've never heard the name Ronnie before."

"Well, I'm glad to be your first. It's short for Ronald."

"We have a Ronald at school, but people call him Ron," she said. "He isn't very nice." She looked away. "Are you nice?"

"I think so. No one has told me otherwise in a long time."

"That's good." She was weighing something in her mind. "Can I ask you another question?"

"The more the merrier," he said.

"What's a mongrel?"

"A mongrel..." He paused. "Hmm, a mongrel is a dog with a mixture of breeds. You have purebred and mongrel—" The man ceased speaking.

Mary's eyes watered. She dropped her dolls onto the pavement and began crying uncontrollably. She was about to flee when she felt two enormous arms gather around her. She opened her wet eyes and saw that Ronnie was on his knees in front of her. He was hugging her gently and rocking slightly. In a soft, singsongy voice, he beseeched her not to cry. For a long time, he held her as she shook and Mary laid her head on his shoulder. Her tears wet his shirt. He rubbed her back and swayed side to side. After a while, she quit shaking and the tears stopped. He sat back on his heels and looked at her. She was a little embarrassed. Ronnie took out a handkerchief and wiped under her eyes.

"Kids at school are so mean to me. I don't even do anything to them," she said.

The man hugged her again and stood up. "Kids are bullies because they are jealous. They are bitter and that's all. The bullies are insecure with themselves, so they take it out on other people. Do you know what *insecure* means?"

Mary nodded, although she had only a vague idea of the definition. "I just wish they'd leave me alone."

Ronnie nodded to her and tussled her hair. "I know," he said. "But, you are better than that. You won't let them get you down. Right?"

Mary nodded and smiled up at the man.

"Do you like ice cream?" he asked.

"Yes, sir."

"I've got three different kinds in the freezer. Want some?"

Mary nodded.

"We are going to have to try all three," Ronnie said. "If we don't, we can't tell which is the best."

Mary smiled and took his hand. She walked with him towards the porch. She set her dolls on the steps and climbed them. They were in much better shape than hers. She didn't have to watch out for the broken or rotted wood. Mary looked in amazement at the little plants growing from brown clay pots on the porch. Tiny green tomatoes grew on a vine that looped around metal stakes.

The porch only made a muted creak as they walked over the strong boards. They didn't rattle or sag. Ronnie unlocked the door and held it open. Inside, Mary was blown away by the cleanliness. She'd never seen a place so nice. It didn't have clothes, trash, or bad things strewn all over. She often felt uncomfortable around new people, but with him, she didn't. He pointed towards a couch and walked to the kitchen. Mary hesitated, not knowing if she'd mess it up. It looked ornamental. Finally, she sat and relished in the comfort. The one in her trailer was ratty and painful. Sharp metal springs stuck out of it and bit her bottom.

Ronnie approached with three tubs of ice cream stacked under his chin. In his free hand, he held two bowls and spoons. Mary's mouth watered at the sight of the containers. Smiling, Ronnie set everything down on the coffee table. He took a seat next to her and pried open the ice cream tubs one at a time. None were eaten from. Mary found this very lonely.

"So, which one first?" Ronnie asked. The flavors were vanilla, chocolate, and mint chocolate chip.

"Vanilla, please."

"Can do."

Mary watched as Ronnie took a spoon and dolloped two spoonfuls into the empty bowl. He repeated for his own. He handed Mary a spoon and held his up. He motioned for her to tap his spoon. They clanked their spoons like swords before battle and started to eat.

They finished their bowls at the same time. Mary watched Ronnie lick his spoon and she copied him.

He turned to her. "So, which next?"

Mary giggled. "Umm, let's try the mint chocolate chip."

"Your wish is my command," Ronnie said lightheartedly.

He doled out more ice cream into the bowls. Mary watched as he held his spoon up yet again. Their cutlery tinged on contact. This time they ate more slowly. Neither spoke as they finished the second bowl. Mary didn't understand why this man was being so nice. She'd never known strangers to be so kind. People she knew weren't like this.

"Last but not least," Ronnie said.

Mary smiled. "Okay, but I don't want a lot."

"Just one scoop?"

Mary nodded. Ronnie placed one scoop in her bowl and put two in his own. She held out her spoon and he clanked hers. They both laughed. Halfway through her third bowl, Mary stopped eating and listened. She thought she'd heard her name being called. The wind had picked up outside and she wasn't sure. It might've been her imagination. Mary ate more. She was getting sleepy. She'd never eaten so much ice cream in her life.

Then, again, the whisper of a familiar voice. Ronnie heard it too because he put his bowl down. A third time, the voice was clear. It was her mother screaming Mary's name. Ronnie looked at Mary and smiled.

"Somebody's looking for you." Ronnie stood up and went to the door. He held his bowl in his hands. He opened the door and turned on the porch light. The sun was setting in the west and twilight approached. Mary walked to the door. Ronnie moved out of her way and she joined him outside. She looked off in the distance and saw fresh stars shining in the dusk. Darkness far off in the east.

Ronnie held his hand up and hollered. "Ma'am, she's over here." He was waving enthusiastically with the spoon in his hand.

Mary stepped forward and watched her mother run down the street towards the trailer. She wore her work shirt. It was unbuttoned and the lapels flapped in the wind. The ocean breeze lashed her hair about in an overwrought frenzy. She looked crazed. Mary had never seen her mother run like that, a terrified and furious expression on her face. Mary watched slack-jawed as her mother cleared the porch steps in one leap. Her eyes were huge and shone with glints of madness. Her mother took two quick steps up to Ronnie and slapped him hard in the face. She was screeching incomprehensibly and clawed at his cheeks.

Ronnie took a step back and turned away from the blows. They sounded like drums as Mary watched her mother's fists hit his back. He slouched and shuffled away. Mary dropped her ice cream bowl and it shattered on the porch. She screamed and her mother raced over to her.

"Did he touch you? Where did he touch you?"

"He didn't, Mommy. Why'd you hit him? He's nice."

"Shut up, he's a pervert!" Mary's mother screamed. She gathered Mary in her arms and faced Ronnie. "You ever come near my daughter again and I'll cut off your fucking balls." Mary's head was around her mother's shoulder. She saw that people were milling about and watching the show. Suddenly, her vision blurred and abruptly flashed back to Ronnie.

The gray darkness shrouded him. Gloom was all about but for the porch light. As her mother carried her down the steps, Mary saw the growing red welt on Ronnie's face. Blood fell in small droplets from three fresh claw marks. She watched the sadness in his eyes as tears streamed from her own.

Chapter 6

Mary was screaming, crying, and kicking her feet against Clara's stomach. The little girl's arms were pushing against her mother. Clara clung tight to Mary with a matriarchal strength previously unknown.

She entered the stinking trailer and walked through a dense fog of meth smoke. The floor beneath surged and buckled with loud groans. Joe was picking at something on his face. He stared up with a crazed look of incomprehension.

"Bitch, don't burst in here like that. I thought you were the cops."

Clara walked past him to the bedroom and set her screaming charge down on the unmade bed. She kneeled in front of Mary. There was sadness in her daughter's doll-like eyes. Clara ran her fingers through Mary's hair and hugged her tightly. Her head sagged forward and she sniffled. The child's tears were subsiding, as were Clara's panic and rage.

"What happened?" Clara asked.

"Mommy, he was being nice to me and gave me ice cream."

"Did he touch you?"

"He hugged me when I was crying."

"Why were you crying?"

Tears flooded back into Mary's eyes. She told her mother all about the teasing and mean names. The cruel taunts and her friendless existence. Clara had no idea. Her daughter had never shared these things with her before. Clara felt plagued as a miserable parent, unable to protect her only child. All the world went silent but for the whimpering of her daughter. She hugged Mary tightly and listened to her recount the complex and simple injustices she faced. Most not wholly unfamiliar to Clara herself. Mary leaned heavily on her mother's shoulders, and Clara sang softly in her ear. Clara listened to Mary recount meeting the neighbor man and their discussion. She told of her shame at bawling in front of the stranger. Mary shared how the man comforted her and stopped her from weeping. She described the ice cream and the spoon clicks. The terror and rage on her mother's face. Mommy hitting her new friend. Clara was crying herself now. She whispered and crooned words of love into her daughter's ear. She rocked her child and continued to softly sing. A tune wholly familiar yet lost in origin. After a long time, she felt her child drift to sleep.

Clara laid Mary down in the bed and tucked her under the covers. Dried tear tracks ran down the side of her sleeping face. She breathed heavily and whimpered like a puppy dog. Her little hands played with her hair as she dreamed. Clara sat down hard on the floor. Her emotions were flooded with uncertainty. Her heart was racing and her head hurt. The chaos of the past hour heightened her anxiety. She needed to get high.

Clara rose and exited the bedroom. Joe was grinding his teeth and watching the television with interest. He didn't acknowledge her presence. She walked over to the couch and sat down. It crunched underneath her and a spring poked her backside. Clara picked out the baggie of meth from her bra and sprinkled some of the crystals into the glass bulb at the end of the pipe. Joe still hadn't looked over. She brought the pipe to her lips and lit the cigarette lighter. It cooked the little crystals and they boiled in the heat. Smoke rose and she inhaled deeply. She repeated the exercise and rolled the glass back and forth to keep from burning the meth. Clara sat back and exhaled a massive plume of smoke. Joe snapped his fingers and held his hand out. She handed over the pipe and lighter. Joe took a hit and handed it back. It was still smoking and the glass was hot. Clara took another hit and set the pipe down on a magazine. It singed the plastic pages, but she quit paying attention. Clara sat back and her mind turned into a kaleidoscope. Her screams reverberated in the ether and her ears sang. She watched the wallpaper slightly mutate and slowly alter. The abstractions of the peeling paper looked like a carousel of nightmares and Clara got up and fled into the kitchen.

"Where's my money?" Joe hollered from his chair.

"In my purse. I'll get it here in a second."

"Don't fucking hold out on me," he shouted.

Clara didn't respond. She opened the refrigerator and spied the contents. The smell was atrocious and everything inside was varying degrees of spoiled. A half gallon of milk was curdled and turned immiscible inside the jug. A piece of cheese was growing another life-form. Various open containers reeked of decay. In the back was a green and furry half-eaten sandwich. Clara took two bottles of beer from the fridge and walked out on the porch. Joe screamed about the money, but Clara didn't look back. She walked down the steps and across the yard towards her neighbor's house.

A quarter moon hung in the sky. Tree frogs and crickets sang out inharmoniously. Clara wandered with ease barefooted across her neighbor's manicured grass. Her tongue felt swollen and a dire stench radiated from her pores. The drugs set her heart pounding and she felt it pulsing in odd places. Orange light shone from the few unbroken street lamps. The interior of his trailer shone like a beacon, but his porch light was off. Clara walked up the steps cautiously and quietly went to the door. She put her head against the wood and listened. She heard a guitar playing. A soft voice singing. She stood for a while and listened. Then, she knocked. The guitar paused for a moment and began again. She rapped on the door a little louder and the music stopped. Creaking noise from inside. The porch light turned on and the door opened.

The man stood facing her and wore a look of confusion. It wasn't anger like she'd expected. The scratches on his face were covered in band-aids, and he smiled down at her with a strange benevolence. He held a scratched and poor-looking guitar by the neck in one hand. He leaned it against the wall.

"Good evening," he said.

"Hidy," Clara said. Her eyes skittered around and she felt nervous. The man looked down at the beers she held that were beading with condensation. Clara offered them up. "I wanted to give you these and say sorry. I shouldn't have acted that way. I thought someone stole my daughter and I lost my mind a little bit." Her eyes finally settled on his and she noticed a warmth deep within his gaze. A simmering niceness formed in his countenance. The tropic breeze filled her hair and blew it crazily. A vision of a snake-haired woman flashed through her mind. The man took the beers and stepped out onto the porch.

"Already forgotten," he said. She didn't respond. "I want to apologize myself. I didn't think about how scary that would be. Having your daughter go into a stranger's trailer. She was just so upset, and I thought ice cream would help. I'm really sorry."

She waved her hands. "No, you were nice to her. She told me all about it. I guess I'm not used to a little kindness. She likes you. She'll probably be over all the time now."

"That's just fine," he said with a chuckle.

Clara stood with her hands oddly rubbing together. "I better head on," she said.

"Wait a bit," he said. "Have one of these with me." He held out one of the beers and Clara took it. "Let's sit over here on the swing." He walked over and sat on the metal glider. It bobbed back and forth slightly. Clara took a seat next to him and opened her beer. It fuzzed and she sipped the neck. The two rocked and were silent for a time.

"I'm Ronnie, by the way. Ronnie Wells." He held out his hand and Clara shook it. "We've been neighbors for months, but I haven't introduced myself."

"I'm Clara Bennett. You've met my daughter, Mary Bennett."

"Lovely little girl."

"She's my whole world," she said. "You know, I never thought I could love something the way I do her. Never in a million years did I think it even existed." She smiled and looked him in the eyes. She noted sadness. It was faint and hidden. She looked out into the night as they both sipped their beers. The swing swayed back and forth rhythmically. Clara felt safe for the first time in what felt like ages.

Over by the door, a collection of moths swarmed the porch light and scattered the illumination into a million little shadows. These were breaking and changing and alive. A car horn sounded in the distance followed by unintelligible shouts. Both sat waiting for the dull pop of gunshots. Only the screeching of tires followed. Clara's beer tasted wonderful.

She turned and looked at the man. He watched out across the road at nothing in particular, searching out the unordered and unembellished. Ronnie twisted and gave her a faint smile. They chatted together for a long time. Long after the beers were gone, they spoke of all matter of things. Secrets and dreams. Hopes and fears. They shared their pain and plans. By the time the night was over, these two complete strangers were friends.

Chapter 7

Ronnie woke with the towering crimson sun rising in the east. Red light shone through a gap in the blinds. His alarm clock rang and he reached over and shut it off. Ronnie lay for a moment staring up at the ceiling. The fan above his bed rotated silently. He felt his face to examine the claw marks. Nothing but the rumor of bumps. He got up and opened the drapes. Clouds ran across the sun, creating bizarre creature-shapes on the concrete.

He'd grown fond of sunrises and sunsets—daily occurrences that he had missed for thirty-three years. Ronnie never noticed them before going to the penitentiary. Surprising the little things you missed and the small things taken for granted.

On an electrical pole, the small glow of the street lamp shone on and looked under attack by an endless horde of insects. Ronnie saw the man who lived across the street stand naked from the waist down and piss off the balcony of his trailer. The arch of urine steamed in the dawn. Ronnie smiled and went down the hall to make coffee. While it percolated, he jumped in the shower. He stood under the scorching faucet for a long time, letting the water loosen his weary bones. The whole bathroom was enveloped in condensation by the time he finished washing himself. He exited and went into the kitchen for a cup of coffee.

He walked out on the porch and lit a cigarette. His footsteps were enormous and amplified in the emptiness. He felt the sun burn into his neck. Off in the distance, two thrushes sang to one another, and a squirrel scampered up an electrical pole. The wind blew the leaves, rustling the branches like soft whispers. There were bugs in rancorous multitudes. The breeze brought the faint odor of wildflowers and freshly cut grass. And a hint of putrefaction. Everything looked animate and was imbued with small life. Narrow crannies and spaces filled with incertitude. A dog barking drove two doves out of a trailer's roof who pirouetted in the sky and returned to the gutter. Their wings echoed in applause. Ronnie stood looking out over the scene like some great judge and proclaimed it good. He smoked his cigarette and enjoyed the coming of day.

Ronnie heard Clara's door open and saw little Mary step outside. She flapped her arms enthusiastically, which Ronnie responded to in kind. Clara came outside and waved as well. Ronnie lifted his coffee mug and watched them walk together down the street. He heard low muffled voices carried through the warm morning air. Mother and daughter were holding hands. A flock of birds flew overhead, and he studied their movements until they disappeared. He heard a little girl's laugh reverberate from down the road.

Across the street, his neighbor lay snoring on the porch with a small hand towel to cover his crotch. Two cats raced over the pavement in a running fight, screeching and yelling of old scores. They disappeared under a trailer. Ronnie spied Clara's boyfriend exit their trailer and mill about in the yard digging amongst the grass like an ape. Prodding for anything of substance. The figure scrounged about in such a manner that he looked like a thing seen through old and poorly glazed glass. He searched uncertainly and skittered about crazily. The man paused and looked to the heavens in calculation and then returned to his investigation. This lone reprobate was in a heated argument with himself. His words were of mounted panic, rage, and indignity.

Ronnie studied this crazed specimen. The spiderlike madman was combing through the dirt. Hunting something that Ronnie figured, for an absolute fact, wasn't there. After a few minutes of watching the show, Ronnie shook his head in bemusement, put out his cigarette, and went inside.

A short time later, Ronnie exited his home fresh-looking and ready for the day. He smiled at the sight of his truck sitting in the driveway. The sun was warming and he couldn't remember a finer morning. Even the air smelled better. A little less toxic. The morning dew was burned away. The scratches on his face were nearly unnoticeable. The wasted scene next door wouldn't sour his day. The keys felt strong in his hand and he sighed with relief at not having to worry about catching the bus.

Ronnie's jeans were freshly pressed, and he felt a new man as he walked towards his truck. Clara's car was gone, and squirrel boy was nowhere in sight. Ronnie waltzed over and slid into the truck. It was hot inside, and he cranked the engine. Ronnie rolled down the windows and sat fiddling with the radio. When he looked up, he saw the dilapidated bike lying along the side of Clara's trailer. He'd grown accustomed to seeing it. Yet, sitting in his new transport, the disused bike was calling his name.

I can fix that for little Mary, he thought.

Ronnie got out of the truck and crossed over into Clara's yard. It was full of cast-off things. Little bits of antiquated and ruined goods. He spied the claw marks left by the boyfriend in the sandy clay. They were crisscrossed at odd angles and he saw two empty baggies in the grass. Ronnie shook his head. He went over to the bike and lifted it up. The front wheel was smashed and the back tire was flat. The frame looked sound, but the handlebars were bent and the brake cable was cut. The suspension fork looked okay, but the bike was completely without a chain. The saddle was rotten and cracked. There was only one handle grip. The disc brakes looked fine and the gears were rusted but cranked and rotated without a problem. Ronnie carried the bike to his truck and set it in the bed. Satisfied with a day's mission, Ronnie headed off down the road to work.

Ronnie drove down the gulf highway with the windows down. He leaned towards the door and let the wind rustle his hair. The tires made a rhythmic hum from the road. Every so often between the sand dunes, he watched the waves break along the beach. A few cars passed going the opposite way and Ronnie waved to each. Most drove on as if in a trance. He drove with an inescapable purpose and a sense of vocation for the day. He'd fix that bike for Mary. A kind gesture for a sweet girl.

He hoped she was having a better day. Her and her mother.

The sun was bright in Ronnie's eyes. A few white wisps of clouds hung in the air. The road poured out ahead and he tapped his fingers on the doorsill. A green iguana raced across the blacktop on two legs like something out of a cartoon. It wore an expression of appalling surprise with its tongue stuck out.

As Ronnie drove on, he felt what he'd long expected. Scenes flashed in his mind of that night many years ago. Bearing down on the unsuspecting barman with unmitigated rage. The night his life changed forever.

The sun burned down upon his clenched fists. They gripped the steering wheel and he was sweating. Pain moved from his chest down to his gut. Bile retched to the back of his throat. Ronnie dry heaved several times. He saw the boneless looking face of the barman looking up at him. The horrible death grin and the leech sucking away. A rubbery expression of incomprehension. He closed his eyes and prayed for the vision to vanish. Ronnie shoved his thumb and forefinger into the sockets until it hurt. Finally, the face dimmed and was gone.

He opened his eyes and through blurry double vision saw his work on the right. He pulled into the parking lot and shut off the engine. Ronnie sat in the truck for a long time. It was quiet but for birds in the distance and the muffled barking of dogs. His face was wet with tears. He tugged at his shirt to wipe his cheeks. In the mirror, blistered eyes looked back. After a time, Ronnie gathered himself. The tear stains dried slowly on his shirt. The clock read 8:10 a.m.

Ronnie paid Tim one hundred dollars to fix the bike. At first, his boss protested and tried to convince Ronnie to purchase a brand-new bike. Tim had some in the back that were in good condition. He'd make him a deal. But Ronnie held firm. It had to be this bike. Tim was reluctant at first but eventually took it in the back and began to work on it.

Every so often, Ronnie walked into the workshop and viewed the progress. Tim took the whole bike apart piece by piece. Ronnie watched in awe as Tim greased the components and laid them out in a sort of ordered chaos. At one point, he saw Tim using a tube and pipe bender on the frame. As Ronnie collected an order of spark plugs, he saw his boss dismantling another bike for parts. Tim wore a look of intense concentration. While helping a woman pick out insecticides, Ronnie heard the distinct sound of the buffer machine from the back. After three hours, there was the sound of a small bell. It echoed around the warehouse. Ronnie and Sue Ellen exchanged glances and were greeted by the sight of Tim riding the bike into the front of the store. He rode up one aisle and down another. He was smiling hugely and parked in front of the cash register. Ronnie walked up and stared wide eyed at the bike. It looked brand new. Tim flicked open the kickstand and stood back with arms extended.

"Well, what do you think?" he asked.

"It looks brand new," Ronnie said with enthusiasm.

"A lot of it is new. I took parts from other bikes. I couldn't do anything with the old, rotted seat. Now it rides like a dream."

"It looks pretty," said Sue Ellen, who glanced at the bike and returned to her magazine.

"It's great," said Ronnie.

"I'm glad you like it," said Tim. He turned to Sue Ellen. "Ring him up one hundred bucks for parts and labor."

Sue Ellen clicked the register without looking. The drawer slid open and she held out her hand. Her eyes never left the page.

"More than that, Tim," Ronnie said hesitatingly. "You spent a lot of time on it."

"I know, but it's in house. I won't take a penny more."

Ronnie handed the money to Sue Ellen. She put the bills in the drawer and slammed it home. Tim patted Ronnie on the back and started towards his office.

"Tim," Ronnie called out. "Can I head out early today? I want to give it to the little girl when she gets home from school."

"Absolutely," Tim said and waved his hand.

Ronnie watched the clock. At two thirty, he wandered to the back and said goodbye and thanks to Tim. Then he drove to the Palms with his surprise in tow. He couldn't stop smiling.

Chapter 8

Mary wandered through the school cautiously. The time between classes was torturous and she navigated the halls as discreetly as possible, wanting to blend in with the paint or just disappear. Certain hallways she avoided altogether, dangerous places where her bullies always congregated.

She thought about Mr. Ronnie, how kind he was, and the wise words he shared. It heartened her and she wasn't as afraid. As Mary walked to class, an ugly boy barked at her while his friends howled in laughter. The words of her neighbor echoed in her mind and she hurried along. She'd long stopped going to the playground for recess and instead sat in the library reading various books or magazines. They took her to a different world where mean children didn't exist. Without a doubt, though, lunch was the closest thing to hell without getting burned.

Mary wandered into the large cafeteria and walked with her head down over to the free lunch line. There were two entrances to get food. One carried the fare of chicken nuggets, pizza, hamburgers, and French fries. These for students to purchase. The other was for the poor kids who received a tray of questionable meat, greasy vegetables, and a thin slice of white bread. Mary collected her lunch and a small glass of punch and sat at an empty table. Other kids walked past and stared at her sitting all alone. They avoided her table like she had a contagious disease. Mary picked at her food and pushed it around the little plate. It looked like someone had thrown up on her plate. The food smelled vaguely like her refrigerator at home, but warm.

The table across from her was full of rowdy older boys. She heard them shout about the incomprehensible size of their gorged members and other sexual swears that they only vaguely grasped. The boys spoke of things that she had no imagination to understand. After a while, something shifted in the air and their attention turned to her. They shouted lewd and rude phrases that she struggled to comprehend—acts that her family engaged in that her mind knew but didn't want to recognize. Mary stared down at her plate and strained to keep from crying.

Suddenly, two shadows appeared on her table. She looked up and saw a pair of mean-looking bullies staring at her. They both were smiling and kept turning around to laugh with their tablemates across the way. All the boys were turned and faced her. All of them grinning like half-wits. It was like a show. The audience was raptly anticipating the next move.

A tall toothy blond boy spoke. "So, what kinda dog food you eating today, mongrel?" The other boy was slapping his knee and grinning while the other boys erupted in a fit of laughter. He'd practically screamed those words.

Mary glared at him. "I know what that word means." Her eyes were fiery.

"Good doggie," the other boy said, doubling over.

"Go away," Mary said forcefully.

"No," said the blond boy. "Don't talk until I say so. Stupid mongrel thinks she's got the right." He was no longer smiling. "I've got to ask you a question." He turned as if addressing the room at large. "Which part of you is the nigger? Is mommy the nigger or daddy the nigger?" The blond kid wasn't laughing. He was staring at her with pure meanness in his eyes. "I bet the bitch is the nigger." The table of boys were falling out of their chairs. They slapped each other on the back and guffawed like a troupe of imbecilic monkeys.

Mary looked around and noticed that practically the whole cafeteria was watching the spectacle. It was preternaturally quiet. Students even quit chewing their food. Mary gripped the plastic glass of fruit punch tightly. Her knuckles were white and her arm was rigid and tense. She looked down at her pathetic food tray, which was a bleached grayish metal. Something welled up inside her. It was rage. She didn't know where it came from.

Mary took the cup of red punch and tossed the contents at the blond boy's crotch. The juice splashed all along the front of his pants. The blond boy stared wide eyed at himself while his dopey friend started laughing uncontrollably and pointing. The growing dampness flowered all across the front and down towards his knees.

Just as the blond boy was about to hurl abuse at Mary, his friend grabbed him by the shoulder and twisted him around. Mary saw him cross his hands over his crotch. The whole place erupted in laughter.

"Look, everyone," shouted the other boy. "The mongrel made Jacob piss himself!"

Students were standing up in their chairs and everyone was laughing. The table of boys were howling like animals. One fell out of his chair. The blond-haired boy screamed and beseeched his classmates to listen. It was only juice, but his cries were drowned out by uproarious laughter. The blond bully turned on his heels and sprinted out of the cafeteria. He was pleading for understanding and cried the whole way out the door.

Mary got up quietly and left through the side door. She wandered to the back of the school. No one was around and she found a small shade tree. Mary plopped down hard on the ground and sobbed uncontrollably. Her heart was heavy. Seeing that mean boy cry was both satisfying and heartbreaking. Mary was uncomfortable with the fact that it made her feel good. That bully was mean, but it didn't make what she did okay. It wasn't right. She never wanted to upset anybody. All she wanted was to be left alone. Why was that too much to ask?

A bell sounded in the distance marking the end of lunch. Doors opened and students wandered the grounds. Mary felt a fresh wind. She got up and went to class.

The rest of the day breezed by. She didn't see the bully again, but people left her alone. No one yelled mean things to her or laughed at her. She passed a group of boys who normally teased her relentlessly. They just stood and stared. There was a cold aura about them, and it made her uneasy. At the end of the day, Mary gathered her things and raced out of the school.

She was the first to her bus. She went all the way to the back and sat very small against the window, praying that no one saw her. Eventually, the bus filled. No one said anything or bothered her. Several kids turned around and watched her but didn't say a word.

The school bus rumbled to life. The windows were down and the wind blew away the trapped wet Florida heat. Beads of sweat on Mary's forehead cooled with the air. Mary looked out the window and saw small birds pinwheeling in the crystal blue sky against the backdrop of the sun. She felt the lumbering bus bounce over holes in the road. The cheap metal roof shaking noisily overhead. She placed her head on the cool glass of the window and watched the world pass. Trees, fields, and houses slipped past that were blurred and conjoined along the landscape. Ahead, she saw the entrance for the Palms. Mary breathed heavily and stood. She made her way down the aisle and saw every face watching her. They looked at her like she was of a different species. It made her uncomfortable and embarrassed. Mary hurriedly stepped off the yellow bus.

Walking down the pockmarked streets, Mary felt safe. She passed a group of men lounging in ratty lawn chairs passing a bottle. They waved and smiled at her. A pair of mockingbirds sat on a wire and chittered. Heat radiated off the blacktop, and Mary quickened her pace. There was an illusion of sudden haste and she was unsure where it came from.

Tentative chords of music played somewhere and it warmed something within her. She continued down the main road and finally reached her street. Mary looked down the drive and her heart surged. Ronnie was sitting on the back of his truck's tailgate. He waved and Mary started to run.

Mary's shoes slapped along the concrete. Her bookbag bounced and slid atop her shoulder. Mary noted his happy patience. She saw Ronnie step down from the tail gate and move around the side of the truck. He seemed unhurried. There was a giddiness about him that excited her. Mary extended her arms. She wanted a hug. Ronnie was smiling hugely and he held up a hand to stop her progress.

"Stay there, Mary," he said jovially. "I have a surprise for you."

Her eyes lit up. She couldn't remember the last time something like this happened. "Okay, Mr. Ronnie."

"Close your eyes."

Mary shut her eyes tightly. She was squinting and her nose scrunched tightly. She didn't dare look. A rolling commotion tempted her—a metallic clicking that she couldn't place. The noise stopped in front of her.

"Okay, you can look."

Mary opened her eyes and saw the pink bike from her yard. The broken bicycle that one of her mom's boyfriends brought home smashed and destroyed. He swore he'd fix it, but it laid to rot. That boyfriend was gone and replaced by others who left it as before. Mary had long given up on learning to ride. Now, she stared at the bike in its newfound glory. She ran her fingers over the handlebars and seat with an uneasy gentleness, as if it might collapse into pieces with her touch. Tears came to her eyes and warmth flushed her cheeks. She felt something foreign and joyous in her heart that bubbled like a wellspring. Mary bobbed up and down on her tip-toes.

"Well, what do you think?" Ronnie asked.

"I love it. You say it's for me?"

"Absolutely."

"What do I have to give?"

"Not a thing in the world. A girl needs a bike."

Mary hesitated. She didn't know how to broach the subject.

"Everything all right?" Ronnie touched her shoulder.

"Yes, sir, I think so." She looked around to make sure no one was in earshot. Mary leaned in close and Ronnie dipped his head. "I don't know how to ride," she whispered loudly. Mary saw Ronnie purse his lips and her heart sank.

"Well, guess what?" Ronnie said.

"What?"

"This bike comes with free lessons."

Mary smiled and hugged Ronnie around the waist. "Thank you, Mr. Ronnie."

"No problem at all," he said. He pointed to the seat and she climbed on.

She put both feet on the pedals and stayed upright. Ronnie stood behind her, holding the seat. He told her about balance and pushed her slowly along the street. She didn't pedal, but let it coast. Then, Ronnie taught her how to steer. He ran alongside her with a hand on the seat and followed her as she circled down the street. His steps locked in sync with hers. Next, Ronnie taught her about pedaling and stopping. She wobbled a little, but he held her upright.

Mary's confidence grew. She was getting better at steadying and stabilizing the bike. She rotated the pedals and picked up speed. There were times Ronnie wasn't holding onto the seat at all and just followed her closely. She worked on turning the bike and felt comfortable with the balance. It wasn't before long that Mary was riding up and down the street without his help. With each pedal, she felt a joyousness that was beyond her comprehension. Now and again, she glanced over at Ronnie, who stood beaming from his driveway. She tested her speed and turned with greater accuracy. Mary wasn't wobbling anymore. She noted the family across the street on their porch, watching her ride. The little boy stood in shocked amazement. Like he'd heard of it, but had never seen a bike ridden before. Mary pedaled down to the end of the road and back. The wind and her speed whipped her hair across her face. It was warm and she felt sweat bead across her forehead. She felt like she was under a canopy of wet heat, but she didn't care. Mary pedaled harder until she was red-faced and breathing heavy.

She saw Joe crouched on the trailer porch watching her over the railing like a spy. When she passed by again, he was gone. Mary kept circling and came back around to find Ronnie sitting on the tailgate of his truck, tuning a guitar. It made strange noises and he kept fiddling with knobs on the headstock. It looked battered and ancient. It was scratched and worn along the body. The polish was gone where his hands went. Ronnie was strumming it softly as she pulled over to a stop.

"What'cha doing, Mr. Ronnie?"

He jumped a little at her approach then smiled down at her. "I'm messing around with my old guitar."

"Wow," she said. "I didn't know you played. Where did you learn?" Mary was straddling the bike and holding it expertly between her legs.

"I learned where I was living before. Took me a while, but I got the hang of it."

"Sorta like riding a bike."

Ronnie chuckled. "Yes, but not as quickly as you learned."

"Will you play something for me?"

"Absolutely, what do you want to hear?"

"I dunno."

"Okay, well, I know a song titled 'Mary.' Would that work? It's by an Irish band."

"Sure," she said with hesitation. "What does Irish mean?"

"It means they are from the country of Ireland."

"Is that far?"

"Very," he said. Ronnie fiddled with the knobs again. He clinched his fists and released. He began playing and to her it sounded great. Mary bobbed her head slightly to the music. It sounded enormous and she watched his fingers dance along the neck, while his other hand stroked the strings. Ronnie's eyes were closed.

Mary used her shirt to mop the sweat from her neck. She noticed movement and saw a collection of children hiding in the tall grass watching intently. They wore solemn looks on their dirty faces. Mary held a hand up to block the glare of the sun. It sat low in the west and surrounded Ronnie. It was sliding into faint traces of indigo along the edges. From her perspective, he looked like some celestial being descending from heaven, except playing a guitar instead of a harp. She listened to him play and then he started to sing "Mary."

She didn't understand a lot of the words but enjoyed the music. He kept playing and sang with his eyes closed. There was an intensity in his voice and a serious look on his face. When he finished, she asked him to play it again. And again after that. Ronnie was sweating now and it dripped off his nose onto the concrete below. It quickly evaporated and left only a faint stain. The shadows of the trailers grew as the sun descended. The sky turned the color of burnt orange. The glob-like sun dripped away. Mary watched Ronnie set the guitar down. He was breathing heavily. She'd not moved the whole time. He took out a pack of cigarettes and lit one.

The blue smoke he exhaled danced in the breeze and was gone. There was a glint of sadness in his eyes. Like the guitar was both soothing but also an augury of something else. She couldn't tell what. Ronnie looked off in the distance and didn't seem to recognize her presence. As if, he was peering and searching for a thing unknown. Whatever it was, he gave it reverence.

Everything was silent. Mary didn't move. Then she heard the sound of squealing tires on a curb. The cry of a motor straining and rattling painfully. A green jalopy turned onto the street. It made the noises of a doomed animal that needed to be shot. Loud music clattered the already suspect automobile. Parts of the car looked like they were held together by some string. It pulled up to Mary's trailer and the brakes howled piercingly. Mary covered her ears against the cry. She snuck around the side of the truck.

Ronnie watched the car. He placed his hand on her head to reassure her that everything was alright. She didn't like those men. They were scary and mean. She always felt uncomfortable with the way they stared at her. As if she was something they wanted to carry away. Mary looked up at Ronnie and noticed that his expression had changed. He had transformed from the caring old man to a guardian.

She bent down out of sight and her legs began to cramp. She heard them scream something unintelligible. Joe's voice echoed in return. There was shouting back and forth. The yells didn't sound like an argument, but the voices were tinged with restive violence. A dog started howling at the noise. Others answered until the yapping was general. The chorus of dogs barking spread throughout the trailer park. Someone in the distance hollered for them to hush. This only encouraged them to cry out with greater invective.

Ronnie got down from the truck and walked around to Mary. He held her tightly and whispered softly. He asked if she wanted him to order a pizza and she nodded. Ronnie pointed and she started for his trailer. Mary was slow at first, but quickened her pace. Something was wrong. The very environment seemed sinister. As if, the very dirt and rocks spawned the sense of unease. She practically jumped the steps up onto the porch. Mary was wide-eyed in her retreat. She turned around and saw Ronnie carrying the bike over his shoulder. He looked like some sort of knight hauling forth a prize. He set it down next to the front door and went back for the guitar. She stood watching him from the doorway. He kept looking over at her trailer.

One of the men yelled something to Ronnie that Mary couldn't hear. He waved and kept going. His face was bloodred and his mouth was taut. There was a hint of recognition and shame on his face. Twilight appeared far to the east. The lunar world beyond was frightening, but, here, Mary was safe. She watched Ronnie enter. He looked occupied. Upon seeing her, he smiled. Mary instantly felt better. She sat down on the comfy sofa and watched him. He set the guitar in the corner and went over to the phone. He was whistling softly and Mary joined him. He rummaged through a drawer and brought out several brochures for pizza delivery places. He flipped through each and held them up for Mary to choose from. She pointed to the Godfather's Pizza coupon.

"Hooray," Ronnie said. "That's my favorite. What kind do you want?"

"Pepperoni, please, Mr. Ronnie." He gave her the thumbs up and dialed.

Chapter 9

Something burned inside Clara like molten lava and spoke in hushed tones. She had to get away. She fled the motel with a fierce urge to use. Yet a terror set deep in her bones had forced her to flush the meth baggie and all. Clara pulled out of the motel parking lot and drove towards downtown Pensacola.

The guardrails on either side of the coastal highway were pockmarked and bent in certain points where wayward drivers had beat them brittle. Places that looked like crushed cans where folks met with death. She tasted something metallic set deep in the back of her teeth. Spasms of phantom pains raced up her spine at a deliberate pace, like a tone set to music. She was trying not to use today, but the lingering urge kept up the mental obsession. How did others keep the monsters at bay? She needed a long line of meth to take her away. Make her feel normal.

She passed waving dunes of white sand on her right. Beyond was the vastness of the Gulf, at times a beauty without measure. With withdrawal taking over, Clara imagined stripping naked and wading out into the cool surf. Letting the endless tide take her away. Like a great anti-baptism that wrought none of the forgiveness. Instead stole her and allowed the eternal darkness to settle. Peace, finally, anointed in death.

She watched scavenger birds ahead dissect and devour a rotted and crushed thing along the side of the road. They whipped and took flight at her passing but soon returned to gorge some more.

She had to go to someplace where her mind could shut off. Quit twirling and beckoning the bad. Clara pondered what sobriety might look like. What form it might take. She'd fled work without telling anyone where she'd gone. She stared ahead as she neared the outskirts of Pensacola. Gas stations and pawn shops fleetingly caught her eyes. She drove like someone caught inside a dream and without any semblance of control. There was a glimmer of reassurance when she mechanically slowed and took two lefts and a right and pulled into the parking lot of her old high school.

A large sign out front read *Sign Up for GED Classes*. Pulling into a visitor parking space, Clara pondered why she was there. In the back of her mind, she'd always thought about taking the equivalency exam and getting away from Joe. Breaking from the cycle of her addiction and taking Mary to a safer place. Using the GED as a stepping stone for better things. Who knows, maybe even attending a community college. Yet, she knew that was beyond the pale. Still, it didn't hurt to dream.

Resting her head against the steering wheel, Clara imagined a multitude of possibilities. Her heart raced with giddy anticipation and painful withdrawal. She needed to get high and she felt a wave of nausea sweep over her. She swallowed several times to keep the bile from swift evacuation. The bitter taste sat on the back of her tongue. Finally, she shut off the engine and wiped the sweat from her palms. Now or never, she thought. She walked towards the school's entrance.

A pack of girls huddled near the door whispered and laughed as Clara approached. Each turned to watch and snigger at the strung-out maid. The spectacle thrust her back to long ago when she hugged the hallways and prayed for invisibility. The relentless teasing that drove her away from school and into the welcoming arms of addiction. A flash of that terrible vision passed through Clara's mind. Gaggles of girls throwing trash in her face as Clara rushed to her next class. Even teachers joining in on the fun. Clara pinched herself hard to drive the vision away.

Her pace quickened as she entered the high school. It was much like she'd remembered. A few minor changes, yet mostly it had stayed the same. She noted a surge of fear travel up her spine. Trophies from bygone eras sat austere behind glass. Pictures of athletes who were now long past glory days. She smelled the ghost of old perfume that hinted of ancient troubles. The stench of bullies. To the right was the administrative office. She quietly crept towards the door. A steady chomping sound from her grinding teeth followed each footstep.

There was a woman with enormous glasses sitting behind a tall desk. Clara's appearance did not stir the woman from the magazine she held. Clara all but crept up towards the woman. Finally, there, she waited with her hands behind her back. The woman still hadn't noticed the outlander until Clara cleared her throat.

The receptionist looked up and, for a moment, stared bug eyed at this drug addicted interloper. The heavy-set woman frowned at Clara like she was someone beneath her and it would always be so. Not even a feigned look of respect. Just a baleful stare with cold and contemptuous eyes.

"What do you need?" the woman asked.

There was a pause. Clara felt like she couldn't speak. As if someone filled her mouth with cotton. She swallowed several times and finally croaked, "I'd like information on getting my GED. Do you have that here?"

A bizarre smile crossed the woman's face. Almost like someone stifling a laugh. She looked Clara up and down. Perhaps she saw the strung-out look of a junkie and was pondering her next move. Then, something strange happened. The woman's countenance changed. Morphed into someone genuinely trying to help. Perhaps seeing something that Clara couldn't. The woman opened a drawer of her desk and brought out a stack of papers. She started to lay them out of the desk.

"Sure, just let me get ye a packet ready."

Clara took an awkward step back and watched the woman closely. She feared it might be a trick of some kind. Instead, the woman stapled a stack of papers and placed them inside a school folder. She smiled and held it out for Clara to take.

"This is all the information. You can take the test twice a year. We have preparation classes here two nights a week, or you can sign up for ones at Coastline Community College."

Clara clutched the packet to her chest and nodded.

"But, I'd encourage you to take them here, because they are free. We also provide the study books for you to use. At CCC, you have to pay a small fee." She tapped her fingers on the desk. "You can also try and take the test without the class, but I wouldn't encourage you to take that route. The test can be hard if you haven't been in school for some time. When were you in high school?"

Clara looked down at her feet. "It's been some time. I left after my freshman year. I attended here."

The woman smiled. "That's okay. We are here to help. It's important to get some type of qualifications. When do you plan on taking the test?"

"Oh gosh, I dunno. I just wanted to get some information…"

"I encourage you to think long and hard about it. You never know what good might come of it. Getting your GED could change your life."

A strange realization flashed across Clara's mind. For these few short minutes, she hadn't thought about the withdrawals. She'd not wanted to use. There was something akin to excitement in her life. Prospects of something better. She thanked the woman and left the office.

The sun was starting to set outside and the girls were gone. The parking lot was nearly empty but for a few cars. Clara looked down and saw that she was still clutching the packet of papers hard against her chest. Her knuckles were white. She released her grip and hustled to the car.

Sadly, once inside the car, her addictive yearning returned.

Clara pulled out of the parking lot and returned to the coast road headed towards the Palms. The withdrawal set her teeth to grinding, and enameled bits crumbled on her tongue. She spat the powdered crumbs into the floorboard. She watched the ocean and the curves of the swells. The rising and falling of the greenish water breaking along the beach.

Clara cruised along just under the speed limit. She thought about Mary and her uncertain future. Her mind flashed with daydreams of escape. Taking her daughter and driving away. Across the state and country. Settling in California. Far away from all this. No more drugs or prostitution.

Yet, she was disheartened. The idea was so ludicrous that Clara felt silly for dreaming it up. It felt nice to hope for, so she sat with the fantasy the whole ride home.

Clara turned into the Palms. She continued down the main thoroughfare and regarded the familiarity all around. The residents were like animatronics so regimented was their schedule of slovenliness. There was a sort of comfort in that. The sameness was like a warm cloak.

Her car made an unnatural sound as she turned onto her street. It bucked and sputtered but kept going. Steam billowed from the gaps in the hood. Every single light blinked on the dash like a Christmas tree. Finally, the car died and she coasted behind the ratty vehicle parked in front of her trailer and came to a stop.

Clara grabbed her purse and got out of the car. It stank like burnt rubber and something else. It was a smell she couldn't place. All she knew was that it wasn't good. The smoke was black and acrid.

I'll never hear the end of it from Joe, she thought. Her only mode of transport was now echoing a metallic, clanking death rattle that reverberated down the street.

Suddenly, her trailer's porch light turned on and Joe appeared in the doorway. He looked bad even in the fading light. He'd scratched open the sores on his face. He was shirtless and his crude and ill-placed tattoos looked just as ridiculous from this vantage point. His eyes skittered about at everything but her. Looking around like some petrified little creature in a world full of terrors. Joe held his hands up and swore. He balled his hand into a threatening fist. Clara ran up the gravel drive and went into the trailer.

The white meth smoke hung thickly throughout the sitting room. You could cut it with a knife. Clara coughed and her eyes burned. Joe, his supplier, and an enormous stranger sat on the couch facing the little television.

The newcomer glared at her body lustfully. He wore two teardrops tattooed on his face. She could smell the trouble. The supplier was wearing sunglasses and appeared rail thin. He looked like spandex filled with wire hangers. A manikin of bones inside loose fitting clothes. Their faces looked wasted and thin. Skin pockmarked with sores and wrinkled to look like paper. Overall, they were a motley collection stacked together like sardines.

On the little table was a large sandwich bag full of meth. A small pile of crystals was on a mirror next to a blackened glass pipe.

"Gimme the money," Joe said with his hand out.

Clara reached into her little purse and handed over the wad of folded cash. He never even looked at her. Joe was counting and the other two watched him intently, almost salivating.

"Where's Mary?" Clara asked.

"Over with the killer," Joe said with a stupid, sly smile.

Clara was confused. Did he mean Ronnie? Startled, she asked, "What?"

"I'll tell you after."

"After what?"

The supplier spoke up. "Ole Poopsie here just got out of the pen." He nodded at the large man next to him.

"And you're going to fuck him," Joe said, pointing to the bedroom.

"A welcome home gift." The supplier cackled.

The humongous man rose and licked his lips. He was already erect and his crotch was swollen and bulging. He was rubbing himself violently. The man watched her like something inanimate. A tool of some sort. No humanity in those evil looking eyes.

Joe snapped his fingers. Clara tentatively walked to the bedroom. Poopsie came up behind her and grabbed her painfully. His hands were like mitts. He pulled her dress up and she felt his crooked and calloused fingertips. Inside the bedroom, he turned on the light and pulled off her dress. She stood naked and trembling before this giant of a man. He roughly grasped her shoulders and forced her to the ground. Her already rug burned knees felt on fire. He abused her in every way possible. He used no protection and tossed her around the room like a doll. When he was done, he threw her over the bed and Clara's head hit the thin metal wall. It dinged loudly and the man guffawed.

"You liked that, didn't you, whore," he man said while gasping for breath. "Good little skank bitch. You should be proud."

Clara didn't respond at first. The pain inside her was so intense that her crotch felt like something cooking. Some sort of new disease communicated instantaneously. His filth was splayed all over her. He tossed her a filthy shirt.

"Wipe me off you," he said.

Clara did as she was told. He stood watching her as before. She cleaned herself and put back on the black dress. It slid over her and she felt safe.

"You knew Ronnie, my neighbor?"

"Oh yeah. We were in the same wing at Marion Correctional." He smiled strangely. "He was in for murder. Killed a boy with his bare hands." Poopsie sat on the bed. "They said he was a badass in his younger years, but he'd calmed down when I got there. Mostly kept to himself." He licked his lips. "But you got a killer next door."

Poopsie stood and grabbed her by the hair. He occupied an enormous space in that little room. The man was a vulture in human form. "One more go and you can get." He spoke slowly and with conviction.

Clara tried to push his hand away. He pulled back her head and glared into her eyes. His were hollow and vapid. The sight of them made her shudder. A coldness almost unbearable. She felt her pulse beating in the veins of her neck.

"Don't do that, bitch," he said as he slapped her arms away. "I've tried to be nice. You are bought and paid for."

Clara tried to speak, but he pulled harder. Her eyes were looking at the chipped and ruined ceiling.

"I was supposed to beat the shit out of your boyfriend. He's been using more than selling. Teach his dumb ass a lesson. You're the only reason his arms aren't broke. So be grateful, you stupid bitch."

A single tear ran down the side of her face.

"Now, take that dress off before I rip it."

She did as she was told.

A short time later, Clara hobbled across her yard towards Ronnie's trailer. The lights were blazing on his porch and it was full dark outside. She struggled with each step and shockwaves of pain traveled up her spine. Her whole concentration was on his front door. She needed relief.

After Poopsie, she'd smoked meth, and her head felt scattered into a million little pieces. A world of order that the drug reversed. Like watching something through old and warped glass. She trudged on with watery vision. Her jaw felt funny and she unhinged it with a great deal of effort. There was a snapping sound in her ear. She was barefoot and didn't notice until the sharp pain of glass burned her big toe. Clara picked up her foot, pried the glass out, and tossed it away. Her tiny spindle legs kept going with one foot in front of the other. She remembered Joe and the supplier leering at her with amusement. Poopsie leaving the bedroom like some great victor. Yet, they all knew she didn't have a choice.

The air outside was clear and thin. The stars created a lovely ambiguity of promise. The constellations seemed to swarm amid the eventide. Whippoorwills called out, breaking up the silent night. Echoes from far away slowly diminished.

It gave Clara comfort to hear their song. The smoky moon was a cradled crescent in the east. She was a woman of chaos and mystery, yet the lunar light evoked a sense of symmetry that her life missed.

Her legs felt heavy. Her pace quickened as she moved from something sinister. She walked precariously around tiny trash obstacles. She looked between the trailers to a clearing and the darkness beyond. There was a faint light in the distance. It hung in the blackness with solemnity. Or, perhaps, it was apoplectic like the watcher.

Clara climbed the steps cautiously and saw the pink bike leaning against the railing. It looked new and nothing like the broken mess it once was. Clara shook her head. She'd known Ronnie for twenty-four hours and he'd done more for Mary than anyone else she could think of. She knocked on the door. A television played inside and she heard footsteps approach. Ronnie opened the door and smiled.

"Good evening, Clara. Come inside." He stepped back and she entered. The room smelled like pizza and Clara looked around for Mary. "She's in the bedroom. She fell asleep on the couch after supper and I carried her back there." He was whispering and had pizza sauce in the corners of his mouth.

Clara hugged him and walked towards the rear of the trailer. She cracked the door and the thin ray of light shone inside. Mary was sound asleep on the bed. Clara silently closed it.

"She's out," she whispered.

"Yeah," Ronnie said with a chuckle. "She wore herself out riding that bike."

"You taught her?"

"I sure did. But, she mostly picked it up on her own. Smart girl. I hope you don't mind that I fixed that bike up. It was a shame to see it going to waste."

"No, not at all. I'm glad you did." All of this was so strange. He was being nice and Clara was confused as to why. No one was this kind. He must have an ulterior motive. Something in return. Clara knew exactly what.

Ronnie was pointing to a box of pizza. He held the lid open, and Clara saw that half of the pepperoni pizza was gone. "Would you like a slice? Mary had two for her supper." He was laughing a little. "She scarfed them down. I was afraid they'd make her sick."

Clara shook her head and said no. She went over to the couch and Ronnie followed. He sat down in front of the television. She stood awkwardly in front of him. He watched her with a puzzled look, his head cocked to the side like a dog investigating a foreign sound. Clara knew this would hurt. Her crotch was already badly swollen. Even her own skin-to-skin contact ached. It didn't matter. She'd persevere. Clara reached up and took ahold of the shoulder straps from her dress and slid them off. The loose material slipped down her body to the floor.

She looked at Ronnie and saw him turn away. He held up his hand over his eyes in protest. Clara immediately felt ashamed and dirty. She covered herself and started to cry. She put her dress back on and was about to flee when Ronnie stood and gently took her by the elbow. She'd not really looked at him until now. There was a mixture of benevolence and understanding in his eyes. He smiled at her and held her hand. She walked with him over to the couch and sat down.

"Why are you being so nice to me? Nice to Mary?"

He seemed to study her query. "Because, it's the right thing to do."

"There is always more than that."

He nodded. "Also, I guess, because I missed out on so much with my own daughter. I've never even met her. Not once." He blinked several times and looked very sad.

"Your ex-wife never took her to visit you?"

"No." He exhaled. "I haven't seen her neither. Not since the trial."

Clara reached over and hugged his neck. She sat back and looked at him. This benevolent old man who was an antagonist in other men's tales. Ronnie turned sideways to face her. The television played softly and she heard Mary snoring. This made Clara laugh and it felt good. Ronnie joined with her.

Then, Clara got very serious. "They told me what you did to get sent to prison."

"Yeah, I figured Leonard might spill the beans."

"Leonard?"

"Yeah, that big ugly feller."

She chuckled. "They called him Poopsie."

"Good God." Ronnie started laughing in a whisper. "That fool is about as dumb as they come. He shot himself in the foot during a robbery. That's how come he got caught. Idiot left a bloody trail all the way to the hospital. The cops just followed him there."

Clara was covering her face. She'd not laughed this much in a long time. She swatted him playfully. "He said you were tough but calmed down later on."

"I guess that's fair." Ronnie smiled. "I was very angry when I first got locked up. I blamed everyone else for my incarceration but myself. I had an enormous chip on my shoulder and took it out on people around me. It was so stupid. I spent the first year plotting my escape. First thing I was going to do was kill the judge who handed down my sentence… He was just doing his job, but I felt I'd been wronged somehow. There wasn't a guard in that prison who I didn't try to fight. That includes the women." Ronnie sighed. "I guess that makes me tough. I don't know. I cried myself to sleep more times than I'd like to admit."

Clara held his hand and rubbed the back of it with her thumb. It was large and misshapen. There were scars from old wounds. They were wrinkled and disfigured. Almost like broken, deformed things put back together randomly. She spoke very softly. "Did you mean to kill that man?"

"No," he said. "I never meant to kill him. I was just drunk."

Ronnie turned away and stared at the floor. He wiggled his feet in an uncomfortable manner. The phosphorus glow of the television created a spectral light across the floor. She saw the hairs on his hand stand stiff, and Ronnie looked like he was shivering. He shook his head slowly. "I shouldn't say that."

"What?"

"Say that I was just drunk. It takes away from the enormity of what I did. Sorta tries to rationalize it. Or make excuses. The fact is that I killed a man. There's no other way to tell it. No other way to state what happened."

Ronnie kept speaking as if Clara wasn't in the room. Like he was spilling out his soul to a higher being and she just happened along as a spectator by accident. He spoke like a man imbued with a weighty burden. His words sounded like a benediction. His red eyes rapidly tracing something that wasn't there. As if he was reading a script against the wall. Clara watched him closely. She tried to discern what he was thinking.

"It only gets heavier," he said. "The weight of it." He pointed to his heart. "I think about it every day. I try to imagine what his life would've been like without me in it… He had a twin brother. I learned about it at the trial. I saw him walking in and nearly fell over. I saw this living version of the man I stole away. For a long time, I wondered if God planned this all along and so he made a spare. I know that's silly, but it made me wonder."

Ronnie shook his head. "Truthfully, I think about his family more than my own… I can't change what I done. But, maybe, I can do some good in this world yet. Prison changed me. It was good for me in a way. I don't know if that makes any sense."

"It does," Clara said.

He smiled at her. "Sorry to kinda unload all that on ye."

"It's perfectly fine. You have a good heart. It doesn't matter what happened in the past. Not you or anyone can change it. What matters is where you go from there."

Ronnie nodded. Outside there was whooping and hollering from next door. It sounded like mocking echoes from a madhouse. The hackles rose on the back of her neck. She and Ronnie were silent and listened reticently, each trying to puzzle together the intent. Wind from off the Gulf picked up, and the trailer creaked faintly, moving slightly back and forth by the tentacle-like ocean gales from far away.

Next door, it sounded like a fight was set to commence. Clara's heart sank. Then, just as the bickering reached its apogee, there was the unmistakable roar of laughter and whimsy. Madness and self-loathing hilariously intertwined. Their meth-induced rage subsided and Clara heard the group reenter the trailer, Joe the loudest of them all.

Clara stood slowly. She dreaded the prospect of leaving Ronnie's trailer. Her skinny frame made a silhouette of shadow across his face. He looked up. Ronnie was watching her and was considering something. She knew it by the look he acquiesced. Then a smile spread across his face.

"Go on back there and sleep with Mary. I've got the couch," he said while patting the pillow. "No need for you to get back in that craziness tonight." His hands motioned vaguely towards her trailer. "They'll be carrying on all night."

"I don't want to put you out," Clara said.

"It won't. You'd be surprised how often I fall asleep here watching the television."

Clara noticed his eyes were heavy. She wasn't tired. The meth she smoked earlier electrified her mind. Though her body was weary. Everything still hurt. She bent down and kissed Ronnie on the forehead. There was a blanket across the back of the couch. Clara unfolded it and draped it across him. Ronnie mumbled thanks and goodnight. She smiled and recorded a mental snapshot of this old man sleeping. A stranger who showed her and Mary kindness with no ulterior motive. None of it made sense, but, thankfully, it didn't have to.

Clara walked back through the trailer to the bedroom. She heard little Mary breathing softly from under the covers. She kicked and whimpered in her sleep like a puppy. Clara reached to take off her dress but remembered she wore nothing underneath. She slid into the bed and pressed herself back-to-back against Mary. After a while, she heard loud snoring from the other room. It was labored and without rhythm. She looked out the window to the crystalline sky. The stars were plentiful and austere. The bright moon reflected a blue glow across the landscape. She saw it fade occasionally through the passing clouds. She watched as soundless wings passed over the pale orb. It rode low in the distance. The twilight evoking all but muted light. Clara thought she felt her blood pulse. She smiled with a suggestion of joy on her face. Here she was safe. With Ronnie to watch over them, everything felt right.

Chapter 10

A union of friendship blossomed. Not a day went by without contact. Ronnie changed his schedule at work to meet Mary at the bus stop after school. Each day, Ronnie made Mary her new favorite after school snack of fried bologna and cheese sandwiches. Old man and young girl always found something fun to do. He took Mary fishing and watched her ride the bike. They'd go to the ocean and walk along the surf with their pants rolled to the knee. Pretending to be protagonists in fairy tales with knights, princesses, and story book monsters. Or, making up games with bizarre rules and names that Mary always won. There, the gulf winds swirled her hair into wild bouffants that they both found amusing. He taught her how to play the guitar. He'd sit on the swing in the sunshine and listen to her pick away at the strings. Ronnie showed her the chords and bought her a little instructional booklet. Mary learned quickly. She was soon playing simple songs and making up her own.

Often, Victor would slur ad-libbed lyrics and dance crazily. They'd spend the afternoon together until Clara got home from her labor of men and cleaning. The maddening efficiency of selling herself and drawing a paycheck continued unabated. The repetitive false words of endearment lustfully shouted in her ear. Legs violently forced apart and pure regret entered.

Daydreaming of spectral landscapes to flee from the reality. Clara's work infused her into a world that she wanted nothing of, yet couldn't live without. She always came over to Ronnie's trailer and relaxed with a cold drink. Try and clean the taste of strange men from her mouth. Together Ronnie and Clara listened as Mary recounted her day. She seemed happier and more confident. A province of glad destinies. The other children had stopped bullying her after the lunchroom incident. Her anxiety was alleviated. Most important, Mary finally had found a best friend in Ronnie. She no longer felt distant and all alone.

Ronnie had found a family he'd never had. A little daughter much like he imagined all those years in the penitentiary. He remembered those countless nights staring at the irrevocable concrete and wishing he might will himself beyond the dungeon. Yet, the evocative beseeching for God never reached beyond the guard towers. Mechanistic accretions that eroded in the ether and died shortly after the moment of conception. This world incubated and full of things that you have no control over. Windless air in the tomb that perpetually stank of a milieu of filthy men and toxic bleach. That was now gone. Finally, Ronnie had what he prayed for those many nights. A plan that was based off more than the basic human contingencies. A reason to live that was outside of himself.

One night, while Mary was in bed, Ronnie and Clara sat on the porch relishing the autumn cool. A dusk immutable for the changing weather. Clouds passed unnoticed and thunder boomed faintly from off in the gulf. Ronnie rocked in the swing and enjoyed her company in the silent evening. But, he noticed that Clara was strung out and crashing. Four days without sleep and her body was nearly extinguished. Her eyelids quivered and hands trembled. Ronnie knew she was hurting, but was unsure if she wanted help. He'd learned that without admission any chance of breaking the covenant with addiction was impossible.

Now was the perfect time. Yet, in the end, Ronnie lacked the courage to speak. She might have no room for such heresy. He was too frightened that he'd lose them both by upsetting the status quo.

So, in the end, he watched as Clara struggled ahead in the wrong direction. Wandering down the erroneous path. All along were signs of warning that she missed or ignored.

Chapter 11

Ronnie cooked supper for Mary each night and Clara when she was home. They'd sit at his small laminate table and eat. Clara hardly ever touched her food. She pushed it around the plate. She looked strung out and in bad shape. This life was taking its toll. She often mumbled that she wasn't crazy, despite knowing that such denials spoken aloud were tell-tale signs of insanity. Her dim view of existence was provisional and deeply suspect. She feared good things because they always led to something bitter. There were times at dinner when she'd shake with tremors. Sweat beaded on Clara's forehead and it rolled down her forehead and stung her swollen eyes. Her heart raced uncontrollably. She hallucinated bobbing orbs and corpse candles waving in the air like spectral nightmares made real. Ethereal shapes of the dead floating translucent and whispering angelic words of murder and mayhem. A heightened sense of reality subtly deviated from the truth. Clara pretended like nothing was wrong even when she witnessed the sickness herself. Everything was shaded with a warped view. She felt vicious little spasms in her gut and waves of nausea wash over her.

Sometimes she sat in her drugged state and gave no acknowledgement of Mary nor Ronnie's existence. The whole known world dimly reflected out of her glassy and bloodshot eyes. Anything of importance was vanished and gone. She was haunted by shapes and shadows from which she found no respite. Some were meth induced terrors with no hold on reality. Yet, there were others where she wasn't entirely sure. Her mother, long dead, returned and whispered news more horrible than the worst Clara might possibly imagine. A future of desolation and signs of things to come. Making the realm of the living nothing she wanted any part of. Everything Clara believed was subtly altered into strange mysteries. All she knew as fact viewed with suspicion. Her mind playing tricks that ravaged her like a fever. She searched out meaning for what these terrors were and the purpose they served. The most troubling was that conversation, no matter how simple, seemed full of cryptic messages. She was a beat out of sync from the rest of humanity.

This was the curse of her condition.

Ronnie noticed and always tried to shield Mary from it. To fight the withdraws, Clara shut herself away from all she remembered. Often encroaching precariously close to the boundaries of hell. The ways of her existence were difficult at the best of times. Life, for her, was mostly all but unendurable. A series of ever increasing incidents of calamity. Little heretical things she believed were shattered and unadorned in her addicted mind. Everything was a new set of troubling events stacked one on top of the other. Soon, whatever was holding it would break. She was ill at ease and uncertain of what her next movements should be. Not just coming or going but the overarching narrative of her life. Something needed to change, but she was too scared and tired to meet it. Overall, a presage of doom followed Clara everywhere.

It was all a folly, she thought, and too late to turn back now. There were times she felt negated of this world and wished to vanish. Yet, those were only the malevolent embodiment of dreams she could never aspire to. She was fastidious in willing them away. Mostly, she feared her perception of sobriety. Apprehensive of any type of change. A self-imposed exile to an island all alone. Her yellow and cat like eyes never turning towards the lighthouse beacon that was abstinence. Despite the chaos of her life, there was a twisted kind of logic to all her actions.

Joe was seen less and less, but became more volatile. Often only showing up in a scrutinizing role. He watched everything with contempt through narrow and bloodshot eyes. Those windows to the soul were vapid and hollow. Evil things set in motion that couldn't be stopped. A growing sense of acrimony and resentment. Any sort of ostentatiously displayed jollity and cheer was meant to mock him. Yelling and vile threats permeated the night. His insanity was tantamount to inmates in an asylum. Almost anything induced blubbering howls of rage that echoed into a coronach or requiem for Clara's proverbial death march. Ronnie would take Mary inside and turn on the television. He tried to keep her interest and attention on anything else.

Joe was using more than selling. Smoking and injected the meth for more bang. Joe lived constantly in a world unfeatured and often wandered around unsure of where he was. Violence growing inside him that spread unfettered in his cruel heart. Face turning beet red at the slightest hint of indignity. The liquidity of his rage seeped into his blood stream. A malefic monster who grew more volatile by the day. Mean looking men showed up and demanded money. Clara was forced to sell herself almost every night.

Mary stayed over at Ronnie's trailer, while Clara prostituted. Doing whatever she could for more white powder. He let Mary have his bed and he slept on the couch. No more nights of sleeping rough in the car.

Clara's addiction still incubated much of her waking decisions. It was a terrible enterprise. To get more product, Joe morphed her into legal tender for suppliers. To keep from getting beaten, Joe threw Clara to the wolves. He was a malevolent interloper who was ruining her life one trick at a time. She did not fall, but her declination was apparent.

Chapter 12

The days turned cold. The sky darkened earlier and warm ocean winds were replaced by an infectious chill. Everything grew stonier and the clatter of the broken trailers never ceased. They moaned against the wind in a chorus of agony. Even the wild animals stayed away. During the third week of October, it rained nonstop. The storms in west Florida were events that happened suddenly. It was sunny then the air rank with rain and the tempest poured down. The sky was perpetually dark with the only slight differentiation being the blackness that night beheld. The gulf gales carried the water in sideways. The wind brought violent acceleration that bent the trees. Sometimes, the stinging rain even seemed to come up from the ground. It beaded the windows and covered everything. Windblown sheets of water would strike the trailer at once like concussive gunshots. Stepping outside for a few seconds left you wet all the way through. Eventually the pounding rain was so general that it seemed silent. You got used to the noise.

The park's poor drainage system blocked up and whole streets were deluged with trash and other bits of strewn awful. The water was clay colored and vast collections of everything bobbed in the swollen flood. On the last night of the storm, a maelstrom of riotous wind blew with such ferocity that the trailer shook violently. Mary huddled in the corner and cried. Ronnie cradled her in his arms and crooned soothing words. The next morning it was all over.

The sun shone brightly and the sky was crystal blue. The flooded streets were completely calm. An empty liquor bottle floated statically in the middle of their street. Streaks of oil and filthy foam collected in certain places. Across the street, the porch steps marched directly into an enormous pool and out of sight. The air was hot and steamy. It was the beginning of an Indian summer day. The weather station calculated that in seven days it had rained nineteen inches. Ronnie told Mary that he thought that number was too low.

Mary dreamt of horses. It was so vivid she almost smelled the wet mane and heard the grunts and chittering of the anticipatory and myth-laden colt. She rode a pale white horse that galloped across a vast plain. The sun beat down upon her neck and her hair danced crazily in the wind. She saw all of this from above. The horse cut and skittered like a bird. She stood up in the saddle and pushed her feet hard against the horse's flanks. It glided upon the vast range. She heard the hoofs beat rhythmically into the dirt. Mary leaned down and spoke into the horse's ear. It picked up speed and she rode on. Mary felt a freedom most profound. She rocked gently back and forth. Then, she heard her name.

"Mary. Good morning, Mary. It's time to wake up," she heard Ronnie say. She groaned a little in protest at the assailing sound. "I know," he said softly. "But, I've got a surprise for you."

Mary opened her eyes and smiled up at Ronnie. He had a cup of steaming coffee in his hands. The aroma of it filled the room. A bitter smell she'd grown accustomed to. She sat up and saw the rays of sunshine track across the bed. There were blades of light coming through the gaps in the blinds. She stared at them in amazement. Like sunshine was something only rumored about until now. She shot up and raced to the window. Her excitement was palpable. They could go trick-or-treating tonight.

She'd never before trick-or-treated on Halloween night. Her mother always worked, so she was never able to partake in the festivities. When Ronnie found out about this, he jumped at the opportunity to take her. They'd gone to Walmart and bought costumes. Mary had selected a witch's getup complete with a hat, fake nose, and little broomstick. For Ronnie, she had picked out a pirate's outfit that included a red bandana, a plastic sword, and an eye patch.

Mary hopped out of bed and ran down the hall. She ran out onto the wet porch in her socks. They became saturated, but she didn't care. She watched the flooded world and the vaporous mist rise in the sunshine. A collection of spume twirled slowly in the murk. Yellow bubbles eddied and swirled. The light burned fiercely in the sky as if making up for lost time. The heavens were clear and the sun was well up and shone enormously in the east. The air stank of mold and decay. It tickled her nose. The place looked of desolation, but, also, promise. She heard Ronnie's footsteps and he put his hand on her shoulder.

She looked up at him and saw concern. Her heart raced. There was a solemnity on his face. He leaned over with his elbows on the railing. Something felt empty in her gut. She envisioned the thing she cherished taken away.

"I've got some bad news, kiddo," he said. Mary put her head on the railing and groaned. She raised a soggy foot and lightly stamped the porch. "I know," he said. "But it can't be helped. We just can't go trick-or-treating here. We'd drown." Mary rolled her head side to side.

Then, she heard sniggering. Mary was about to admonish him for laughing at this grave injustice, when she saw him red faced. Ronnie covered his mouth. "We'll just have to go to someplace else." He was laughing now. Mary's whole countenance changed. "I have some places in mind. Does that sound good?"

She playfully slapped Ronnie on the arm. "That was mean."

He jostled her hair. "I know. I'm sorry. Go on and get ready for school. I'll have breakfast ready here in a minute."

Mary hurried back into the bedroom and took out her clothes from the little overnight bag stashed in the corner. She dressed quickly and combed her hair in the little closet door mirror. The humidity had already set it, so Mary gave up and put her hair in a ponytail. Before going for breakfast, Mary laid out her witch's costume on the bed. She looked it over with a growing excitement. She ran her hand gently over the outfit and beamed. She heard Ronnie holler something from the other room. He was sitting patiently at the table, waiting for her. She said she was sorry and hustled to her seat. In front of her was a fried egg, a piece of bacon, and toast lathered with butter. A bottle of grape jelly sat next to her glass of orange juice. Ronnie held out his hand and she squeezed it. After that short benediction, they started eating breakfast.

Ronnie said he'd drive her to the bus stop. She gathered her school bag and the sack lunch he prepared. Mary saw a funny sight when she exited the trailer. Ronnie was standing in the water with his pants rolled up to his knees. His boots were slung around his neck and tied together from the laces. She couldn't help but laugh. The water was pooled up past his ankles. He stood near the bottom step with his arms out.

"Your chariot awaits," he said and bowed slightly.

Mary approached and he scooped her up over his shoulder. He carried her around to the passenger side of the truck. A dead rat floated past and Mary screamed. Each step sounded guttural and a slushing sound accompanied his footfalls. Mud churned and waves radiated out across the street. The stillness broken and made alive. A bitter smelling rot attended the churned stagnant water. Mary held her nose tightly and breathed out of her mouth. The stench was so mighty that she tasted it on her tongue.

Ronnie set her in the passenger seat and walked back around. He got inside and smiled at Mary. He cranked up the truck and backed out of the driveway. She heard the great commotion of swirling muck in the wheel wells. She turned around and watched the coursing trail of receding rhythmic arches. She'd never seen anything like it before.

School sped by in a flash. Many of the kids wore their Halloween costumes, but Mary was glad she hadn't. There were witches of varying sorts. She critiqued them with caution. Looked upon them balefully. She was certain hers was the best. The lunchroom was electric with talk of hordes of candy and locations of treasure troves. Neighborhoods that gave out full sized candy bars and horrific localities where school supplies replaced treats. She sat and ate her lunch quietly. She was just happy to partake in the holiday.

Rarely did she get jealous of the other kids. Mary knew that she was poor and didn't have a father. It had always been that way. She didn't know a life that was any different. Yet, not being able to celebrate Halloween was always one of the few things that made her envious of other kids. It wasn't so much the free candy. It was the experience she craved. Dressing up and going door to door. Screaming trick-or-treat and racing to the next house. She'd peer from the trailer window and watch with solemnity as the other children traipsed around in their ghoulish or fool's regalia. Or, listen with jealousy as tales of the night's events were recounted at school the next day. So, Mary was beside herself with excitement. When the final bell tolled, she rushed out to the bus and sat in stirring anticipation. It was still muggy and humid, but Mary wasn't concerned.

Mary watched out the window as the bus chugged along. Everything looked spongy and wet. The distant woods seemed smoky with murk. The tires sprayed massive circular wheels of water up against the glass. The burning sun created mist that hung stationary above the blacktop. It created a haunted aura of menacing fog. When the bus drove through it, the steam swirled and vanished like an apparition. She saw three black ravens sitting on light wires scouting the bloated runnels for dead varmints. Sweat beaded on her forehead and she felt nervous for some reason. Something portentous that she couldn't place.

Ahead, she saw the sign for the Palms and Ronnie's truck parked across from the school bus stop. He waved enthusiastically. She noticed he was wearing his eye patch. She raced over and hopped in the cab.

"How was school?" he asked with a strange pirate accent.

"Great," she said, laughing. "How was work?"

"Boring. You ready to get ready?"

"Argh, matie," she said.

Ronnie raised an eyebrow. He gave her a cunning smile and put the truck in gear.

Mary rushed to the bedroom and slipped out of her school clothes. Her costume was on the bed just as she'd left it. She put on the black tights and black undershirt. Next came the witch's dress, which hung loosely with little strips on the sleeves and hem. These were outlined in orange, as was the belt and hat. Mary faced the mirror. She turned from side to side and admired herself. She carefully applied the fake nose and admitted to her reflection that it looked great. She held the broom up and struck several poses.

Mary could hear Ronnie in the kitchen cooking their usual after school snack of fried bologna sandwiches. When she appeared in the doorway, he jumped in pretend surprise. He let out a little yelp and Mary laughed. She sat down at the table and Ronnie handed her a plate of steaming bologna. Mary took two slices and put them on her bread. He took the mustard and drew a little smiley face on the meat before she closed the sandwich. She got a handful of chips and set them on the plate. Mary waited for him to sit down. Ronnie handed Mary a glass of grape punch and sat across from her. With slow grace, she reached across the table and clasped his hand. He reciprocated with a faint squeeze and lifted the sandwich from his plate.

Mary often watched him eat in amazement. He ate a lot and quickly. Almost like he was attacking his meal. She asked him once why he ate that way. Ronnie sat back and pondered her query for a time. Finally, he responded that, where he lived before, it was better to eat as much and as fast as you could. Or, you might go without. Mary couldn't fathom such a place but didn't broach the subject again.

He scarfed down three sandwiches and a plateful of chips. After, he watched Mary eat. What she didn't finish, Ronnie ate. She listened to Ronnie explain their plans. His boss was letting them park at his house and trick-or-treat in their neighborhood. He explained that it was enormous. They'd trick-or-treat until nine o'clock.

With the pale sun drifting slowly downward, they prepared to embark. Mary had a little orange plastic jack-o-lantern to hold her candy. Ronnie was dressed in his pirate's costume and carried a flashlight. Mary's nose kept falling off, so

Ronnie took pliers and tightened the clamps. She stood in front of the mirror and laughed. The nose was a different color than herself. He told her that it didn't matter. It would be dark and no one would notice. This satisfied her. Standing before their reflection, Ronnie took a disposable camera and snapped their picture.

They waited on the front porch for Mary's mother to get home from work. She wanted to show her mother their outfits. In the meantime, Mary picked away at the guitar and Ronnie sat watching the road. The water was receding leisurely. She noticed that Ronnie looked strangely noble in his pirate outfit. Like he was a real swashbuckling raider from stories she'd read. She watched a blue tailed lizard run across the deck and over his feet. Bugs droned noisily over the stagnant water. There were laughter and distant voices from several streets over. The kids from the Palms were beginning their trek. Mary's heart sank. Her mother wasn't coming.

Ronnie stood up and touched her shoulder. "You ready, kiddo?"

Mary nodded and stood. "I reckon Momma ain't gonna make it."

He shook his head. "We'll see her tonight after our big catch." He let out a laugh. "You'll have so much candy that you'll pop if you try and eat it all."

Ronnie carried her to the truck and got in the driver's seat. He cranked it up and they drove away. She watched children running to different trailers with water almost to their knees. Most wore costumes of their own making. She looked down at hers and felt bad. He'd paid for it and she forgot to say thank you.

"Thank you for the costume and for taking me tonight. It means a lot."

Ronnie smiled at her. "It's no problem at all. I never went trick-or-treating either. So, this is a first for me as well."

"Why not?"

"It wasn't really a thing when I was growing up. Some kids might've, but I never even heard of it."

Mary chewed her bottom lip. "Mr. Ronnie, why are you so nice to me?"

This question seemed to take him aback. He watched the road with concentration. "I never had a father either," he said. "Well, I did in a way. He died before I was born. He was killed during World War II. I never met him, nor him me." The truck made a pneumatic hiss as he turned onto the coastal highway. "My mother never remarried, but my father's ghost was ever present." Mary's eyes widened. "Not a 'boo' ghost, but she mentioned him all the time. Like he was really there. Or, just away on a trip and would return at any moment. My mother was sixteen when she got married. Seventeen when she had my sister and eighteen with me. She was just a kid when she was widowed. Her life was hard. Whenever I was bad, she'd mention my father and how disappointed he'd be. It hurt me to hear her say that. It gave me unreal expectations of what it meant to be a man. I needed someone tangible to set me on the right path. A real person. Anyone would have done, but she never allowed it. It was always, 'your father' this and 'your father' that. My mother even talked to a big old picture of him she had in the sitting room." He paused his soliloquy. "I don't want to see that happen to you. Does that make sense?"

"Yes," she said. "I'm glad you're my friend."

"Me too, darling. Me too." Ronnie slowed the truck and approached a long red brick wall. "Yonder it is," he said with a smile.

The neighborhood was guarded by a huge brick wall that ran the full length of the road. Mary sat up in the truck and saw the enormous roofs rising from houses several stories high. The fence was vermiculate and coasted like a never-ending wave. The movement of it was like something from another dimension. The bricks were a dull red, but looked well kept. Mary saw her mouth gaping in the reflection of the truck window.

The entrance to the neighborhood was gated and Ronnie spoke to the guard who let them through. He slipped on his eye patch and made a pirate noise.

The size of the houses nearly took Mary's breath. They were the size of several trailers stacked on top of each other. She saw a bluebird skim the road ahead and fly away. Felled leaves blew in loose swirls over the blacktop. The homes were brightly lit in the fading twilight. Children scurried with parents following behind. No one dared cross over the grass.

She'd remember that.

Ronnie made several turns and Mary lost her bearings. He knew where to go and she was shocked by the enormity of the neighborhood. After a time, Ronnie pulled into the driveway of a huge house. The front looked like something out of a magazine. There were short palms strategically placed and the grass was well manicured. Ronnie parked the truck around back and they exited the truck. The garage doors were closed and she heard a dog barking from within. A man appeared on the back porch and waved. Ronnie raised a hand and hollered a greeting. He switched on the flashlight and turned to Mary. "You ready, darling?"

"You bet," she said excitedly.

"All right," he said while setting off down the driveway. "Don't forget what I told you. Always say thank you. Right?"

"Yes, sir."

Children's laughter and voices trailed through the air. Mary looked into the darkening sky and saw a shooting star.

She pointed for Ronnie, but it was gone. There was not a cloud in sight. The night turned black beyond darkness. There was no chill. Ronnie began whistling and Mary joined him. His flashlight and those of other parents bobbed along as if carried by ghosts. The beams of light playing across the walkways with minds of their own. Children with masked and painted faces raced by.

As they went house to house, Mary felt like a pilgrim wandering in a strange land. The homes were enormous and the insides extravagant beyond Mary's understanding. Everything so inviting. Her bucket grew heavy with candy and she remembered to always say thank you. Ronnie offered to help carry her pail, but Mary declined. She rotated arms. It was all part of the experience.

They trekked side-by-side to the last house before heading home. It was large and set far back from the road. It looked so distant and far away in the night. The house was lit like a beacon. The driveway was winding and lined with dwarf palms surrounded by mondo grass.

There were little faint ground lights on either side leading up the drive. Approaching the flagstone walkway, they saw the path was ablaze with floodlights and the interior shining brightly. The ground cover grew with a sort of ordered chaos. There was an eerie silence that Mary noted. It gave her the creeps even in this most perfect evening. Ronnie reached down and held her hand. He shone the light at her feet despite its unnecessity. Mary climbed the steps. She rang the doorbell.

She heard two sets of clicking heels from within. The noise grew louder at their approach. The door opened, and an older woman and a young lady stood smiling with a bowl of candy.

"Trick or treat," Mary said.

The younger woman bent down, smiling at Mary. Just then, Mary heard something crash to the ground behind her. She turned and saw Ronnie reaching for the flashlight, his hands fumbling for the light.

Mary turned back to the young woman and noticed a strange familiarity. There was something about her eyes and the structure of her face. The way she stood and her countenance were recognizable. Something Mary saw every day.

"Hello, Ms. Witch," the young woman said. "Don't you look scary." She crinkled her face in mock fear. The same look Ronnie had made in the trailer earlier. "I love the nose, sweetheart."

The older woman stared past Mary towards Ronnie and clutched her breast. Mary thought she was pretending to be scared of the pirate, but she wasn't so sure. The older woman's hands were shaking, a look of shock on her face.

"Here, honey." The young woman offered Mary a candy bar. The manner of her voice sounded identical to something.

Mary tentatively took the candy bar. "Thank you."

"Have more than that," the young householder said with a smile. "We won't have many more visitors tonight, and I'll just eat it all. Get a handful."

Mary reached in and grabbed a fist-sized bundle of chocolate.

The woman looked up at Ronnie. "How about you, Mr. Scalawag? Do you want some candy?"

"No, thank you," Ronnie said quickly.

A baby started crying from within. The woman smiled with a hint of exacerbation. "Goodnight. Ya'll be safe," she said before shutting the door.

Mary turned to leave and noticed that Ronnie seemed visibly distressed, like his lungs were incapable of holding in breath. He was trembling and his hair lashed about in the wind. Mary took his quivering hand and turned to face the driveway. Ronnie hefted her up upon his shoulders and started down the path. He held onto her knees and she pointed the flashlight in front of his feet. They walked on quietly with only the trundle of the candy shifting in her bucket. She pointed the light ahead and Ronnie wandered with his feet stepping into nothingness. They were back on the road and heading home. Mary's eyes were heavy and her legs ached. Something was wrong with Ronnie. She almost heard the mechanisms ticking away in his mind. An aura of something nameless permeated from him.

"Mr. Ronnie," she said. "That woman looked an awful lot like you."

"I thought so too, sweetheart. I thought so, too."

They walked on.

Chapter 13

Clara slept little. When she did, her dreams were beset with nightmares. Her sleep was riddled with peril and Mary was ever present—her child lost and crying for help. Clara would wake up screaming. Very rarely, she dreamt of goodness and happy times. She and Mary walking through a flowering meadow in the sunshine. Everything so rich in color. Amazing frescos of lush landscapes. Yet, these were terrors all their own. She'd gone so long without happiness that even the faintest hint of it frightened her. It was a phantom stirring. Like a false flag for crueler things to come. The lingering smell of flowers morphing into the acrid stench of paint cleaner. Grainy bits of match heads. Visions of corpses and dead things. Her days as gray as ash. Practically every waking hour was stress filled. Everything was happening so fast and she couldn't keep up. Her daily tasks were evocative of a terrible incubus. She pleaded with the gods for a respite.

She'd been gone with Joe for three days. Or maybe four. Clara wasn't quite sure. The very air of her was the stench of meth. The taste of it never left her mouth. She was smoking it more to give her nostrils a break. Her eyes were red, strained, and filled with muck. If she didn't wipe them, bits crusted along the edges.

All she knew was that it had finally stopped raining. They were holed up in a dingy crack house. She didn't know the town or state. They might've been on the moon.

When they'd arrived, Joe had put Clara on a filthy cot in a bedroom. He sold smack and her from the living room below. When Clara would venture from the bedroom, she'd see the mummified dead strewn about waiting for their next fix. People moved about silently like cats. Flies swarmed and bugs skittered without notice. There was no working bathroom and people defecated painfully into corners. Occasionally, she heard the moans of copulating couples from somewhere in the house. Men came and went from her room.

Of them, she had no memory.

The butcher, the baker, the candlestick maker. At one point, Joe entered and injected her with crystal. She'd never felt so alive. Every cell in her body leapt and microscopic beings crawled under her skin. She felt the earth beneath her feet rumble like the coming of an earthquake that wasn't there.

In her drugged state, Clara inspected the rooms like a crazed archaeologist. The floors were buckled. The plaster was damp and areas of the ceiling were exposed. The crown molding was cracked or missing altogether. Free wires hung loosely and Clara thought she heard them humming. Parts of the flooring were blackened from what looked like small fires. Writing and crude drawings covered the piss-colored walls. Phallic symbols and shit house poetry scrawled about without order. Words scribbled by the addicted crying out for help. Childish balladry that was true to her heart. *I'm sure you must be weary dear, with soaring up so high; will you rest upon my bed? Said the spider to the fly. There are pretty curtains drawn around, the sheets are fine and thin, and if you like to rest awhile, I'll surely tuck you in.*

She scratched her arms until they bled. Torturous noises radiated from behind the walls. Menacing shadow figures danced provocatively. Souls left to wander these dreary halls to haunt the haunted. Everything was covered in soot and dust. The windows were brown looking with film and hardly let in the light. The colossal and continuing storms wrecked the already ruined roof and there was a constant flow of water. It pooled onto the floor and stank. The whole house was wet and pungent. The rich and sweet smell of mildew. Clara was rank and couldn't remember the last time she'd eaten. Such trivialities were far from her mind. She was too busy trying to comprehend what the voices whispered. The constant hushed droning in the rafters. She spoke earnestly to the invisible specters but heard no response.

When Clara came to, she noticed the rain had stopped. The dripping continued, but something resembling sunshine illuminated through the sooty windows. A word dragged her out of the drug-fueled irrationality. It rested on the tip of her tongue. She moved her mouth woodenly to bring it to life. Her jaw cracked with a painful snap as she whispered, "Promise."

From far away, perhaps down the street, tiny voices echoed faintly. The giggling of children at play. These weren't the demons who crooned words of love as before. Not the angelic words encouraging self-harm. Nor the sweet whispers encouraging mindless violence. The children's laughter was migratory and roving. The pluralism of sounds reverberated and wavered, drawing Clara to the warped and cracked window. The view was like something from a funhouse. Everything covered in mist and crazily distorted. Clara blinked, but the perspective didn't change. Her unfocused eyes found a semblance of order and what she saw took her breath.

All about were nightmare creatures who'd escaped from hell and set free to wander the earth. A threadbare world where the fabric split and ruinous beasts now ran riot. Clara closed her eyes and whimpered. Then, unmistakable laughter and beguilement. She wiped away the soot and looked again. A princess dressed in purple and pink wandered across the street. A gaggle of ninjas snuck past. Clara placed her head against the sill and groaned.

Clara hurried to the door and entered the hall. At one end, she saw a junkie furiously tugging at himself over a lifeless woman. He made inhuman noises and was violently masturbating at a drooling, withered crone. Eyes glassy but animate. Clara quietly crept down the hallway hoping not to disturb the erect beast. A vision of him chasing after her with his member flapping made Clara shudder.

She went down the winding stairs to a room of chaos. A fog of meth fumes hung stationary in the air. It mingled with the reek of humanity about. Clara scanned the room for Joe. The smoke was so thick that it distorted her view. Her eyes welled with tears. She heard droplets of stale rain that pattered softly on the floor. She wandered among her fellow fiends looking for her pimp lover.

Clara found him sitting under a blue tarp with a half-empty vodka bottle in his lap. She said his name, but nothing registered behind his dead eyes. They looked sunken deep into his skull. Two cold gray stones buried deep within. Almost like a schoolhouse skeleton. The drum of water repetitively crashed onto the tarpaulin. She screamed his name and jostled his shoulder. Joe turned and looked at her drunkenly. He seemed confused as to Clara's very existence. Then, his eyes flicked of memory.

"Is he done already?"

"Who's done?" Clara asked.

"The guy I just sent up."

A vision of the hallway onanist flashed through her mind.

"Yes," she said hurriedly. "All done. We need to get home. I promised Mary I'd help with her costume."

"Hell no," Joe hollered. "We aren't leaving. I've made a killing here." He pulled out a huge wad of cash and flashed it in her face. "This is profit on top of the money I owed."

"Okay, we can come back," Clara said nervously. "But, let's just go home. I need to clean up and change anyway. I'm filthy." She held out her crusty shirt.

"Find a faucet!"

"I already tried," she lied. "They don't work. And I've got monthly issues to deal with."

Joe pursed his lips. "Okay, but we are coming right back."

"Fine," she said.

He held out his hand and she helped him up. There was a deadness to his weight despite his tiny frame. A damp puddle of stinking piss was left where his seat was. He stood uneasily and staggered along with intoxicated precision. Every labored step meticulously thought out. Like an old processing system playing catch-up. The bottle swung loosely in his hand and Clara hauled him forth with the other. Joe was ripe and smelled sour with a mixture of liquor and urine.

The sun descended and children ran up and down the street laughing. The trick-or-treaters gave the crack house a wide berth and watched it nervously. It played host to their greatest fears and urban legends. Childish ghost stories abounded.

How right they were.

On the street, none of the children fled from her, as Clara looked like any other holiday harlequin. Old makeup ruined and gaudy. They stumbled to the car and Joe tried to get in behind the wheel but fell over. She took the keys and stuffed him in the passenger seat. The car cranked and died twice. Clara smashed the dashboard with her fist. On the third attempt, the car sprang into life. Clara drove around the city and searched until she found a geographical marker. They were in Fort Walton Beach. A sign said Pensacola was fifty miles away. She took the coastal highway and headed west.

They traveled through a drifting haze of steam from off the blacktop. She caught Joe out of the corner of her eye. He was sleeping with the bottle between his legs. Clara took the bottle and drank. It burned her throat and she fought back tears. She turned the bottle up a second time and wiped her mouth with the back of her hand. The sky was a dull sulfur yellow, reminding her of the color of the chipped walls in the crack house. A flock of migratory birds crossed before the falling daylight. She watched them go until they were just specks and vanished from sight. Clara wished them safe travels. She drank again and the vodka felt warm in her gut. The lids of her eyes grew heavy.

In her half-drunken state, she remembered long ago, the man entering her bedroom. The shuffling of his feet as she clinched her eyes shut. How the bed moved and suddenly he was sliding in beside her. His breath stale and stinking of beer. His scruffy beard cutting into her skin. He had put his hand inside her pajama bottoms and whispered, "If you tell anyone about this, I'll kill you and your mommy."

Clara was crying. She pondered the late hour and her promise. The bottle of vodka was nearly empty. She drove on and tried to think about good things. Yet she was left wanting, because her life held so few. That monster had been the first of her mother's boyfriends to molest her, but he wasn't the last.

Now, she felt his phantom grip, and her body recoiled spasmodically. Then she felt nothingness. By the time they reached the outskirts of Pensacola, it was full dark.

The moon rose beyond the distant woodlands. She knew where to go and was shuddering violently. She drained the remaining vodka and threw the bottle out the window. An ephemeral crash of the glass breaking on the concrete. Her tear ducts were filled with murk and she wiped away the dried filth. It was like she was driving with her eyes shut. Everything seemed without dimension. A passing car flicked its high beams. Then she realized her car's lights were switched off. She turned them on and continued through town.

Joe remained slumped and looked dead. She saw his brown and rotted teeth. The clammy and pus boiled flesh. They drove down West Main Street and passed the standing palms that grew on either side. Erect and well placed. Purely aesthetic and nothing like the real west Florida arecaceae that bend and grow much to their own choosing. The plastic bag window flapped noisily and she wanted to scream. She looked in the rearview mirror at the way they'd come. Adults dressed in costume strolled along the sidewalk holding hands and entered different bars. These revelers were outfitted wondrously in every description. Living lives Clara couldn't even imagine. Hers was chaotic and she constantly feared how it would end. Although, in truth, she didn't want to know. She looked again and the band of partiers vanished. Yet, the troupe strangely remained in the mirror as an afterimage of something Clara could never aspire to.

Ahead was the sign for the Palms. Clara slowed the car and pulled in. She watched the street for passing children but nothing moved in the street. All about, costumed critters sat on porches eating candy. The burn barrel posse were passing around a dirty pillowcase picking out treats. A ghost boy sat on the ground pointing and squalling. She passed a gaggle of boys clustered around a trailer window. A woman was changing in full view and the adolescent boys gawked at her enormous swinging pendulum breasts. The smiling old maid was well aware of her audience.

Further on, Clara saw a single piece of clothing break free from a clothesline and dance in the breeze until out of sight. Water stood in enormous puddles, and her passing car created great spewing waves. Something childlike within Clara caused her to hit the standing water head-on. Joe lurched forward crazily in the seat and shrieked at the noise. Clara quickly pushed this happy feeling away.

She returned to numbness and despair. Life as it really was. A shrinking world of waiting terrors followed by nameless oblivion. The animate life of the Palms left her encumbered with the fact that she'd have to return to the crack house in the morning. Everything gnarled and black in her heart. Clara turned down Seventh Street. She heard the sounds of Joe snorting a bump of meth and the terrible rattling tick from deep in the car's engine. She hoped for a message or warning in the tableau but was left wanting, as always.

Ahead, Clara saw Ronnie and Mary sitting on his porch swing.

They looked settled and Mary was picking through her bucket of candy. Ronnie was playing the guitar and watching her. Blackness of night was all around, but under that beacon there was something tangible. A vision of the last vestige of goodness in her life.

Come jail or death, would he care for her? Would anyone?

So much of Clara's life was dedicated to making Mary's better than her own. An existence that was a step up from

Clara's childhood. In truth, that wasn't so hard. Especially when it consisted solely of protecting her child from molestation. As if that served as a fantastic accomplishment.

Clara saw Ronnie and Mary stand at her car's approach. Both were smiling, and she laughed a little at Ronnie's eye patch. Mary looked adorable in her witch costume. Joe was wide awake and wild-looking. His head made movements like a bird, as if he was in perpetual mortal danger. Perhaps he was.

Ronnie stood with his hand raised in a stately attitude. He shook a little plastic sword and waved it like a victor after battle.

Mary shouted a warning about the mud, and Clara ventured cautiously over the damp ground. It squished under her shoes and she nearly lost her footing. Each step was followed by a nasty sucking sound. Dead leaves and small twigs littered the yard. This strange scene was oddly intact. There were bits of sediment left from the high-water mark on the porch steps.

The vodka felt heavy in her empty gut and her legs were wobbly. Her stomach seemed bloated and her vision was blurry. She sensed her insides gurgling. She'd not slept properly for days and the weight of it bowed her back.

Mary on the bottom porch step holding a handful of candy. Clara wanted to stop and rest, but knew she wouldn't start back again. Mary's twisted and wiry nose looked cute. Joe was making a racket behind her, but she didn't turn around. He shouted something unintelligible that she ignored. Her feet were weighty with caked sludge. She stood before the costumed duo.

"Hi, Mommy," Mary squealed. "I got a whole bag full of candy." She was trying to force a chocolate bar into her mother's hand. Clara gently pushed it to the side and hugged her daughter tightly. Beauty grew on that little face. A goodness in her child not yet ruined by the world. A miniature reflection of herself before the horrors of life snuck into her room. She felt her child's warmth and the rhythmic moving of her chest. Almost hearing the faint pounding of her tiny heartbeat.

"I can see, baby. Did you have fun?"

"Yes," she said, nodding enthusiastically.

"Did you thank Mr. Ronnie?"

"Of course," she said with a charming sort of annoyance.

"She did just fine," Ronnie said. He gave Clara a hug. "Come on inside." He stood back and Mary made for the door. Her bucket jostled with candy. A few empty wrappers were on a little table that Ronnie pocketed. She'd felt faint, but the smell of Mary revived her.

As Clara started up the steps, she felt hands grab and tug at her arm. She turned and saw Joe staring at her crazily. His skin looked papery and all but translucent. Face so sunken that his cheekbones looked sharp, as if they might pierce his skin.

For a flickering moment, Clara saw the absolute truth of her pimp and the world he prescribed. She viewed the cold and relentless future with him. A cyclical life of tragedy. An implacable darkness where she lived on borrowed time. A place she'd be loathe to go. The succeeding a land of violence and incarceration where her child was gone for good.

Clara yanked her arm free and tried to step away.

Joe swore viciously and attacked. He latched onto Clara's elbow and hurled her off the porch steps. She felt weightless and panicked with presaged doom. The moon and stars filled her sight. Blackness about. For a moment, time stood still. Then, she slammed headfirst onto the muddy ground.

An enormous white light flashed through her vision. She blinked rapidly several times and the glare faded away. Clara tried to breathe but couldn't. She strained to inhale but her lungs felt blocked. She heard an echoing of harsh words, an argument that sounded far away. Suddenly she was struck by the stench of wet clay and grass. She looked up towards the porch and saw Joe dragging Mary by the hair.

Clara held her hand out and tried to speak but was voiceless. She saw blades of grass and mud covering her fingers. Mary looked terrified and watched her mother. Mary's fists were clutched tightly to her chest and she dropped her bucket of candy. Clara saw her daughter's mouth was ajar and she was screaming, but Clara registered no noticeable sound. She blinked and, in an instant, Joe was gone. He was on the porch one second and then he wasn't.

Clara rolled over onto her knees. She saw Mary hunched down, all alone on the porch. Clara stood and slipped in the mud. It was slathered all over her and she felt heavy. Mary ran to the railing and was hopping up and down with her hands on her head looking desperate. Clara's hearing hadn't returned and she saw the child's mouth moving rapidly. It seemed like a strange dream.

Finally, Clara righted herself and labored around to the other end of the porch. What she saw was Ronnie holding Joe by the throat against the wall of the trailer. Joe was kicking his feet and flailing his arms to no avail. There was a huge indention in the mud where they'd gone over the side. Clara didn't know what to do. Ronnie's enormous arms were extended and tightening. The veins pulsed along his forearms. Clara hadn't noticed how strong the old man was. She ran over to him and saw his face. His eyes were burning with rage. His teeth were clenched and his jaw firmly set. Joe's eyes bulged and his face turned purple. He'd soiled himself and the stench of shit permeated off him.

Clara touched Ronnie's shoulder and the old man turned his head. His face softened and he lowered Joe to the ground.

Joe coughed and tears streamed down his face. Ronnie hadn't let go. He pulled Joe close and uttered something in his ear. Clara watched his mouth move unhurriedly. He spoke with a calm and slow precision just out of hearing. A menacing whisper and a smiling threat. Joe nodded quickly in response. Ronnie continued his benediction. Joe's eyes were huge and filled with horror. After a time, Ronnie stood back and let go. Joe slumped into the dirt and shook a little. Then, abruptly, he shot up and sprinted away. Joe didn't look at anyone. He just took to his feet and fled.

Clara turned and watched Joe skitter across the yard to the street. He ran out of his shoes and kept pumping his legs as fast as he could. His bare feet slapped the slick pavement. The back of his pants was dark from the mud and sagging with shit. He didn't stop, and he never looked back.

A hand touched Clara's shoulder and she jumped. Ronnie put his arm around her and held her close. He spoke to her, but the words were faint. She placed her head on his chest and sobbed. She cried like she hadn't in a long time. Emotions flooded out. Her life of rape, abuse, and prostitution was finally finding a release.

Mostly, she was tired of feeling like a pilgrim or gypsy left to wander the earth with only Mary as her charge. Drifting with no set destination and without enterprise. No true place to call home. She'd always wondered if there was a fissure in the earth just for her that leaked terrors long past understanding.

Yet, all of that seemed to slowly drain away.

She smelled the dank mud on Ronnie's shirt. His shoulder was drenched where she'd cried. Clara felt Mary grab hold of her leg and squeeze it tightly. The girl was trembling. Clara stroked Mary's hair and smoothed it. Her daughter flinched where Joe had grabbed hold. Clara let go of Ronnie and knelt in front of Mary. They were eye level. Clara tried her best to wipe her hands clean. She stroked her daughter's hair and kissed her wet eyelids. She sat back on her heels and held Mary's hands.

"I'm so sorry, sweetie," Clara said. "That never should've happened. Some things in this world can't be helped, but I could've kept him far away. I was blinded into thinking that my actions wouldn't affect you. It never occurred to me that you'd get caught up in all this." Clara hugged her daughter. "I should've looked out for you better, but I didn't. For that, I'm sorry."

Ronnie gently took Clara's arm and lifted her up. All three watched the street to make sure Joe hadn't returned. It was empty save refuse and no one was coming. Ronnie led them up the stairs onto the porch. Clara was slathered in mud and stood like something escaped from a bog. Ronnie was little better.

"I'm going to get a towel for you. You can have first dibs on the shower." He took off his shoes and placed them by the door. He entered and Clara looked at Mary. She was gathering her candy that had spilled. She held up one and cut her eyes at her mother.

"Go ahead, sweetie," Clara said. "Can I have one?"

"Sure, what kind?"

"Any, whatever you don't want."

Mary studied the bucket for a long time and handed her mother an Almond Joy. Ronnie exited the trailer with a large bath towel. He held it up like a great partition. Clara stood behind it and stripped down to her underwear. He wrapped it around her. She turned to enter the trailer but paused. "I don't have anything clean to change into," she said, a little embarrassed.

"Just pick something," Ronnie said. "It's all right."

Clara went down the hall to the bathroom. She flipped on the shower and waited for the water to warm. She slid off her panties and watched her reflection. She looked like a prison camp survivor. Just bones and skin. She was so thin. Blisters and bumps festered across her chest. She stared at herself until steam covered the mirror. She stepped under the faucet and scrubbed herself with Ronnie's soap and lathered her hair. The water about the drain was filthy and bits of dirt created a ring around the bottom. She let the hot water burn her skin. Like a scalding baptism washing away her sins.

After she dried herself, Clara went into the bedroom and searched for something to wear. She collected a white t-shirt and boxer shorts from Ronnie's dresser and put them on. She felt funny in his outsized clothes.

In the living room, Clara found Mary sleeping on the couch. She had a blanket draped over her and a pillow under her head. She still wore the witch's nose. This made Clara laugh, and it felt good.

Clara stepped out on the porch and saw Ronnie sitting shirtless, smoking a cigarette. Their muddy clothes were in a heap by the door. She sat down next to him, but he looked preoccupied. Like he didn't recognize her presence. After a time, Clara placed her hand on his shoulder, and he jumped a little in recognition that someone was there.

"Sorry, I didn't mean to startle you," she said.

"No, you're all right. I just let my mind wander a bit." Ronnie looked at her and chuckled at her outfit. "Hey, you could've gone trick-or-treating with us."

Clara playfully slapped his shoulder. She felt silly in his clothes.

"Wait a second," he said with mock anger. "Them's my only clean pair of drawers." Ronnie was openly laughing now and she joined with him. "What am I supposed to wear tomorrow? Guess I'll have to go commando."

Clara was smiling and looked Ronnie over. She cringed at the sight of an enormous scar. It was a foot long and spanned the length of his abdomen. The old wound was jagged and crude and made by no trained hand. Well, perhaps someone skilled in a craft of taking human life. The scar looked like an enormous centipede with the suture marks on either side for little legs. It seemed very old. She ran her finger across it. "What happened?"

"I got into a disagreement with some pretty bad guys over the ownership of my commissary. They were pretty adamant that it should be theirs. I thought differently. Some words were said. One decided that he wanted to see what my insides looked like."

"Oh God."

"Yeah, they got my food and left me in a cell trying to keep my guts from falling onto the floor. I nearly died. All over a damn bag of potato chips…" He lit another cigarette. A soft breeze picked up in small drifts. He exhaled blue smoke that wafted and disappeared into the night. "I had a come-to-Jesus moment while lying in the hospital bed. I'm not religious, but I made a deal with the almighty. Don't let me die and I'll start living my life right. He kept up his side of the bargain. And I'd like to think that I have too." He sighed and stared down at his feet. "I feel like I let God down tonight. I let the anger get the better of me. I saw that son-of-a-bitch toss you around and yank Mary's hair… I lost it. I saw red. I would've killed him if it weren't for you stepping in." He rubbed his legs with the palms of his hands.

"I think you're the finest man that I've ever met," she said earnestly. "I really mean that. I've never met anyone quite like you before."

Ronnie smiled at her. "Thanks…" An owl crossed the face of the pale moon with enormous wings outspread. It eclipsed the blue light until it ascended into a black dot and was gone. There was so much she wanted to say. Perhaps he did as well. When he finally spoke, he said, "I think I met my daughter tonight."

Clara's eyes widened. "How?"

"Trick-or-treating. I saw my ex-wife and a young woman at the door who was a dead ringer to me."

"Are you going to try and meet her?"

"No. I don't think that would be a good idea. For either of us. She lives in a huge house with a family of her own. Best to let her live her life." He stared off down the road. "I'd better get cleaned up."

Ronnie stood and held out his hand to Clara. She took it and rose. They entered the trailer and Ronnie locked the door. He shut the blinds and turned off the light. Everything shadowlike and without feature. The world outside passed trackless and unaccounted for. A nameless offing in the dark beyond. He walked down the hallway and into the bathroom. Clara looked at her daughter sleeping soundly in the dark. Small little breaths. The lost moonlight shone through the blinds and danced across her face. It created the faintest visible shape. Mary hadn't moved. Clara stroked her daughter's hair gently. She felt things falling into place. Everything before was predicated on expectation. Now, there seemed a new chapter.

"He's already given you a better world," she whispered. "Both of us."

She heard the shower turn on. Clara walked down the hall and stood outside the door listening. She placed her palm on the door and whispered heartfelt thanks. She turned and went into the bedroom and slid under the covers. She was asleep just as her head hit the pillow.

Chapter 14

They formed a sort of blended family. The next day Clara and Mary moved permanently into Ronnie's trailer. Joe had returned sometime in the night and stole away anything of value from Clara's old trailer. In a fit of irony, he slashed the tires to her car, but he possessed the only set of keys. He trashed the place, but an outsider wouldn't have noticed. The television, kitchen appliances and cookware, the stash of drugs, and most of the money was gone. Clara had hidden a thousand dollars, which was taped behind a rotting piece of plaster that, thankfully, remained. He'd urinated over Clara's clothes and pooped on the bed.

Ronnie and Clara picked over the goods like scavengers. Badly used cutlery and a ruined cast-iron pan were all that remained in the kitchen. The two salvaged what they could and took the items over to his place. Mary's little bed from her cubby closet was carried forth and put into Ronnie's spare room. The room wasn't exactly large, but enormous in comparison.

Later, as a little latter-day family, they painted her new bedroom an electric pink color that Mary picked out. Ronnie and Clara spent two whole days cleaning the junk out of her old trailer. It took fourteen large plastic trash bags to remove all the useless odds and ends. Ronnie joked that it'd be easier to set the thing alight and start over. He wasn't entirely wrong.

Finished, they sat on Ronnie's swing and looked at the huge pile next door. Senseless artifacts waiting for the dump. Twilight overcame them. The faintest shape of a crescent moon overhead. Under the pale light, Mary circled the street on her bike. Clara and Ronnie were covered in sweat and soot. They swung lazily without communicating. There was no need to. The whole endeavor felt right.

That fateful night, Joe had stabbed and cut most of Clara's clothes. Her outfits looked like the apparel of murder victims sprawled across the trailer. Ronnie, Clara, and Mary went to the mall and purchased a whole new wardrobe. This time, she bought practical apparel. Clara felt weird, because she didn't know the style of women her age. She wandered among the racks of clothes very skeptical and everything seemed suspect. Slutty clothing was all she knew. Something to attract men for sundry purposes. Turning her into an object for their use.

An old ex-con and a seven-year-old weren't exactly hip to the latest fashion. They looked through magazines to cross check and picked out whole new outfits for her to wear. Clara felt funny trying on clothes in a designer store, but Ronnie and Mary clapped with approval. She looked like the thin shape of something unknown reflected in the mirror. A thing disinterred and set loose to wander among the gravestones. Most of the clothes didn't fit her. Her spine and ribs showed, but her breasts remained firm.

It's the little things, Clara thought.

Ronnie sat and waited outside the changing room in a comfy chair. Mary came and went bringing different sizes. Clara noticed Ronnie slouched and sleeping. She watched her daughter kiss him on the cheek. He opened his groggy eyes, smiled, and snored again. Mary sat in the changing room and watched her mother in wonder.

When they counted up the purchases it was clear that none of it was affordable. So, the trio went to a thrift store and tried the process over again. Here, they found similar yet slightly dated apparel. After clothes shopping, all three went for ice cream before heading home. It was a wonderful day. Another in a growing list that were better than the one before.

Clara swore off prostitution and drugs. The former was easy. She had tried to go back and work at the motel, but her boss demanded they keep their sexual arrangement. When she balked, he fired her on the spot. On her way out, Clara saw the two Hispanic cleaning ladies. They watched her cautiously with nervous eyes. Clara walked downcast towards her car, when she stopped and turned back. As she approached them, their hands were wild and both looked afraid. Clara hugged one and then the other. Both were stiff as boards. Clara asked to pray with them.

She put her hands together and looked to the heavens. Their expressions changed and they nodded. One took Clara by the hand and led her into an empty motel room. They kissed the tips of their fingers. Clara copied them and watched their rituals with wonder. The two women got down on their knees and brought out precious rosary beads. Clara had never seen them up close. These objects imbued a sort of supernatural power. They were beautiful and hand crafted. The crucified Christ looked austere and pained. That was not lost to Clara. They prayed an incantation in Spanish. They spoke with a vengeance.

"Angel de Dios, mi guarda querida, a quien el amor de Dios me compromete aqui, jamas este dia o noche estar a mi lado, a la luz y protector, guia y regla. Amen."

Clara kissed them both on the cheek. In broken English, one said she'd keep praying for her. Every day. Vaya con Dios. Goodbye.

Sobriety was much harder. The first night, she slept for nearly forty-eight hours straight. There were times she felt something almost recognizable in her altered state. Foul beasts visited her in nightmares and she screamed in her sleep. A pale monstrosity that was almost luminous crouched in the shadows. A thing waiting and biding its time. A nightmare manifestation of her addiction. Sometimes she heard the soft patter of feet and smelled the faint aroma of her daughter. Little whispers from within and laughter from without. A blurry vision of Ronnie sitting beside her and wiping her forehead with a wet towel. She dreamed of Mary playing the guitar and woke to the sound of her daughter singing softly by her bedside. Clara stirred in the middle of the night shaking and vomited across the bed. Ronnie cleaned her with care. He watched her sleep all night.

The sound of pans and the smell of bacon carried her from the slumber. Clara felt bad and her stomach ached. There was a ravenous twitch in her belly. She was feeble and walked weakly out of the bedroom. Ronnie and Mary sat at the little table and smiled at her. Clara said she needed to shower and Ronnie asked Mary to go with her. Her mother still wasn't feeling well.

She ran a warm shower and Mary watched her mother carefully. At one point, she wobbled and Mary hugged Clara's legs to keep her upright. Regaining composure, she lifted Mary and hugged her tightly. She looked at her daughter in the eyes and told her how much she loved her. Mary kissed her mother and said she loved her too. Clara set her down and turned off the shower. She watched her daughter dry her curly hair.

I know there is a God, she thought. Because something greater made you.

She started going to Narcotics Anonymous. Ronnie hid or dumped all the alcohol out of the trailer and went to meetings with Clara for support. While attending, she learned about her condition. She learned that drug addiction was just a symptom of her problem. Staying off drugs only dealt with part of the issue. To stay clean, she only needed to change one thing, which was everything. She'd long believed that she was far past saving, but those meetings showed her otherwise. They told her to keep coming back, it works if you work it, keep it simple stupid, this too shall pass, and a whole host of other bizarre phraseology that made no sense to anyone outside of the rooms. By coming to grips with her past, she could find a solution.

The last day of her physical cravings, they went to the beach. It was a sunny Sunday and the fresh air soothed the final stages of withdrawal. She watched the mighty seascape and felt the soft southern wind. It blew and shifted the dune's grass. A thing both elegant and synchronized like the beauty of a dance. She wore a yellow sundress that became her. Gulls glided stationary in the wind or bobbed casually atop the rippling ocean. All three walked out and stood barefoot in the sand.

Mary strode into the pale surf and let it roll and crash around her knees. Her hair blew wildly in the breeze and she threw her head back and laughed as the swells swayed. They wandered the shoreline hunting for shells. The white sand of the gulf reflected the sun and burned away the autumn cool. The wind blew and they tasted salt on their lips. Mary had a shirt full of shells that she carried in front like a little basket. They walked up the beach and sat on the towel and drank cherry Kool-Aid. Mary lay back and sunned herself. She rolled up her shirt into a makeshift bikini top.

"Sweetie," Clara said. "You'll burn. Let me put some lotion on you."

Without moving she responded, "But Mom, I don't need lotion. I'm already tan."

Ronnie snorted.

"Yes, but you can still burn and it will hurt terribly."

Mary flipped her shirt down and rolled over to face the two. She was looking down and looked lost in thought. A heaviness on her mind. Finally, she spoke.

"Mr. Ronnie," she said very seriously. "I've been thinking... If it's okay with Mom, I'd like for you to adopt me. Love for you to adopt me. We talked about it a little. And she said I had to ask you."

Ronnie turned crimson and Clara looked down smiling.

"You are the nicest boyfriend my mom has ever had."

Clara lay back on the towel laughing.

"Is that so," Ronnie said.

Mary shook her head up and down enthusiastically. "Then we could be a real family. Like on paper and everything." Mary cocked her eyes and tried to be sly. "And, you and mommy can have baby. I could be a big sister!"

Clara was shaking with laughter and Ronnie was smiling and shaking his head. "That so? What a turn of events."

"Yes," Mary said proudly. "I know how that all works."

"Good grief," Ronnie said. He looked out across the great expanse of ocean. "How about we get some seafood?"

"Yes, please," Clara said, sitting up.

They stood and Ronnie collected the towel. Clara put her arm around Mary and they walked back to the truck. Ronnie walked a little behind them, laughing.

Chapter 15

That night, Ronnie lay on the couch and Clara exited Mary's room. She'd tucked Mary into bed and said goodnight. He expected Clara to go down the hall to her room. Instead he heard her faint footsteps approach in the dark. He heard the couch creak. She straddled him and leaned in to his ear. She kissed his neck and he was frozen. He tried to speak, but there were no words. Ronnie lifted his arms to her waist and found she was completely naked. A scene of his ex-wife from their wedding night flashed through his mind.

How beautiful she looked in the candlelight. How she stepped so gracefully out of her clothes and let them fall delicately to the floor. He couldn't take his eyes off her as she slipped naked into the bed. Their bodies were side by side and she was so soft and cool to the touch. The scent of Clara was intoxicating, but he pushed that feeling away. She whispered in his ear. "I've been thinking about what Mary said earlier…" She reached her hand down and grasped inside his underwear. She took hold of him with both hands. "Whoa," she said. "That's impressive."

Ronnie moved his arms and stopped her. He saw a look of concern reflected on her face in the moonlight. A slight quivering of her lips. She seemed an animal caught in headlights. Terrified and calculating a host of decisions, but the most important one: to move. Clara sat up and blades of light crossed her naked chest. "What? What's wrong? Am I dirty to you?" She spoke in a quaking whisper. Almost on the verge of tears. Ronnie gently caressed her thighs. They were hairless and tracked with goosebumps. He shook his head side to side. He slowly moved his hands up her side and pulled her close. Their lips locked in a moment of unadulterated passion.

He envisioned his ex-wife and the moistness of her loins. She was so small and delicate that he feared he'd hurt her. She cried out in little whimpers and pleaded with him not to stop. The picture in his mind took him back to her even after all those years. You, he thought. It was always you. Their hips thrusted in tandem. The young and the old. Away from it all.

He placed his hands on her backside and lifted her. He stood and she wrapped her legs around him. He walked her past Mary's door and into the bedroom. The shades were open and the moonlight illuminated the room. He placed her gently on the bed and stood. He felt damp and clammy. Her legs were open and she looked beautiful. Ronnie saw flashes. His ex-wife and Clara over and over. They were the same age. He took off his underwear and lay on top of his imagined wife. The vision eternally young.

As they set to commence, he heard the faintest snore from the other room. He opened his eyes and saw Clara in the twilight. Ronnie shifted out from between her legs. Uncoupled and untangled. He slid over and lay watching her. She folded her arms under her head and watched the watcher. He gathered the blanket and pulled it over them. Clara slid close to him and their bodies touched. Something was in the air. A sense of understanding. They tottered knowingly through perfect blackness. Sightless as the blind, but wandering lost while holding hands. They lay in the dark and communicated in silence.

Finally, Clara started laughing and she sighed. She rolled over and faced the ceiling. From night that forward, they shared the bed. It became their room, but nothing sexual occurred. Too much was at stake. True love. Real love. It sustained them.

Chapter 16

The days turned chilly. The temperate west Florida winter was upon them. The three went and purchased light coats. Black, navy, and maroon. Time marched on. Clara worked as a cashier at a dollar store and Mary made new friends. The child growing more confident by the day. Like the stability at home awoke something within her. Ronnie continued working at the hardware store and life was good.

Then one day, the twin brother of the man he killed appeared and life went askew. Ronnie was hauling a box full of door hinges from the storage room to stock in the storefront. Different colored and varnished fulcrums ready for sorting. He turned down the aisle and saw him.

The twin was bent and speaking to his own twin set of boys about screws. Two matching little boys were hugging either leg staring at the collection on the bottom shelf. The screws were different sizes and shapes. He told his sons about the Philips and blade heads. Flat and raised. Metal and wood screws. Bolt, drivers, and anchors. He shared this fatherly information with his sons and they looked transfixed and bored with this new knowledge. Acumen that they too might pass on.

Ronnie approached warily. The doppelganger did a double take. Ronnie knew he was holding his breath. Both frozen. The twin's twins played with the screws. Their little hands moving and misplacing the merchandise. A short time passed, but it seemed like an eternity.

It was Ronnie's worst fear made real. A scene he had played over in his head a thousand times. His selfish play was far different from what occurred. He imagined something with great pomp and circumstance. An event with great bearings. Tears, forgiveness, and understanding. An egotistical performance where Ronnie was the hero. Yet, life doesn't work like that. He created a picture of how the meeting would be in his head and that was all he saw. But, he learned the hard truth that his fabled reality wasn't real.

There was nothing special about it. No grandiose exchange. Just one second and he was there. It hit Ronnie like a ton of bricks and nearly took his breath. A terrible vision of that night returned. Nowhere to run and nowhere to hide. A twisted timeline formed in Ronnie's head. The ancient grinning corpse he remembered brought to life. Older and grayer, but very much alive. They saw each other at the same time. Ronnie pushed away the urge to flee. Perhaps the twin did also.

The twin slowly bent down and whispered something to his children. They nodded simultaneously and walked down the aisle to the door. Sweat beaded on Ronnie's lip and his mouth dried to stubble like sand. He licked his lips, which only made it worse.

The store was preternaturally quiet and they might have been all alone in the world for how distant it felt. Ronnie felt the muscles in his back spasm from the tension. His cotton work-shirt felt damp. The back of it wet and he felt droplets fall from the neckline. Ronnie knew there wasn't going to be another time. This was his only moment to ask forgiveness. See if there was any way to make amends. It was as close as he'd get without falling in. What do you say to the twin brother of the man you killed? They shared a womb and knew each other before anyone else. Huddled together in comradery against the unknown outer world.

Now, there was no trace of his brother but bones and dust inside a box. Ronnie made that so. It was his fault. That was the truth. There was no other story to tell. They stood like two duelers waiting for the sun to reach high noon. Ronnie felt awkward with the box in his hands. He set it down on the floor and looked up. The doppelganger hadn't moved. His arms were taut and fists clenched, yet his eyes were calm. No telling what was behind them.

Now or never, Ronnie thought. He felt the raw glare of the florescent lights overhead. He was faint. He wiped his hands on his work pants. Ronnie stepped forward and spoke. "I reckon you know me."

The twin nodded slowly.

"I want to say that I'm so sorry for what—"

"Save it," the man hissed. There was unmitigated rage in his voice. It was like a malevolent whisper. A darkness clouded his face. "If you want to apologize," he said very methodically, "meet me where it happened at six o'clock tonight."

"Okay," Ronnie said.

The man turned on his heels and walked towards the door. He dropped the screws on a random shelf. They bounced and skittered across the aisle. Ronnie went to pick them up. He heard the door open and the bell ring. He stood and watched the doppelganger lead his sons across the parking lot. One swinging along in each hand. He moved with a sort of determination and the boys were jogging to keep up.

Ronnie studied the scene. He saw them get into a large black sport utility vehicle. He kept looking at it until the SUV pulled onto the highway and drove away. Ronnie wasn't sure what he expected or what was to come. What Ronnie knew for certain was that he was afraid in a way that he couldn't comprehend.

It was two-forty-three and the store was all but deserted. Sue Ellen was so captivated by the latest celebrity romance that she'd missed the whole encounter. Tim went home early as was his managerial prerogative. Ronnie left the box of door hinges and went to the kitchen area in the back. He took a styrofoam cup and filled it with coffee. He sat down at the little fold away table with the cup steaming in his hand. He studied his predicament for a long time. The coffee cooled and remained undrunk. Countless probabilities crossed his mind. Various risks that meeting the twin would accrue. There was potential for danger and the odds of leaving that swamp unharmed were slim. Murder was in that man's eyes. It was a thing Ronnie had seen before. Also, a reality he lived. Yet, the promise of curing his weary soul was too great. A small chance of reconciliation.

Are you willing to risk it, old man? Most likely die for a chance to sleep well at night? He drummed his fingers atop the cheap plastic table. How motivated are you for redemption?

Ronnie shook his head and rubbed his temples. He exhaled with a shudder and his eyes welled with tears. You are thinking about this the wrong way, he thought. This is your selfishness and self-centeredness talking. You lost that right. It's not about you anymore. The family deserves satisfaction. Whatever form it takes.

Ronnie rose from the table and walked over to the wall mounted telephone. He dialed Clara's number. He placed his head against the cool metal wall. The phone rang twice and she answered.

"Hey… I'm okay…I saw the brother of the man I killed… Yeah, he came into the shop with his sons…Just about as surprised as me, I suppose...He wants to meet me...Where I killed his brother...Yes...I don't want to, but I need to...I think he wants to kill me...No, no, I don't...I shouldn't have said that...I don't know...It's fine, don't worry...I'll be home after while...I love you and Mary...Okay, bye."

Ronnie picked up the coffee cup and dumped the contents into the sink. He took care of the screws and watched the clock. Time slowed, reminding him of the jungles of Vietnam all those years ago.

At five o'clock, Sue Ellen went home and Ronnie stayed behind to lock up. He turned off the lights in the stock room and went to the cash register. He took out the money drawer and went to the safe. He placed it inside and spied the other objects hidden away. Several stacks of cash waiting for deposit and a small thirty-eight caliber revolver. He sat down on his heels and looked at the gun. It was dark blue with a cherry wood handle. Lethal despite its size. There was something comforting about that. He fought the urge to pick it up.

You take it, you'll have to use it, he thought.

Ronnie stood up, shut the safe, and spun the dial. He locked the office and went to the keypad by the door. He set the alarm, turned off the light, and stepped out into the empty parking lot. His truck was parked at the far end. He checked the time. It was five thirty. You could get there first.

No, Ronnie thought, he'd be there. He's been there. This is his moment. His accounting.

Ronnie got in his truck and lit a cigarette. He rolled the window down and watched the light flow of traffic. Finally, he cranked the engine, tossed the cigarette away, and reversed out of his parking space.

"This is stupid," he said under his breath. "Yeah, but that's never stopped you before."

Ronnie pulled out onto the coastal highway. The sun was setting. A crystal blue world directly overhead. The clouds in the sky burned dancing shadows across the blacktop. The shapes hurried down the length of road ahead. The white lines pulsing like a thing alive. He continued past the outskirts of Pensacola. He turned to watch the sea. The Gulf looked gray and the dune's grass flittered in the wind. The sun's continued descent into dusk set the seascape ablaze with a blood orange and crimson vista that seduced Ronnie to the incredible vastness. The ocean grew dark and changed its hue with each break and was swallowed back only to spit forth again.

He passed a boarded-up gas station. Crude words and strange symbols were painted on the plyboard. *Christ Is Coming, Everyone Look Busy* was sprayed in red. Ronnie didn't know what to make of that. There was a faded and dangling Keep Out sign. He spied the birds perched on wires scanning the road. He drove down the straight highway with a heavy heart. Raw visions of forgiveness euchred in his thoughts. He was chain smoking. Despite the years, he knew exactly where to go. Staring at the ceiling of his cell, he drove that road. Pleading with himself to keep on down the highway. Yet, he never did.

After fifteen minutes, he saw the turn off. It was faint, but very much there. Ronnie exited the blacktop and steered down the clay baked path. Patches of it looked volcanic. Something familiar even after all these years. Real life of his terrible mien.

He continued driving down the dirt road. The light was fading. There was just a bit of red mixed with twilight in the distance. He was encroaching on a place he'd visited many times before in dreams. Now, he was in the waking world.

Ahead was a gate that stood ajar. Ronnie parked. He sat with the engine shut off and the window down. The chain link fence strung into the woods and out of sight. A sign read

Warning Keep Out. The entrance rocked back and forth. The lock holding it closed was cut. Ronnie thought about that. He got out of the truck. He shut the door quietly and looked around. The moon was as bright as quicksilver and the stillness of the environs chilled him to the bone. He had a bad feeling. He was a trespasser in more ways than one. His elongated shadow was the only animate thing about. Ronnie listened for any sound that resembled footsteps. He turned slowly and spied the country. He walked over to the fence. He crouched and studied the cut lock.

The bite was hot where the bolt cutters clipped it free. It proved to Ronnie that the twin was determined. He threw the useless catch into the woods. He rose and got back into the truck. He lit a cigarette and continued down the dirt road. The ember reflected his face off the windscreen. He kept driving until he saw the dark shape of the sport utility vehicle parked near the swamp's edge. The deep guttural churn of his truck rumbled underfoot. The tires bounced over the rutted ground. He followed what looked like fresh tracks. Ronnie's eyes skittered around looking for movement. He found none.

Ronnie parked next to the black SUV. He left the lights on and glanced at the swamp in the failing light. It was beautiful. He turned off the engine and listened. Everything was still. The water looked ink black. The smell was the exact same. No forgetting that. A darter cawed from the depths of the twilight. Something large crossed the swamp above the headlights. All Ronnie saw were the faint shapes of feathers. The predators were hunting in the waning moments of day. He felt strangely akin to the unsuspecting prey. Ronnie tapped the steering wheel. He felt a coldness enter his bones. The scene morphed into something haunted. He wished he'd brought the gun.

Too late now.

He opened the truck door and got out. The fierce headlights burned across the sandy bar partially lighting the way. Ronnie stood oddly erect by the door. If he were to die here, he felt a sense of calm knowing that he held some sort of agency in his own destruction. He spied the SUV and it looked empty. He heard nothing and no one was about. A haunted place that was profoundly still. He held his breath and concentrated. Only the sound of the swampy inlet. Nothing of men.

The water was still and motionless. It reflected the moon and reminded him of glass. The stars close enough to touch. His forehead beaded with sweat. He scanned the area and saw nothing. He begged for some type of disturbance. Ronnie felt something akin to regret. Every man was accountable for what he did, he thought. He wondered momentarily how much this place had changed. Or, he himself. It was getting too dark to see tracks in the sand. There was a flashlight in the glove compartment. Can't get it now.

Ronnie walked to the front of the truck and leaned against the grill. He almost felt the ghost of the slain brother watching him. He spied the tire treads in the sand and noted that the SUV had approached and exited several times. There were hints of uncertainty. Ronnie didn't know what to make of that.

Toads, crickets, and other beasts sounded from the outer dark. The rattle of branches in the wind sounded like frozen trees or a skeletal percussion. He heard something snort that might've been an alligator. That was the least of his worries. He reached for his cigarettes, but thought better of it and left them in his pocket. He considered that he should be at home.

"Matthew," Ronnie hollered out. "Matthew!"

He listened closely. There was no response. The idiocy of his next move was apparent, but he'd long passed the point of no return. He walked towards the black vehicle and spied the rocky sand around the driver's side door. There were dozens of boot prints going all different directions. A purpose in the chaos. Finding the last set was impossible. No way to gauge which way the twin went. He felt cold. Ronnie didn't know if it was the weather or his soul manifesting itself physically.

He approached the SUV and looked inside the window. It was empty. Nothing moved but the rustling of leaves overhead.

"Mathew!" Ronnie stepped back and listened. He might be taking a piss, he thought. That wasn't likely. He's holed up waiting for you. You don't have the slightest inclination what sort of trouble you're in.

Ronnie swore under his breath. He followed a set of boot tracks to the rear of the SUV. He tried to see into the backseat, but the windows were tinted and all he saw was his stupid reflection. A look of primal and elemental terror on his face. He was quiet and hardly breathed. He felt his heart pumping in his chest. He even tried not to blink. Then, he heard a noise. What seemed like the unmistakable sound of steps in the sand.

By the time Ronnie saw the empty beer bottle lying on the ground, he knew it was too late.

He was hit in the shoulder and the pain raced down the whole length of his body. He let out a groan. The wind swooshed overhead and he was struck again in the collarbone. There was a loud snap and Ronnie dropped to one knee. He stared about but saw nothing. A phantom attacker from old fairy tales. He struggled with each breath. The next blow smacked him square in the back. It stung like a thing on fire. He turned and watched his silhouette reflect off the side of the vehicle. He saw the crowbar come out of the blackness and rain down between his shoulder blades. He cried out in agony. Then, there was a loud crack and his vision went. His world went haywire and Ronnie forgot where he was. He felt another faint pat on the crown of his skull. There was numb movement around his ears. His nerves were shot and it deadened the ferocity of the second blow. There was a piercing ringing in his ears.

This is where you die, old man, he thought. I welcome it with open arms.

Fresh pain from his ribs knocked him out of his stupor. He wiped his eyes and saw his hand was slick with blood. It ran off his forehead and pooled into the sand. His mouth tasted metallic. He felt something break in his side and it took his breath. Ronnie winced and fell over onto the ground. He lay in the fetal position, trying to suck in air.

Matthew hadn't said a word. This was done with professional precision. Like he'd planned it all his life.

Ronnie stared off towards the lights of his truck. The he turned and watched the bayou until everything lost shape. He closed his eyes and received blow after blow. Ronnie vomited blood and rolled over onto his back. There wasn't a place on his body that didn't hurt. He held up his hands and mouthed something. The crowbar fell against the side of his head a final time. Ronnie felt rubbery, and when he spoke, blood bubbled in the corner of his mouth. He spat out a bloody tooth and turned to his attacker.

Matthew stood with the light behind him, breathing heavy. He held the crowbar above his head.

"Wait," Ronnie said weakly. Warm blood flooded his mouth. "Wait, please. Hear me out."

"What was his name?" the shrouded figure said with a calculated and calm rage.

"Michael," Ronnie said weakly. "His name was Michael." The dead brother held claim over both of them. "Kill me if you want, but let me speak to you first." Ronnie was wheezing between each torturous breath. There was no response, but he saw the faintest nod of the head against the light. "I won't blame you. But you do this and you'll regret it your whole life. Not a second will go by that it doesn't haunt you… Think about your boys. If you kill me, you won't ever hold them again." He felt blood dribble from his ears. "Closest you'll get is behind glass… I've done enough harm to your family. Forget about me. I'm nothing… Don't waste another second on me. Go home."

The figure lowered the crowbar. What was a few seconds seemed to Ronnie like an eternity.

Matthew stepped around to the door of his car. Ronnie followed him with his eyes. The twin got behind the wheel of his SUV, started the engine, and slowly backed down the drive. The lights bobbed with the road, and Ronnie watched them until they were gone altogether. Only the pale lights of his own truck to illuminate the inlet. Now, the ghost of Michael haunted Ronnie and Ronnie alone.

He lay on the ground for a long time. He felt nauseous and blood kept running into his eyes. Ronnie tried to roll over, but yelled out in anguish. His scream echoed throughout the empty expanse. He'd known agony, but nothing this bad. His head was throbbing and he felt the blood pump from the crack in his skull. He lay back and looked up at the night sky. Thousands of tiny lights blinking in the blackness.

You could just go to sleep and it would all be over, Ronnie thought.

He sweat his shirt through despite the cold. Ronnie clenched his teeth and rocked back and forth like a turtle. After a few tries, he flipped over onto his stomach. His shoulder made an ungodly sucking sound and then popped into place. He shuddered and arched his back against the pain. He moved his hips like a woman in the throes of contractions. He looked ahead and saw the black water not five feet from where he lay. It took him ten minutes to crawl to it like a slug. He inched along and rested often.

The water looked delicious, but he dared not drink it. Ronnie dipped his whole head into the ice-cold swamp water. He washed the gore from his face and his eyes. He cupped a handful into his mouth and rinsed out the blood. Ronnie thought his collar bone might be broken. After much maneuvering, he sat up on his knees. Moving brought more blood and he felt the warm river run down his face. There was a constant tremor in the upper half of his body and he was struck by a wave of chill. He thought about the girls at home and it gave him some resilience.

When he stood, his knees cracked like the breaking of limbs. He screamed in agony and outrage. Self-loathing and physical pain manifesting itself. He thought he was going to vomit. He stumbled towards his truck like a drunkard. He was tottering and faint. The mechanisms of his body were misaligned and firing incorrectly. His vision cut out and he felt like falling. Everything went black, but he willed himself forward. He wasn't firing on all cylinders. Ronnie seemed like a child who'd lost his way.

Was it worth it? he thought. Yes. A fair exchange. The world seemed righted and rotated appropriately on its true axis. May Matthew sleep better at night. Let me be nothing more but a distant memory.

Ronnie got into the truck and rested his head against the cool back window. He studied the almost muted world from the safety of the truck cab. His hearing was partially returned and the chorus of crickets sang out. The suddenness of it surprised him. It reverberated like a great noise echoing down a long corridor. Or, a great clamor wrapped in thick cotton.

All these years, he thought. They led to this. Blinded to other hazards. You were afraid and that's okay.

Ronnie adjusted the rearview mirror and stared at his face. He looked like he was wearing war paint. He picked up a napkin from the door pocket and wet the tip. Ronnie wiped the blood away as best he could. He looked like a horrible clown. A feeling of death warmed over. He touched the wound on the top of his head and felt serum. It was congealing, which was a good thing. He was already thinking of excuses if he got pulled over.

Finally, he cranked the engine and turned on the heat. Dull winter chill drifting away. He sat with it running and he thought about his life. The warm cab calmed him. He was very tired and scarcely breathing. After a long time, he put the truck in drive and steered slowly down the dirt road.

Chapter 17

Clara tried to remain calm in front of Mary. After her daughter went to sleep, Clara paced the floors of the trailer for hours. She sat in front of her GED study books, but nothing on the pages distracted her swirling mind. She knew something was wrong. I should've gone with him, she thought. I should've demanded it. Damn. Stubborn old fool.

Clara went into the bedroom, put a pillow over her face, and screamed. She felt like a war wife or mother waiting for the postman. Terror and longing at the same time. The slightest noise dragged her to the window. Her hands wouldn't stay still. Her feet ached from the countless steps. Finally, she went out onto the porch and sat in the darkness. She listened intently to the world about. Grackles cawed from trailer gables and a mockingbird retaliated in kind. Clara clasped her hands and prayed. She didn't know what to do or say. A couple of words in Spanish. She was a novice of things ethereal. She whispered pleading words to the almighty. Her eyes were clinched tightly. Sweat beaded along her furrowed brow. She raised her eyes and stared into the heavens.

Please God, she said, bring him home.

Her hands wouldn't stop fidgeting and her knee bobbed up and down involuntarily. She checked the time on her cellphone.

It was a quarter to nine. Scenarios played in her head as to where he was. They might've gone for a beer. Or, he was lying dead in a ditch somewhere. Haunting scenes of seeing his lifeless corpse flashed through her mind. Nightmare visions of him dying all alone.

Clara went inside and got her keys. She'd give him until ten o'clock before going out and searching for him. Back on the porch, she listened to the sound of the Palms. Then she heard it. The truck motor was faint at first, but grew louder. She went down the steps and closed her eyes. A rumble and slow revving. She walked into the middle of the street and stared down the lane. There it was. The truck turned on number seven. Tears welled up in her eyes. He wasn't dead.

When he drew closer, she saw the pain on his face. When he pulled into the little driveway, she was by the driver's side waiting for him. She opened the door and looked at his pained face.

"Oh, Ronnie," she said softly. "Ronnie."

He smiled brokenly. "Good evening, darling."

"Oh, Ronnie," she said again. She touched his face and he flinched.

"I'm going to need some help."

Clara nodded and struggled to extricate him from the cab. He cried out in pain several times, but she held on. He limped towards the porch and she felt the full weight of him. She noted the dried blood and the failed attempts to clean himself. It was hard going up the stairs. He nearly toppled backwards. If he falls, Clara thought, there's no way you'd get him back up. An inner resiliency overtook her and she focused on one step at a time.

Ronnie limped through the trailer and she steered him into the bathroom. Mary was snoring inside her room and

Clara didn't want her to wake and see this. Inside the bathroom, Clara leaned Ronnie against the counter. She collected one of the metal kitchen chairs and put it inside the shower. She turned the nozzle and hot water steamed up the little room. She asked no permission. She pried off his shirt that was practically glued to his chest from the sticky blood. The sight of him took her breath. He had enormous purple welts all over him. They were terribly discolored and would only get worse.

She traced the outlines with her eyes where the object struck him. It looked painful, but the bleeding had stopped. One boot came off fine, but the other was filled with blood. A cut above the knee soaked everything through. Taking off his socks was like pulling and band aid. She placed his foot under the water and slowly pried it off. She sat him down in the chair and let the water wash over him. He winced at first, but slowly the warmth soothed away the pain.

Clara hurriedly stripped out of her pajamas and entered the shower. Although the water burned her, she paid it no mind and used a hand towel to clean off the blood. Ronnie placed his chin on his chest and went to sleep. She continued to wash him and cleaned off the gore. The bottom of the shower looked grimy and pink. The cut on the top of his head was congealing and looked to scab over. His elbow badly discolored and swollen. Ronnie's left shoulder hung funny and he woke with a cry as she moved it. She whispered it was okay and he nodded.

Clara turned off the shower and dried him sitting in the metal chair. It took a long time. She struggled getting him to stand up. He fought against her weakly. Finally, she had him on his feet and walked him to the hallway.

Both were naked and started towards the bedroom door. A noise sounded from behind and Clara turned. Mary poked her head out from her room. She was watching the spectacle with huge eyes. Clara whispered that Ronnie wasn't feeling well and for her to go back to sleep. Mary shut the door while giggling.

Clara and Ronnie took one step at a time. He was mumbling something unintelligible. Clara didn't know what all was wrong with him, but that he was hurt bad. She walked him over to the bed and laid him down. He cried out in pain, but soon settled in to sleep. Clara covered him with the comforter, got dressed, and sat on the bed. She watched his breathing. It was labored and he winced when taking deep breaths. Despite his appearance, he slept with a smile on his face. Like an enormous weight was lifted from him.

Old words of his reverberated. *Life is nothing but what you make of it. The past can own you, but only if you give it that right. Most people are unaware that you can say no.*

He'd cared for her while she was getting off drugs. Now it was her turn. She gently stroked his hair and studied him. There was nothing else she could do.

Clara woke with the sun shining through the windows. Dust danced through the beams of light. The ceiling fan ticked softly as it turned. She was tucked in bed and heard voices and dishes rattling in the kitchen. She heard Mary laughing and smelled the aroma of hot pancakes. Clara sat up and felt a pull in her back from carrying Ronnie the night before. She turned over. The sheets on his side of the bed were pulled up to the headboard. She moved the comforter and saw that the pillow was covered in blood. It was still wet and had stained the sheets as well.

Clara stripped the bed and pillowcase. She balled them up and put them behind the door. She'd wash them after Mary left for school. She went and opened the curtains to let the light in.

She felt something in her gut. A strange sense that this was the start of something new. Usually change evoked fear, but this didn't. Strangely, she welcomed it. She knew who she was and where she was. No greater feeling in the world.

Clara found her daughter sitting at the kitchen table, a huge stack of steaming pancakes in the center. Ronnie stood with his back turned and was pouring batter into a frying pan. He wore a long sleeve sweatshirt and a hat. Hiding the pain. His movement was stiff, but he tried to look normal in front of Mary. Her daughter was slathering butter between the flap jacks and smiling. She gripped a huge syrup jar and poured liberally.

"Good morning, Mommy."

"Good morning, sweetie. How are you?"

"I'm great! Ronnie is making a special breakfast to help with the sad day."

Clara tried to think of what she meant. Ronnie turned around with the spatula in hand. He had an enormous grin on his face. Clara walked over to the kitchen table and sat before an empty plate. She rubbed Mary's arm. "What do you mean?"

"Remember? Today's the anniversary of when Grandma became an angel."

Yes. December first was the day that it happened. Her mother had been living with Clara's sixth stepfather, one on a long list of lunatics who fed her mother's addiction. Taking more each time and destroying her soul. Her mother's only sober breaths were when she was asleep. If even, then. Clara wished her mother died an alcoholic death. Something at least peaceful in that.

No, instead it was a violent end to a tough life. No getting around that. The painful truth was that her mother died cowering and afraid. Her last husband was wanted for child pornography charges. Such was her mother's type. He'd unwittingly shared pictures online with a police detective. The next day they showed up and pounded on the door. A hostage situation ensued. Her drunken mother was the only captive.

It all occurred without Clara's knowledge. She was stripping that night and only found out after the deed was done. Senseless. Completely senseless. There was no negotiating with him. After several hours, with no response, the police breached the small scrabble house and found the bodies. He shot her in the face before turning the gun on himself. She was lying on the ground and tied with duct tape. The caliber was such that no open casket funeral was possible. In a sick twist of horrific irony, the murderer's family buried them side-by-side. Clara had no say.

"Mommy gets sad on this day, Mr. Ronnie. She visits her grave. When I don't have school, we go together." Mary turned to her mother. "So, Ronnie said he'd go with you." She stuffed an enormous bite of pancakes in her mouth and chewed. Clara watched her daughter in complete amazement. The ways of a child's mind.

"Yeah," said Ronnie. "I'd love to go. I'm not going to work today. Already called. Still not feeling well enough."

"He's in a bad way," Mary said between bites. She was mimicking someone and mockingly tried to speak several octaves lower. She didn't look up from her plate.

Clara laughed. "Where did you hear that?"

"That's what Ronnie said about you after we moved in. He said you were 'in a bad way.'" She imitated him again and laughed before taking another huge bite of pancakes.

"Eat your food," Ronnie said with pretend outrage. "You have to leave in fifteen minutes."

Mary nodded with a sly smile and finished her breakfast.

They walked down the street and to the front of the Palms. Other children milled about in various groups and Mary stood waving at her only friend. She looked up at her mother who said to go on. Mary set off running. Ronnie and Clara stood watching and waiting for the bus. She watched her daughter laughing and she thought briefly about her life. Never could she imagine that this was in the cards. She was always trying to keep up with living, but reality was never in her purview. She was miles behind.

We'll all find out in the end. Clara hated hearing that.

By then, it'll be too late. She long tried to second say the workings of the world. Yet, there was a strange calmness in letting go. A sense of clarity in giving up the scrupulous search for purpose. The road that led to here was fraught with peril. Trying to keep account of it was tedious. It couldn't change. Or wouldn't. Only her outlook shifted. Questioning what lay ahead was a pointless endeavor. You only get vague notions of what lies ahead. Nothing more. There was a peace in knowing that.

The school bus pulled up and the children boarded. Mary waved goodbye from the steps. A happy start to a new day. Seeing this in her daughter warmed something within her. Something she thought died a long time ago. Ronnie and Clara walked back towards the trailer. With her daughter gone, she noticed that Ronnie's fortitude waned. He strode slowly and limped along. His shoulder hung low. Every few steps, she heard him wince. They locked arms and took their time. It was tough going.

Halfway back, Clara said, "We should stay home. Help you heal."

"Nonsense. I'm fine. A little worse for wear, but I'll survive."

"No, it's fine. I don't even know why I do it."

"I think it's a good idea. I'd visit my mom if I knew where she was. She died when I was in prison and I can only guess where she's at." He put his arm around Clara's shoulders. "I think it's nice that she's remembered. I hope I am." He stopped and laughed. "Now, I don't want to be a urinal for disgruntled well-wishers. Maybe be reminisced in a good way." Clara felt him shake with a guttural laugh. He winced a little and they walked on. The two created a shadow of agony along the pock-marked roadway. They passed a dirty toddler playing in a puddle, splashing stagnant water at their feet as they trudged past. The reeking smell of his diaper permeated from yards away. Paper white gulls passed overhead who called out brokenheartedly.

Back at the trailer, Clara ate breakfast and showered while Ronnie watched the news. She heard him sigh woundedly and change the channel to a morning gameshow. She dressed quickly and entered the living room. Ronnie was gone. She went to the window and spied him outside.

Clara walked out onto the porch and sat down next to him on the swing. He was smoking a cigarette with his head resting on his chest. He seemed to stare at his shoeless feet. She looked at his phantom pinky toe that was left in South-East Asia over forty years before. Clara followed his gaze. He faced a line of ants parading across the porch towards the door. Little black things ignorant of the world besides their purpose. She looked out across the lot towards her old trailer. A cold wind blew dead leaves over the yard. Last week, the superintendent came by and made the place look half habitable. Preparing it for the next set of itinerate degenerates to call it home. Clara sat in reverence next to Ronnie. She could only guess at what weighed on his conscience. The physical pain was real, but perhaps it manifestly healed his heart. His cigarette burned slowly towards the filter. Clara did not want to disturb his musing.

Or, at least that was what she thought. His snoring broke the silence of the morning and she gently shook him awake.

"I was just resting my eyes," he said softly.

"I bet." She laughed.

"You ready?"

"Not really."

"I figured not, but we're doing it anyway," Ronnie said. He tried to stand, but struggled to rise. He tossed his cigarette in the ashtray and held out his hands. "I'm gonna to need some help, darling. Once I get going, I'm fine. It's the starting I'm struggling with."

Clara stood before him and pulled him up. A cracking sound followed and he cried out faintly. They stood side-by-side until he took a distrustful step forward.

"All better," he said.

They stepped into the trailer. Clara went over to her purse and hooked it about the elbow. Ronnie shuffled bow-backed into the kitchen and pointed to a cabinet over the microwave. She'd never seen him use that shelf. "Darling, will you reach up there and grab that bottle of whiskey?"

"Whiskey?" Clara asked with a sly smile.

"Whiskey. I hope you don't mind me drinking in front of you. I tend to stay away from the ole mother's ruin except for certain solemn occasions. Mostly on anniversaries of horrors from Vietnam. I drink to remember my dead comrades. I know it's grim, but you'd be surprised how it helps. It's still there, but not as bad. Sorta takes the bite out of the sorrow."

"It's all right. Go ahead."

Clara went over to the cabinet and brought down a dusty bottle of whiskey. It was half empty and sloshed about. The bubbles beaded along the side. The whiskey was an expensive brand. She handed it to Ronnie, who tucked it into the pocket of the jacket he wore. He limped over to the counter and took up his keys. He turned and handed them to Clara.

"You better drive," he said. "I don't think I'm one-hundred percent."

Ronnie locked the door from the inside and they stepped onto the porch. The sun was shining down. A light breeze gave off a chill and stirred the scene about. Windchime bells tolled off in the distance. They started across the patio.

Suddenly, an enormous racket exploded from the trailer across the street. Something shattered and there was a high-pitched squeal. Clara and Ronnie walked down the steps, but eyed their neighbor's home with suspicion. It sounded like a beast was loose and destroying the interior. A chorus of oaths that sounded vaguely human. Just as they reached the truck a massive crash reverberated in the morning quiet. Suddenly, the spiderlike drunkard burst halfway through the front door of the trailer. He looked like the living dead escaped from a tomb. He clung to the frame and was pulling with all his might. His eyes looked like they would burst. Something powerful held him back. He was practically phosphorescent with dry and cracked skin. After a short struggle, he broke free. He jostled and tripped over his naked feet. He fell onto his back, but rolled through and rose into a sprint. It was graceful and athletic. He soared away and landed among the paving stones. They gained traction and he bolted and tore off down the street. He carried a small pink handbag that he rifled through as he ran.

Clara saw the curtains part and a tiny dark face appeared in the window. He looked afraid and the eyes were hollow. What was behind those glazed orbs? His mouth was wide and there followed a blood curdling high pitch cry. The large woman stepped forth from the dark within and was breathing heavy. She looked flustered and enraged at the same time. A burning disappointment. She banged on the ratty banister and screamed. A flock of birds rose in unison and took flight. Behind the anger was real unadulterated sadness. It hurt Clara's heart.

As Ronnie and Clara walked to the truck, the neighbor woman called out. "Hit that no good son-of-a-bitch on your way out." She was crying and shook involuntarily. "Not a soul living in this world will care… There goes the damn electric bill money. Ass and elbows down the street. Our son will live in the dark because he needs a damn drink." She was sobbing now. Exacerbated and disgusted. Frustrated beyond measure at another burdensome cross to bear. The rage left and was replaced by unmitigated sorrow.

Clara couldn't stand to see it, so she entered the car. Ronnie didn't follow her. She watched in the rearview mirror as he wearily crossed the street. She saw as he reached into his pocket and pulled out his wallet. He took out several bills and palmed them. He stood at the bottom of the steps and spoke to the woman quietly. Her head rested on the banister and she hadn't looked up. Finally, she did and her tear streamed face glistened in the sun. He handed her the money and she slipped it into her bra. She walked down the steps and hugged him tightly. Clara knew that had to hurt, but he didn't let it show. After a long time, the neighbor let go and went back into her trailer. Ronnie limped back to the truck.

"Who are you?" Clara asked as she backed out of the driveway. "What planet did you come from?"

"What?" Ronnie said with a chuckle.

"Giving that lady money. Being good to her. You didn't have to do that."

"I know. But, it's going to get cold and Christmas is coming. I couldn't have them go without power for the holidays. It wouldn't be right."

"Well, she should kick that man out."

He turned his whole body to face her. He gave her a shocked look. "What a novel idea! Deary me... That's rich. It took an almost act of God for Joseph to get gone." Clara smiled and smacked his leg. "Ah, abuse," he hollered.

"Here," he said, pointing to the side of the road. "Pull over for a second."

Clara saw the pink purse and its contents scattered by a trash can. Ronnie exited the vehicle and gathered it up. He walked back to the car woodenly and slid inside. It was filled with various cheap knick-knacks. Little objects only important to her. A small child's drawing of the woman and her son at the beach. Clara immediately felt ashamed for what she'd said.

"You are just so nice to everyone," she said. "Prison really changed you for the better."

"Yeah, but I wouldn't recommend it for everybody."

The two drove down the main road and headed towards the coastal highway. Ronnie was staring out the window and Clara kept watching him out of the corner of her eye. She knew there was more he wanted to say. So much euchred in the silence. She thought about that. The light looked dusty in the rearview mirror. She spied their neighbor. The drunkard was standing crooked behind a trailer trading for a clear bottle of unbonded spirits. He was crying. He looked like a crouched buzzard. A terrible truth laid bare across his wet face. Complete addiction. The absolute realization that he'd do anything for his fix. His family be damned. Clara knew that look. For it was one she still carried. Ronnie was watching it too.

"You are like an aged hero," she said softly.

"I wouldn't go that far. I think that being nice to someone can have great ramifications. In a good way. Just a little act of kindness can turn someone's day or, hell, even life around.

You don't know what people are facing. Maybe a dying mother or sick child. A little thing you do, can mean so much to a complete stranger. We all wear masks. We meet people every day and we can't comprehend what's going on behind theirs. Little things can make or break someone. We never know what might talk them back or send them over the edge. I used to purposefully try and hurt people. It made me feel better about my useless life. If I couldn't be happy, I'd damn sure try and make everyone as miserable as myself." Ronnie shook his head. "That was the old, angry me. I generally do the opposite of that. I try to remember what it was like as I go throughout the day. Show a little kindness. Always."

Clara smiled at Ronnie. "I still think you're an alien."

"Might be. That would explain a lot." He chuckled.

They took the coastal highway east towards Pensacola. A few cars on the road. The truck kept going and crossed a bridge over an inlet. This marked the city limits. It rattled the cab and Ronnie sat straight up. She watched him retrieve the whiskey bottle and take a sip. He wiped his mouth and returned it within the jacket. The water below looked pale green. There was lush river grass growing along both banks. The wind jostled it back and forth. The sun shone gorgeous in the sky among a few wispy white clouds. Birds sat perched on the electric wires strung pole to pole. The lines looked like vertical sidewinders as far as the eyes could see. On the other side was the beach. The sand looked incandescent in the blazing sun. The plumes of surf were white and filled with foam.

Clara cut north bypassing the city.

The cemetery was far inland and set on a promontory above sea level. She navigated with a keen understanding of what this meant. Ronnie watched the sights and tapped his knee. He took small sips of whiskey to drive away the pain.

They drove on past a peculiar run-down shopping center where no form of human life moved. Along the way, he pointed out an abandoned lot where he and his ex-wife lived. The apartments long gone and only the hulking ruins of concrete remained. They passed other ruined buildings where it seemed all civilization had fallen. Remaining structures serving as abodes for the homeless or indiscriminate lovers. Driving away from the beach they saw the world turn flush with the evergreens. Fetterbush and witchhazel grew among the river birch. Farther off were standing red cedars and bent slash pine. Everything so beautiful amid the onset of winter. Their movements in the wind created little and strange shapes against the blue sky.

After a while, the truck loped along a straight patch of road that ran parallel to a long-corrugated cast iron fence. The stone monuments within stood raised in a massive grouping of lines like ancient sentinels. Some of the stones were elaborate and gaudy, while others were small and reverent. One visible from the road was of an enormous praying Christ holding eternal supplication for the dead. All marked the bones of loved ones gone from the earth, but who live on in the hearts of others. The sign for Rosecrest Cemetery was made of wood and painted white with black stenciled letters. Something plain and appropriate for the hallowed ground. The cemetery was laid out like a racetrack. There was a single oak tree that stood austere on top of the rise. The oak was incubated in this place before white men settled the country. Now a lonely watchman blanketing the dead. A visible sign of life amid the sleeping. Everything else descended from that. Slight decline marked by stone. There was an ornate bench underneath with a few words inscribed.

I am the resurrection and the life. He who believes in me will live, even though he dies.

A place sat on by hundreds of mourners like devotes before a shrine. One driveway circled property and there was a large brick house that stood in the right corner. The gravedigger's purple Mercedes was parked around back next to a green lacquered shed. Just as she remembered it. From that day those six years ago until now. Little changes with the dead. The living make sure of that.

Clara circled past the office and kept driving around towards the far-left. She drove slowly and breathed in her surroundings. Even after all these years, it still pained her heart. She'd never allowed herself to grieve properly. Her mother wasn't much of one, but that didn't make it any easier. She wasn't a bad person. She was sick and couldn't get well. She was murdered by an evil pervert for no reason. He stole her mother's life. After death, her mother visited her in dreams. Not the tiny yellow skinned alcoholic, but a fabled mom that she should've been. In them, she was full of life and a carrier of sage advice. Imparting it while Clara slept. A golden form of a mother who never was. There being something strangely comforting in that.

She parked the truck and exited the vehicle. Ronnie made slow go of it. There was pain on his face as he walked around the rear. Clara waited for him and they locked elbows. They watched two doves swoop together among the gravestones. A picturesque scene of peace. Some of the graves held plastic flowers in cheap vases that to Clara seemed blatantly disrespectful of the dead. The wind had blown most over and no one cared to right them. It was an almost clear demarcation that your loved ones had forgotten you. All about, the air smelled sweet and many of the markers looked bleached from the sun. Being in the cemetery without meth gave her a feeling that she couldn't place. Perhaps it was bitterness. More likely not. Maybe the unease brought by promise. That always instilled in her a real sense of fear. Holes in the greater part of her heart. Yet, she felt that perhaps now there were different parts filled.

Clara and Ronnie were slow going. Their feet settling deeply into the damp and cushiony grass. He was stooped and they walked shoulder to shoulder along the barren landscape. Their shadow grown long behind them faint as pencil markings. Birds nestled in the lonely oak with necks outstretched to view the grievers. She turned down her mother's row and walked by looking at the other markers. Names and dates chiseled in recess. The stones were oxidized with bits of sparkling shards from chemical reactions wrought centuries before. They were taken from mountains far away where the rocks rested for thousands of years. Now, they watched over the dead whose bones will turn to dust.

Clara stopped before her mother's grave. Right next to the murderer. The man who instituted her place among the tombstones. Clara spat on his marker. Ronnie hobbled over and sat on it. He brought out the bottle and took a sip. He then turned it up and drained a mouthful.

Clara crouched and ran her fingers over the indentations of her mother's stone. "Hi, Mom," she whispered. She reached into her purse and brought out a pair of small nail scissors. She trimmed around the base of the headstone. Next, she took a tissue and wet the tip with her tongue. She used it to wipe away the dirt. Finished, Clara sat back on her heels and spoke to Ronnie without looking up.

"I don't know how to pray," she said. "I wish I did, but I don't know the words."

"That's all right. I don't either."

"What do you do?"

"I sorta have a conversation. You could just talk to your mom."

Clara turned and smiled sadly. "Yeah. I dunno what to say."

"Just whatever comes to mind. I'll leave if it helps." Ronnie rose from his perch.

"No, no," Clara said. "I want you to stay."

Ronnie sat back down and looked off across the field.

Clara placed her hand flat against the cold stone. It felt almost electric. She thought there was a humming from within, but it was all in her head. The oak tree created dancing shadows across the marble. They looked like tentacles out of a storybook horror. "Mom. I miss you a lot. I think about you almost every day. I guess you know that. I know you are in a better place. Away from the cruelties of this life. You were dealt an unfair hand, but you did the best you could. No one is perfect. I wasn't the greatest daughter in the world. I certainly didn't make your life any easier. I just want you to know that you are missed and will always be remembered."

Clara looked up at Ronnie. He smiled and nodded, then took a deep swallow that made his eyes water. He wiped his eyes with the back of his hand.

"You know," Clara said, "I used to have this vision in my head of how life should be. That was all I'd ever see. But, now I realize that picture isn't real. How things ought to be is not the way they are."

Clara rose and sat on the headstone across from Ronnie. He drank from the bottle and shivered with each swallow. She felt light headed in this place. Clara noticed that he was watching her closely. As if he knew that something weighed heavy on her mind.

"Have you ever had a thought about something that was so bad that you're ashamed to tell anyone?" Clara said. "Even ashamed to the point you don't want to think about it? Fearful it might take you back to it? I wanted to abort Mary. Really wanted to. I thought I'd lose the baby. I had so many miscarriages before. I didn't have any money. By the time I found out she stuck, it was too late. I was past the trimester where it was legal. Now, I don't know what I'd do without her. I'd probably have killed myself. I'd have overdosed and been right here next to Momma."

"I don't know who Mary's father is. I was walking home from the strip club when a group of men assaulted me. Well… boys. They beat me, raped me, and left me for dead. I would've died, but my panties came lose in the night. They'd tied them around my neck and smashed my head in with a rock." Clara pushed back her hair and showed a jagged pink scar tucked in her hairline. "When she was born, one detective thought her race might find out who did it, but it couldn't. They were black and white. All had a turn. Plus, the police weren't that interested in helping out a junkie stripper. Figured I deserved it."

Clara sighed and wiped the hair from her eyes. "I never knew or understood the consequences. I'd hate to think I could go and relive it. Wanting the abortion, I mean. The thought of that terrifies me. I find that it's healthy to ignore it. Or, at least, I did. I couldn't bear to let it eat away at me. It's not so much as facing it, but letting the thing live on. Why give it breath? You'd run before putting it into perspective." She paused and looked directly at Ronnie. "I guess that makes me some anti-abortion person. I'd be horrified to think people used me as an example. I don't know. It just haunts me to think that I might've done it."

"I have thought about things that were really bad, but I don't think that's what you're asking me," Ronnie said. "I think you're wanting something that I don't have the authority to say." He smiled at her. "As a man, I don't know if I'm exactly qualified."

"Well, I'd still like to hear your say."

Ronnie set the bottle down, took out a cigarette, lit it, and exhaled blue smoke into the brisk air. The marble of the markers burned with a bright reflection in the sun. Several rows over, Clara saw a lizard basking in the heat. The uniform shapes of the monument's shadows looked endless. Clara felt something different here. Like looking through a new set of glasses. She tried to recall her mother's face but it was shrouded in fog. The look of her was remote and alien to her understanding. All she had left were memories that drifted further and further away. She feared that soon she wouldn't know the difference between what was made up or real. Ronnie picked up the bottle and took a swallow. It was nearly empty.

Ronnie watched her and spoke. There was a benevolent and earnest look on his face. "I don't think it's all that good an idea for others to make a decision like that. It's personal. Be it rape or incest or even getting knocked up on accident, folks shouldn't be forced into a situation that they aren't ready for. You made the best of your situation. A child will change someone's life whether planned or not. Might be for good, but might end up causing problems. Hell, even couples who wanted a baby can mess things up. I read about a woman who tied up her kids and drove the car into a lake. Another that lined them up by age and drowned them while the others watched. The papers just recently had it where a man left his kid in the car on purpose and went into work. Cooked his son alive. Might as well have put him in the oven."

Ronnie shook his head and spat. "What I'm trying to say is that your situation was unique. You made the best of it with Mary and it worked out. Might've been the other way. You never know. Whether it be a rape or a condom breaking, other people shouldn't oversee another's personal decision. I guess that makes me some sorta liberal, but that's just common sense. For me at least. While in prison, I had a long time to think. I tried to search out God's hand in everything. Every tragedy I wanted to find the almighty's reason for it being so. Yet, after many years, I concluded that there was no motive behind the good or bad things that befall mankind. There was no other course. Retracing those steps will just lead to the confirmation that our life is purely made of chaotic events strung together."

Clara watched Ronnie turn up the last bit and swallow.

"I remember," he continued, "while in Vietnam we sought to find providence in our survival. After our buddies died we looked for the hand of God in our lives that made sense of our existence. Why it was them and not us. The reality was that nothing in fate brought me back, while others died. It was either luck or training that allowed me to come home. God or his plan had nothing to do with it. Our own personalities were insignificant on that great arch. Throughout the war, I tried to make deals with God and swore promises while getting shot at. But the truth is that you can't persuade God. No manner of pleading or petition will ought to change his mind. He is not one for supplication nor a being of mercy. When I learned that, I finally felt that I understood God."

Ronnie paused and smiled. "So, you want me to say that it's all right you wanting to abort Mary. Even though she ended up being a blessing in disguise. Yes. That's all right, because that was your story. That doesn't mean it's the same for everyone." Ronnie smiled. "But, again, remember that I'm not authority on the matter. That's just my thoughts. Nothing more."

Clara looked up at the sky and saw the sun directly overhead. It was at its perfect meridian. She was dazed with hunger. They both stood up and looked around.

Clara touched her mother's headstone and whispered, "Goodbye, Mom."

Ronnie stubbed out his cigarette on the killer's grave. They turned to leave. A car passed on the road behind them that sounded enormous amid all the quiet. Walking back to the truck, Clara stepped around where she though the caskets were. She didn't know why, but felt it impolite to trample the dead. The hallowed field was freshly cut but the area reeked of loss. The air was crisp and she felt cold. She took Ronnie's arm again and they slowly made their way to the truck. Despite the chilly breeze, something warmed her heart.

Normally the singularity of drugs and solitude covered her like a warm blanket. It didn't take much to encroach on the boundaries of hell. The pain of it came and went like the terrors visited in certain dreams. It would pass and nod in slight recognition as travelers often do on long journeys. The more it happened, the colder it became. Yet, now, the weight of it slowly drifted away. As if her heart was physically manifesting itself. She even felt lighter. The thick fog that obscured her thinking was slowly dissipating. Ronnie's words reverberated too. She'd long believed that all wasted lives were a sin. But, he was right. All forms of existence showed signs of sacrilege.

You just need to know where to look.

Chapter 18

Mary woke excited.

She wasn't tired despite her lack of sleep. She'd lain awake most of the night in anticipation of the onset of day. It was January fifteenth and marked her eighth birthday. She knew Ronnie and her mother had purchased her present earlier in the week. It was hidden somewhere in the trailer, but Mary didn't dare look for it. If she found it, they might not let her have it. Better to be surprised.

That night, they were going out to her favorite restaurant and bowling afterwards. Mary hadn't bowled before and had always wanted to. Other kids at school talked about it and how much fun it was. Mary was giddy at the prospect. She'd heard that after eight o'clock, the lanes were blacked out and it turned into disco bowling. There were neon lights and glow-in-the-dark balls and pins. She couldn't wait.

This would be her first birthday since living with Ronnie. Everything was so different with him involved. Almost bigger. For Christmas, they had decorated the inside and outside of the trailer. All three went to a Christmas tree lot and picked out the largest one. It took Ronnie several hours to get it inside, and he'd had to cut the tip off. Together they strung colorful lights around the tree and dotted it with red and green ornaments.

They made peanut butter cookies and dressed them with icing. Her mother torched the turkey and cried, but the day was saved by a trip to Walmart and they grilled steaks instead. Christmas morning, Ronnie dressed up like Santa Claus. He paraded around the trailer singing carols. Mary had never seen her mother laugh so hard. In fact, she'd noticed something different about her. Hard to place, but she'd changed.

Living with Ronnie was transformative. Even for himself. He said so and Mary wholeheartedly believed him. There was a real sense of togetherness in this mismatched family. A strange puzzle put together and made right.

The sound of pots and pans drew her to the bedroom door. She tip-toed and opened it quietly. Ronnie was getting ready to make breakfast and hadn't heard her. Or, at least that's what she thought. Silently she approached. Then, abruptly, he turned and lifted her high in the air. Mary squealed with laughter as he twirled her around. He attacked her with kisses on the forehead and started to sing "Happy Birthday." She was laughing and wiggling for freedom. He set her lightly on the ground and looked at her. He eyed Mary with a sort of sly suspicion. He held his arms out and made a U with his thumbs touching. Ronnie shut one eye.

"Yep," he said. "Definitely a year older."

"But I wasn't born until noon."

"Well, you've sprouted early." He turned around to the stovetop. "What'll ya have, birthday girl?"

"Two scrambled eggs, please."

"Two?" Ronnie said with mock surprise.

"Yes." She laughed. "I am growing."

"Your wish is my command."

Mary went over to the table where the orange juice carton sat next to an empty glass. She filled it halfway and took a sip.

She moved her mother's GED books to make room and wondered how long her mother had stayed up last night studying. She'd never seen her mother work so hard at something before.

Ronnie broke eight eggs into the skillet and hummed "Happy Birthday" loudly. The door opened to the bedroom and Mary's mother stepped into the kitchen. Her hair was wild and she rubbed her eyes with the palms of her hands. Like a creature escaped from a tomb. She shuffled across the linoleum floor to Mary and kissed her on the cheek.

"Happy birthday, sweetie," she said.

"Thank you, Mommy."

"Are you excited?" Ronnie asked.

"Yes, sir."

Clara sat down next to Mary and rubbed her arm. Ronnie brought over a cup of coffee and set it down in front of Mary. Steam wafted from the rim. Mary leaned back away from the bitter aroma. The smell was almost acidic. She turned and laughed. "No no no," she said.

"Oops. Wrong one," he said and handed it to Clara.

She poured a bit of milk into the cup and stirred it slowly. Ronnie returned to the little table and placed a plate stacked with toast. There was already butter and an assortment of jelly in the middle. Clara picked up one piece and buttered it. Mary followed her mother's lead and selected strawberry preserves. She dressed the toast and set it on the plate. Ronnie still hummed "Happy Birthday" and her mother joined in. The trailer smelled like eggs and Mary's mouth watered. Jagged lines of light shone on the table. It reflected through the jam jar and created a beam of red. Ronnie walked over to the table with a skillet full of eggs. He doled out a quarter each for the two girls and took the other half. Mary lightly added salt and pepper to her steaming eggs. Her mother and Ronnie did likewise. Then they clasped hands around the little table and squeezed. Ronnie dug into his eggs and was finished with his meal by the time Mary ate half her toast. He watched them and drank his coffee.

"Do you feel any older?" Clara asked.

"No. But, I'm not eight yet."

"She does have a point," Ronnie said over his mug of coffee.

Clara rolled her eyes and smiled across the table. "I know. I was there!"

Mary watched them and thought about her present. She tried to figure the opportune time to broach the subject. While she ate, Mary noticed that her mother and Ronnie kept glancing over and smiling. As if they knew exactly what she wanted to ask. Here was the crossroads. It gave her an inner-resolve to wait, which lasted only a few minutes. Mary almost felt her pulse for how anxious she was. The anticipation peaked and she couldn't wait any longer. She stuffed the last bit of toast in her mouth and chewed quickly. She swallowed the last of her orange juice and sat back watching the watchers in turn. Waiting momentarily for any form of guidance. An unmarked look on their faces. Then, her mother smiled and laughed.

"So," she said. "I'm guessing you want your present."

Mary blushed and looked down. "Yes, please."

"Okay," said Ronnie. "But, we have to sing 'Happy Birthday' first."

"Deal."

Ronnie and Clara sang to her. When the song was over, her mother went into the bedroom and came out carrying something behind her back. She was grinning from ear to ear and Mary sat on the edge of her seat.

"Pick a hand," Clara said.

"Right," Mary said, bouncing up and down.

Her mother brought forth a dark purple backpack that was popular and much desired among the children at Mary's school. She practically shrieked. It was a brand originally for mountaineers but over time had morphed into a fashion fad. Clara handed it over and Mary was unzipping zippers and completely forgot about the other hand. She placed it around her shoulders and tightened the straps.

Finally, her mother cleared her throat. "Aren't you forgetting something?"

"Oh yeah!" Mary said, waiting patiently for her mother to reveal what was in her other hand.

Clara brought out a used but new looking acoustic guitar. Mary took off the backpack and left her seat. The guitar was thirty-six inches and made of walnut. It was a smaller and cleaner version of the one Ronnie owned. She practiced on his every day, but it was too large and hindered her hand movements along the struts. This was perfect.

Mary strummed several out of tune cords. She tried to tune it, but wasn't used to the new body and strings. She handed it to Ronnie, who tuned it by ear. The guitar's body was a glossy dark brown. The pick guard was black and the bridge was polished ivory. She noticed a few scratches, but was in awe at the instrument's beauty.

Ronnie strummed it several times and handed it back. She sat with the guitar resting on her right leg with the head angled slightly towards her. She twiddled her fingers and placed them on the frets like Ronnie had taught her.

Clara collected Mary's forgotten bookbag from the floor and stood watching her daughter's enamored face. Mary fit the guitar loosely under her arm. She played a few notes and used the frets with an easy niceness.

"We can play together," Mary said.

"Even start our own little band," Ronnie said.

"Yes," Clara chimed in. "But, after school." She was pointing to the clock on the microwave. Mary had fifteen minutes to get to the school bus. "I'll put your books into the new bag while you get dressed." Mary reluctantly handed the guitar over to Ronnie with a groan. "You can say, 'Thank you, Mom and Ronnie.'"

"Thank you, Mommy and Ronnie," she said and hugged them both.

Ten minutes later, they were out the door and headed down the road to the school bus stop. Mary wore her new backpack and walked between her mother and Ronnie, holding their hands. Mary looked over to a trailer on the corner and saw three ravens perched on a gutter. They were broad chested of posture and flapped their wings and watched the troupe pass. She imagined them as little cartoons that she'd seen. They might've broken into song. A dog lay sleeping in the middle of an intersection. Her belly swollen and rippling softly with inner life. Her teats enormous in anticipation. She slept in the sunshine as flies crawled across her smiling and dreamless face. The soon to be pater familias crouched across the street watching her sleep. The trio gave the dogs a wide berth. Despite full on winter, the weather was warm. A light shimmering heat off the asphalt. The bus was waiting and pulled away after Mary stepped aboard.

The day sped by. Students she thought hated her stopped and wished her a happy birthday. Everyone complimented her new backpack. Ronnie put an extra moon pie in her lunch and she couldn't remember a better day at school.

She almost didn't want to leave.

On the ride home, the sun shone through the windows of the bus and she watched the world pass. She saw the little fronds waving to her on the palm trees. The bus trundled through Pensacola and she watched the townspeople with great interest. She saw a woman in a pantsuit walking reticent and austere down the sidewalk. A businessman standing on the corner waiting for the light to change. An old man and woman holding hands and looking into storefronts. A young man jogging leisurely.

When the bus reached the outskirts of town and slowed to a crawl, they passed a rundown and dangerous looking package store. It was barred across the windows and always looked frighteningly impenetrable despite the neon red open sign. A blond-haired woman stood at the corner with an arm resting on her cocked hip. She was pretty and young, but looked mean. She wore clothes reminiscent of her mother's old wardrobe that left little to the imagination. The woman wore gaudy makeup and looked like an irate clown. The whore's hair was dyed a crazy color that held no true name. Perhaps, just a number along the vast and countless hues that was impossible to imitate. Mary watched her as they passed. A curious sideshow act standing on street corners.

Then, the sight of something else chilled her to the bone. Leaning against the wall was Joe. Their eyes locked and he doffed an imaginary hat. He looked like an exiled being returned to walk amongst us. His hair was greasy and looked glued to his scalp. An evil grin was plastered across his filthy face. He was missing a front tooth. He pushed his tongue through the gap. Joe's skin was red marked and full of craters like the face of the moon. His sunken sockets looked like two evil pale stones. Red irises like hot coals. They were without life and seemed carriers of peril like the weapons of a latter-day medusa. Mary slunk back and hid in her seat. Even with her childlike understanding, she knew that Joe was the embodiment of misery. She shook violently like a terrified puppy and clutched her new bag. She was afraid in a way that she didn't understand.

The bus pulled up to the front of the Palms and Mary saw Ronnie's truck idling by the entrance. She weighed the facts concerning what she'd seen. Her child's mind sought to debate the merits of telling Ronnie about Joe. As she walked down the aisle of the trailer park, Mary composed herself and decided against it. He was out of their lives.

She stepped down and ran over to Ronnie's truck. She saw him watching her from the mirror. There was a huge smile on his face. Mary jumped into the cab and hugged his neck. Far away, she kept Joe in her repository. No need to bring him out. It was her birthday and the past with him was inconsequential.

They drove to the trailer and she watched the pure blue sky. Not a single cloud in sight. The sun glared over everything and bits of light reflected off the chipped painted tin roofs. A few sea birds soared lost and motionless against the wind. Their tiny black eyes searching for anything of value. Two clusters of children were throwing a tennis ball across the street. It passed inches over the hood of Ronnie's truck. He rode the brakes and when the yellow thing passed he locked the wheels and skidded. The children broke and ran. Ronnie was chuckling. He let off the brakes and they drove on. The rules of the game were simple. The children tried to get the ball as close to the vehicle without hitting it. If the kids were successful, they kept playing.

But, hitting the car brought the game to an immediate pause as they ran for their lives in every conceivable direction. Ronnie and Mary both laughed at the youthful frivolity. It made her feel older. Yet, deep down, she thought that it looked fun. She felt like a fugitive against her age. Mary couldn't let it show. Especially now.

Ronnie made them a snack of their favorite staple. He fried up thick pieces of bologna and cut thin slices of tomatoes. With the meat still steaming, he spread mayonnaise over the bread and piled the bologna on top. He then put cheese and two slices of tomatoes on the sandwich and handed it to Mary. It was exactly how she liked it. This poor man's delicacy fit her just fine. She'd eat them just so throughout the rest of her life. He made three for himself. His was overflowing with mayo and he practically inhaled his sandwiches. Ronnie was like a human vacuum. She'd not eaten half by the time he was done. He belched and shoved a handful of chips into his mouth. Mary laughed and rolled her eyes at her grinning friend.

"So," Ronnie said with a mouthful of food. Bits of chips sprayed. "What do you wanna do until your mom gets home from work?"

She wiped away bologna grease and mayonnaise from her mouth with the back of her hand. "Can we play our guitars?"

"I thought you'd never ask."

Mary quickly chewed the rest of her sandwich and went to get her birthday present.

The orange sun shone through the window and created burning light. The dusk in the west looked on fire with malefic light. Bits of red hugged the rim and changed the very view of the waning day. Music radiated from within the trailer. Mary and Ronnie played their guitars for an hour straight. Her lessons progressed and she was quite good. The smaller neck of her new guitar allowed her to reach the frets with ease. They began with *Mary* and moved on to various songs from the 1970s and earlier hits from the classic troubadours. The colorful tableau beyond faded away and the two played on. Mary used a pink guitar pick, while Ronnie strummed with his calloused fingertips. There was safety here.

For Mary, playing the guitar shielded her from the troubles outside. No looming outrage or terror breached the serenity. After a while, she leaned her weight against the body of the guitar and played slower. A little off rhythm with Ronnie. Clearly her fingers were tired. Mary paused and clinched her fists several times. Finally, he called a halt to the proceedings. As if on cue, Clara's car approached and the headlights burned bright through the blinds into the trailer. Mary set her guitar down and rose with Ronnie to meet her mother at the door.

They listened to the sound of her exiting her car and mounting the steps to the porch. She crossed wearily towards the front door. She opened it and saw them standing patiently. About her beckoned the first few stars of twilight. Mary cocked her hip to the side in mock annoyance. Clara blew a strand of loose hair from her eyes and immediately started apologizing. She couldn't leave the dollar store until the shelves were restocked and it took longer than usual.

"Let me change real quick and we'll go," she said.

"It's okay, Mommy. Take your time."

Fifteen minutes later they were out the door. All three piled into the truck with Mary sitting in between. Someone from the park was burning trash and the sweet reek permeated everything. Mary felt excited. Like the night belonged to her.

It was dark as they pulled out onto the coastal highway and headed towards town. The moon hovered above the roadway in the east and it seemed awkward and out of place in the blackness. Beauty in the flawless void of the heavens. The lights of Pensacola looked quiet and innocent in the distance. Mary rubbed her tired hands together and stretched her fingers. Tiny shocks of pain as she pulled them free. The tips were raw. It didn't matter. They were abroad on her birthday and headed for a night of fun. The thought of bowling drifted in her mind like the remnant of a sweet dream. Her mother seemed irritated and harried for some unknown reason. It worried Mary that she'd done something wrong. Perhaps her mother knew about her seeing Joe. She tried to push that away. It was impossible.

They drove on in silence with the sound of the road orchestrating music of its own. As they continued, the landscape changed. The truck trundled along into the city. Main Street was brightly lit and alive with activity. Ahead was the sign for Chili's and Ronnie slowed the truck and parked in the lot away from the front door. It was packed with cars. Busy Friday night.

Inside, the walls were filled with interesting antiques and old signs that Mary found fascinating. Advertisements for objects or products long gone with these as their lasting memory. Things of promise and men's life work, living out their days on a chain restaurant's mantelpiece. Mary loved to look at them. She tried to imagine where they came from and what purpose they served. Ronnie knew most of the answers.

The hostess seated them in a booth. Mary and her mother sat across from Ronnie. He ordered her favorite appetizer, which was the chili queso dip. Ronnie and Clara searched the menu, while Mary sat patiently. When the waitress returned with the chips and dip, they ordered dinner. While they waited, Ronnie told jokes and made Mary laugh.

Yet, Mary noticed something was wrong with her mother. She didn't have anything to say. In the strange light of the restaurant, she looked fevered. Like someone rapt with a dark secret. There was something provisional about her. So, Mary finally asked.

"Sorry, sweetie," Clara said, blinking as if broken from a trance. She turned to face her daughter. "I've just had a strange day." She kissed Mary on the cheek.

"What happened?"

"Nothing at all. I've just had a sick feeling in my gut since I left the trailer this morning. I'm sorry."

"Maybe you're hungry," said Ronnie. "If I don't eat, I get piqued."

"That's probably it. I didn't eat any lunch today." Clara smiled and dipped a chip into the queso. Ronnie stopped the waitress and asked for more.

Mary grew afraid listening to her mother. She couldn't mention Joe. Did her mother have some special sort of powers of perception? Mary decided she'd study the possibility later.

Then, their food arrived. They clasped hands momentarily before they began eating.

Mary looked up and noticed that her mother was staring at a booth across the room. There was a group of people, perhaps her mother's age, who sat around several pitchers of neon ice drinks. They laughed and chatted and drank together. She noticed that there was something sad in her mother's eyes. A longing for something that Mary didn't understand. Then, her mother exhaled sharply and called for a waitress who quickly came over to the table.

"Can I have what they are having?" she said. Clara pointed towards the table.

The waitress turned and smiled. "Sure thing. A pitcher?"

"Yes, please."

The waitress left and Ronnie stared at Clara with a burning intensity. "Wait, Clara," he said. "That has alcohol in it."

"Oh, come on," Clara responded. "One drink won't hurt."

"That's not one drink. And you know what they say in the NA meetings. Any type of mind altering and mood changing substance will take you back to that. One is too many and a thousand is never enough." He reached for Clara's hand, but she pulled it away. A sadness entered his eyes. "You've come too far for this."

"Ronnie, it's fine," Clara said with a tinge of utter finality.

Mary didn't know what to do or say. There shouldn't be tension at my birthday dinner, she thought. Too much has happened already today and this seemed to pile onto the bad. She didn't understand exactly what they were arguing about, but it didn't sound good. Mary just wanted it to stop.

The waitress returned with a pitcher of neon drink and Clara filled an empty glass to the brim. Ronnie just stared at her in total disbelief. In short order, Clara drank that glass down and then poured another. She drank that one as well, but a little more slowly. Mary noticed that her mother's cheeks were flush and a dull expression spread across her face.

Mary was side-eyeing Ronnie with curiosity. As if, he held answers to questions yet asked. The countenance of one beholden to another.

"You've thrown all your hard work away. Just like that," Ronnie said softly. Then he started to cry. Tears dripped onto his plate. His own wails caught the attention of their neighbors and the baby pointed and mumbled a host of incomprehensible words.

Mary reached across the table and took his hand. "Ronnie?"

A welter of snot tracked down his upper lip and hung corrugated in a swinging stalactite of muck. His eyes were puffy and red. Everyone watched this lone elder break down in the middle of a chain restaurant. He struggled for breath and Mary feared his heart would explode. He looked clammy and sweat beaded across his forehead. He wrung his sweaty hands together. A sick fear rose in her eyes. A visitation of something warped and corrupted. Like straining to see through ruined and aged glass.

Mary left her plate untouched and watched Ronnie. He was wiping his eyes. Clara kept drinking. The waitress walked past, and Ronnie asked for the check. She returned and he placed cash on top of the receipt. He pushed himself out of the booth and held his hand out to help Mary. She hurried to his side and held his hand. He hugged her and spoke sweetly to her as they walked out of the restaurant.

Halfway to the car birds cried out and Mary asked what kind they were. Ronnie looked to the heavens and told her they were whippoorwills. He said that it was very special that she heard them because they were rare in this part of the country. He placed his arm around her shoulder and they went on. Her mother was several wobbly steps behind. Mary was comforted by his embrace. The landscape dissolved around her and she believed truly that he'd wouldn't abandon them. Now or ever.

The bowling alley was alive with activity. A magnetism created by the blaring music and flashing lights. Everything shone through black light and the miasma of hues fascinated Mary. The previous events washed away. She looked down and saw that her white shirt radiated light, as did the laces on her shoes. She saw that even the whites of her mother's eyes burned brightly. A few laser lights danced across the scene that scattered her senses. A fake fog migrated slowly across the ceiling and breathed life into the strobes. The bowling balls were of various neon colors and looked spectacular gliding across the wooden floors. The white pins stood majestically at the end before exploding into a phantasm of sparkling lights. Mary involuntarily jumped up and down in anticipation. The noise was immense with music and laughter. It mixed with the unmistakable sound of heavy rolling balls across the floor and the smashing of wood on contact.

Mary studied intensely the movements of the bowlers. Watching the mechanics of their stance to the release. She noted the importance of the follow through. One old man even kicked his leg out crazily, but knocked over all the pins. She'd try that first.

The three walked over to the kiosk against the back wall. An annoyed youth stood in faux expectancy for these newcomers. There was something remote in the way he looked. Behind him were rows and rows of bowling shoes that reminded Mary of a clown.

The place was already like a fairground funhouse. Ronnie screamed something to the waiting attendant who turned and collected three smelly pairs of shoes and slapped them on the desk. Ronnie paid and the worker held up four fingers and the trio set off. Mary passed a woman wearing a tie-dye shirt that in the light made her look like a disaster victim. She walked uneasily as if on a ship. A smile that was matched by a forlorn expression. She sauntered around her friends with a strange colored drink in her hand. It looked neon green. Mary noticed how different many of the parties were. They passed a group of serious men wearing matching shirts playing against others in likewise attire. Only the names on the back differed. Next, were a gangly group of youths who guffawed about and paid the game little mind. There was back slapping and fits of laughter that reminded her of animals on a television program. They only needed to throw poop for a complete picture.

Finally, they arrived at lane four and Ronnie typed in their names on a little computer. It popped up on a screen above their station. Mary took off her shoes and put on the ragged clogs. They smelled horrid and were a size too big. Ronnie put on his pair and asked if they wanted something from the refreshment stand. Drinks for all and off he went.

Clara took Mary over to a rack of bowling balls and helped her pick from the group. She selected a small pink one that was heavy. It was the smallest they found so it had to do. Ronnie returned with an enormous tray of nachos and a bottle of coke. Ordering food after they just ate made the girls laugh, but Ronnie waved them away and shoved a cheesy chip in his mouth. He selected a large yellow ball that was bigger than Mary's head and her mother picked a smaller one that was a burned neon blue.

Mary bowled first. Her ball spent most of the time in the gutter. Copying of the other bowlers wasn't working, so she made up a technique all her own. Ronnie struggled at first, but quickly improved his craft. Clara played little better than her daughter, but it didn't matter. They were having fun. As the night progressed, mother and daughter laughed at Ronnie's mock intensity. She watched as her mother howled when he slipped on the slick floor and went flying. His body went farther than the ball. Mary settled on the technique of rolling the ball with both hands from between her legs. Her score improved.

It seemed the calamitous events at dinner drifted away into a faint memory. Any fear or animosity floated away like the smoke amid the dancing lasers. Then, something far worse occurred.

Mary caught sight of the woman from earlier that day. Just a glimpse out of the corner of her eye. Impossible to miss. In the black light, the horror show lady looked even more menacing. She wore the same ridiculous outfit from before, but the cosmic atmosphere in the room created a wholly new nightmare visage. A painted lunatic escaped from an asylum.

Mary bowled a three and turned in frustration when she saw her. The clown was visibly hiding behind a rack of balls and staring at Clara with a horribly crazed expression. Mary felt her stomach sink. An opened pit replaced anything within. Her head started to ache. She looked around for Joe, but couldn't see him amid the lights and smoke. Ronnie nor her mother noticed the clown. They were enjoying themselves. All while Mary felt something break. She was too afraid to speak. She raised her hand and pointed into the dark. Her mouth was ajar for the thing she couldn't name.

Amid the frivolity, Ronnie and Clara saw Mary's face and both turned. Ronnie looked without understanding, but Clara knew. She squealed a little and bounced up. Instead of fear, there was happy recognition. Her mother held her arms out wide and embraced the nightmare. Hauled to her bosom the lurid creature who frightened her daughter. They chatted and laughed like old friends. Her mother seemed bewitched by the stranger.

Mary was dizzy with shock. She hurried to Ronnie's side and grabbed ahold of his arm. She tried to compose herself. He'd quit watching the two and was concentrating on the nachos. He was completely unaware of the trouble her mother was in. The terrible one leaned in and whispered something in her mother's ear. Clara nodded vigorously and rubbed her hands together. They hurriedly went off into the darkness. The strobes shone pointing the way to the restroom. Mary remembered a proverb Ronnie shared one time. It was imprinted on her young mind. She knew what this woman was. This harlequin whore was the smoke. Somewhere close was the fire.

"Ronnie," she said, "I don't like that woman."

"What, sweetie?" Ronnie yelled over the music.

"I don't like that woman," Mary screamed.

"Why?"

"She hangs around with Joe."

Just the name wrinkled Ronnie's brow. His whimsical expression changed immediately. His face clouded and something akin to rage replaced his smile. He leaned towards Mary and told her to stay put. Ronnie stood and looked around. Then he marched off in search of either party. Mary sat forward and stared at her ugly clown shoes. They were ridiculous and she hated them more than anything she could remember. A mournful realization that her birthday led to this. She held her hands together in a viselike grip and squeezed like a sinner at benediction.

Mary looked up and saw her mother step through the darkness into the neon light. Ronnie was at her elbow and leading her to their station. He sat across from Clara and looked at her with disappointment. Nothing close to anger. It was more akin to sadness or regret. Mary didn't understand what was wrong. No idea of what transpired. Just that a fracture had opened up in their little family. She turned to her mother and noticed something strange about her eyes. They seemed dreadfully familiar. A wild burning to them. Red spider webs tracked along the whites. The pair of irises disappeared and were replaced by enormous black orbs the size of dimes. The little shapes of her jaw bone rapidly churning through her cheeks. A grinding noise that Mary recognized over the obnoxious music.

Mary rose to leave and no one stopped her. She passed through the double glass doors and never looked back. She was nearly to the truck when a clicking noise caused her to stop. She looked around warily. A strange feeling rose within her. Like she was being watched. The winter night chilled her to the bone. Even with a full moon, the scene about looked dimensionless. She felt fear return. She drifted away without any accountability but the fraudulent luminous light behind her. There were no stars. The blue-black sky overhead only burdened her heart. Was she being followed?

Then, Mary took another step, heard the noise again, looked down, and saw she still wore her bowling shoes.

Chapter 19

Clara did a line of meth before stepping into the shower. She was using again. It was like she had never quit. Her love and hate for the drug went hand in hand. During her recovery, the physical cravings for meth had disappeared, yet the mental obsession was always there.

That part never left.

Clara's addiction followed her everywhere. Like the devil's minions that never went away. A thing lingering in the shadows, afraid of what the light might find. Her addiction sat outside the trailer doing pushups and waiting for the almost inevitable return. She never dealt with the underlying problem. The actual manifestation of pain that urged her to use and spiral into self-destruction was left unchecked.

Her addiction waited patiently for the right moment to strike. At the bowling alley, her dependence found an outlet. A perfect time to return when she was most vulnerable. Your addiction loves it when things are going well. It tells beautiful lies that everything is all right. *Just one line won't hurt you. You can handle it this time.* All it needed was one smiling and familiar face to open the door.

Clara's life had been nearing a goodness that was almost completely unimaginable. Her detour into recovery had brought with it a light she'd never experienced. She'd only ever known darkness. The happiness terrified her at first. Then she accepted the change brought by sobriety. She looked around and saw another and better world. Things she'd never known were suddenly made clear. The past and present finally made sense. Her daughter was gaining confidence and making new friends. Coming out of her shell that was for so long calcified shut by years of distrust and heartbreak through her mother's drug use.

In sobriety, Clara accepted a man in her life whose sole purpose wasn't to use her and toss her aside. Everything in her world was looking up. Wholly alien and wholly strange. Yet, the siren song of addiction harkened her back to the existence she swore away. Using again carried her back to the undifferentiated terrain from which she'd fled. Like a refugee returning to her homeland that had fallen into ruin. Something almost completely beyond her recognition yet comfortingly familiar. It summoned a yearning that had lain hibernating.

Clara turned off the shower and stood dripping onto the bathroom floor. The division of day only counted by the change from darkness to light. She felt a vibrating tremor from every cell in her body. The familiar tug of caustic anxiety. A sucking sound with each shift of her feet on the cheap linoleum. She closed her eyes and tried to imagine herself somewhere else. Perhaps, rising out of a river and standing amid the whispering shore willows.

Naked before the clouded bathroom mirror, she watched the return of deterioration. Her body had long begun to heal, but the descent into using brought decomposition's return. Red scars from phantom itches oozed blood. The orbs in her eye sockets were sunken and hollow. Drugs provided an outlet for her remorseful and less soul. She lacked any sort of strength to guarantee confidence. Anything to bring a moment's rest. Something to shake away the horrible truth of her past.

Clara began to hum an old song that her mother used to sing. Along the vein of miracles created in destruction. There were few things in life that she could control, perhaps, her death being one of them. Outside, a dog yapped sharply and on rhythm. The barks created a bizarre, animalistic duet in her mind. She suddenly felt an unbelievable urge to get away.

Clara dressed quickly and snuck out of the trailer into the brisk pre-dawn. The blood red horizon was capped black with thunderclouds. The sky directly above was clear and still gleamed and shimmered with last star light.

She crept down the steps. The cool morning breeze drew water to her eyes as she wandered down the street and lingered by her old trailer. The road ahead so depthless that it looked like a tunnel. Night birds cried out their last to forlorn the breaking of day. Clara felt like a denizen among them. She tried to think, but nothing worthwhile stuck. There was a gulf between her thoughts, and that realization terrified her. Clara turned towards the golden smudge growing in the east. She had no idea what she was doing or why. The biting chill brought on goosebumps mixed with beads of perspiration, but she kept going.

Her bones ached, but her brain was alive. Sanity was scurrying about and she spent too much time playing catch-up. Her mind went haywire and she swore softly into the wind.

Even in this cold, early morning, it was so humid that each breath gave the impression of drinking water. Her glossy eyes stared off into that perfect ruin of sunrise. It seemed foreign. Nothing that distinguished any providing detail. An imagined geographical place that was hostile and unknowable.

In the middle of the road, she picked a wild dandelion that grew from a jutted break in the cracked concrete. She held it closely before her face and tried to imagine its place in the world. The doomed parallels with her own. She stared at the tiny white stalks that rippled softly in the wind. She blew into it and the florets spirited away into the shadows of first light. The breeze carried forth what can never be held. The swift shape of the twirling world loosed them arching away to a new point of origin. Something anonymous passed before the blood red birth of sun. She turned to face it and saw nothing but a single feather fall daintily in the street ahead.

There was no one about. Only the wind and the silence.

Then, the dogs of the Palms set to howling and seemed to waken the known world. Wild cries that morphed into rhythm with her heavy breathing. A rolling chorus that erupted the other sounds of bitter reckoning and brought about full day.

Even after just a few days of using again, she already felt alienated from everyone and everything. What she'd once understood seemed dreamlike and remote. She felt a deep sadness down to her marrow that she was slipping away. She finally let the unfortunate circumstances of her birth dictate and control her course. She'd fought against it for so long, but, now, finally, gave up and let it beat her.

When she watched Ronnie and Mary together, it seemed like a living picture of a real family. With him in their life and her off drugs, everything changed so fast. It was like each morning was the start of a new month, year, or world. A proper future that Clara had long hoped for. Yet, the drugs loomed as dangerous obstacles. She was sucking the life out of their little home. The events of her recent past were fading and she plowed ahead running on rage and grief. Reality itself seemed to change and the world took on the look of a funhouse. There were mirrors everywhere that skewed the very fabric of her existence. Her life using drugs was black as obsidian. Something horrible holding that illustration of domesticity back. With Mary now safe, she contemplated leaving forever, but couldn't bring herself to do that.

At least, not yet.

The heaviness returned to Clara that stretched her into isolation from the others. Her heart was no place that she wanted anyone to glimpse. She hoped Mary carried the memories of her mother's sober moments forever. Like a great thing to be treasured or it might slip away. Clara saw no way to backtrack out of her current predicament. The only thing was to go forward. Ronnie and her daughter wanted something that she couldn't give: a sober friend and mother.

Being alone was better because grief loved solitude. And sadness wrought tears of her bleeding heart that sustained her and only her.

All of a sudden, Clara remembered an ex-boyfriend's fist at her throat. Then, a hand squeezing tightly. His grip constricts. The muscles in her neck convulsing. Each shallow breath getting shorter and shorter. Her lungs felt like they would burst. The smell of ammonia permeated where she'd pissed herself. Clara tried looking into his eyes, but his face was turned away. A cold shiver rushed through her. She smelled the rot on his breath. Her arm dangling strangely from where he'd torn it out of the socket. Clara's face swelling from the repeated punches. Her countenance crying out for love and forgiveness. She deserved it, she pled. It was her fault, she beseeched. All the while blood pooled in her mouth and stained her teeth.

That was just like her addiction. Only it didn't leave the physical scars.

She shook the image out of her mind, squatted and bowed her head. Then, she stared at the sky and noted the explosion of colors that looked like a kaleidoscope shattered onto mirror-glass. Desperation seemed to hide in the darkened shadows and in the deepest recesses of her heart. Below, she noted the sterile muddy clay that never seemed to dry. Perpetually damp and awful looking. After storms, it stank with putrefied rot, only to partially drain and scab over until the next storm. It was as if everything from the very earth upwards was totally worthless.

Words of warning echoes unheeded. Clara was tangled like two old trees grown together. She felt ten-thousand miles away and at a location unknowable. She stood trembling for an awkward moment and surveyed the enormity of emptiness. She was truly an interloper into the waking world of hell. She was a prisoner or, worse, a guard for her own jail of addiction. No matter how hard she fled, it pulled her back with an unbearable force of gravity. It imprinted on her heart like a tattoo.

Clara had the perpetual feeling of being lost, yet, knew what was needed. A building of lies to hold her plummet back into addiction. All lies contained within the predillection to use. Sobriety required faith that she did not have. And never did have. Belief in something was paramount.

She turned back towards the trailer and walked with a new-found hurriedness of someone come to something. She met a wall of shifting sunlight with a conviction of utter finality. Clara caught up in the motion of awful enacted of her own doing. Strangely cheerful in the knowledge of her terrible deed. The landscape felt foreign and awkward. As if, the environs themselves mocked her. The clouds made shifting designs of shadows on the blacktop. These conjoined with dancing memories that created false reminiscences of blissful drug use.

She hadn't lost everything, but certainly enough. In the end, Clara tried to imagine a worse life or place than where she was.

Chapter 20

Ronnie didn't know what to say or do. All he wanted from Clara was the truth, but she pretended nothing was wrong. She was back on dope, he knew that. When he confronted her about it after the night at the bowling alley, she denied it. But he knew. Even Mary knew. For him, that was the worst part.

He witnessed that in Mary when he found her crying by the truck. He saw the terror and disappointment in her little eyes. It was etched in stone over her face. He hated seeing her upset and without understanding. For strength, Ronnie tried to imagine the world like she saw it. A place of goodness, where the bad parts existed solely as an aberration. She'd grow out of that eventually. But, Ronnie wanted Mary to hold on to that for as long as she could. She didn't need to know the universal truth that this world was no good and that's all it will ever be.

It was difficult to watch Clara fall back into her old ways. He tried to get her to go back to NA meetings, but she dismissed the idea with a wave of the hand. He felt like a man beset with nightmares only to wake and find himself locked into a reality that was worse yet.

He'd started sleeping on the couch because Clara's grinding teeth kept him awake. This morning, her heavy footfalls tore him from slumber and he shook his head. It was still dark outside and all was silent but for her. He looked at his watch and exhaled heavily. Clara was pacing back and forth. The creaking clapboards were torture to his ears. He swung his legs over the side of the couch and sat with his elbows resting on his knees. Ronnie swore under his breath and stood. With a pack of cigarettes in his hand, he walked out onto the porch and looked about at the coming dawn. The sky was purple, orange, and red. He didn't consider himself superstitious, but the scene sent a spasmodic shock down his spine. The vibrant medley looked like a globe seeping up from the ground. Soon the collection would slip away and full day would take its place to counteract the cool.

He thumbed a cigarette out of the pack, lit it, and blew the blue smoke into the air. It swirled and danced then was gone. Ronnie was confused as to his next course of action. Ronnie didn't know what to make of that. He remembered something an old timer told him when he first went to the penitentiary. Those initial years, he hated everyone and everything. No self-introspection at that point.

That came later.

He had been enraged and distraught about his dissolved marriage. The thought of his offspring being raised by another had filled him with unmitigated rage and grief. Those were his only emotions, and they filled his waking moments for so long that he was incapable of separating the two. Ronnie made a strange friend in an aged black man who would later die in that place.

Forty years before, the inmate had came home one night and found his wife in bed with his brother. For the cuckold, there was no other course of action to take. He collected his gun from the hall closet and shot his only brother in the head.

His wife started screaming and cussing him. That was annoying, so he shot her too. He set the gun down and went out onto the porch. He sat there for a long time and thought about his life. A thing composed of caustic events that changed everything without your consent. Finally, he stood and started walking. He didn't know what else to do. They had no phone. About an hour later, he ended up in town and walked to the police station. Told them what he'd done. No one believed him. Finally, the sheriff decided to take a look. So, the killer rode out with the deputies and that was all she wrote. Two life sentences without the possibility of parole. The state would've killed him, but for diminished capacity. The aged man laughed when he told Ronnie.

I was too dumb to kill. Let that be a lesson to ye.

Ronnie watched from the porch as the colors drained away in the west. He smoked another cigarette. He could still hear Clara pacing from within. The blinds moved but he didn't turn around. He felt her eyes bore into the back of his head.

Ronnie thought back to what the lifer told him. The past was made up of certain claims. People argue over them until what happened is of no consequence. At that point, the truth is pushed aside in favor of the particular person's viewpoint. By then, the reality is dead. Even those who lived it will no longer trust themselves. Instead they take the view of another. The argument is all that remains. Thus, his child was gone and there was nothing he could do. No way to bring it back. At this, Ronnie was furious and almost beat the old man. But, something flashed through his mind. He studied those words and realized the aged black was right.

Something crashed within the trailer, and Ronnie's mind raced back to the Palms. He felt the chilly breeze. He saw the faint street lamps turn off. Another loud noise erupted and he spat into the dead grass. Ronnie stubbed out his cigarette and looked to the blue sky.

He entered the trailer and saw Clara trying to make coffee. She'd spilled the receptacle and old grounds were spread over the floor. She was on her hands and knees picking each speck with her bare fingers. She spoke softly to herself. Sounded like an argument that someone else was winning.

Ronnie walked towards her in his naked feet and touched her lightly on the shoulder. Clara jumped and turned around with terror etched across her face.

"I'm sorry," he said. "I didn't mean to startle you."

Her eyes were enormous and she looked a bit crazed. "I was trying to make your coffee and the damn thing jumped out of my hands." Her voice was almost a shout. She turned back and continued selecting the black specks a piece at a time.

Mary opened her bedroom door and looked at the scene. She rubbed her eyes and yawned.

"Mommy, why are you yelling?"

"I'm not," Clara said in a screaming whisper.

Ronnie walked over to Mary and gave her a hug. "Good morning, sweetie. Go get ready for school and I'll start breakfast. What do you want?"

"Bacon and eggs, please," she said, smiling.

"As you wish."

Mary closed the bedroom door, and Clara continued picking at the floor.

"Here," said Ronnie. "Let me get a broom and a dust pan." He stepped around Clara and walked towards the hallway closet. As he passed, she looked up at him. He saw something insane in her bulging and fierce eyes. Countenance like someone escaped from a madhouse. Her gaze wasn't at Ronnie, but through him. She looked like an unsightly bird crouching over crumbs. The veins in her neck pumped and she never dropped her gaze. Clara's nostrils flared and she shuddered uncontrollably like a spastic. Her jaw was vibrating and her raking teeth sounded like a horrid instrument.

She was in a bad way. He'd not seen her like this before.

Ronnie came back into the kitchen with the broom and swept around her. He'd gathered a large pile, but she hadn't moved. He whispered her name. His voice was more akin to pleading than anger. After a few charged moments, she stood and went into the living room. She paced back and forth. The coffee grounds were attached to her sweaty flesh and her face was bright red. She seemed unaccustomed to the sunlight and was talking to herself again in an unknown language.

Clara was turning into someone he didn't recognize.

Ronnie threw away the old coffee and started a new pot. He heard the shower running and Mary singing. She was incredibly talented. He placed the skillet on the burner and started breakfast. He doled out a dollop of bacon grease into the pan and watched it melt away. He placed two long strips of bacon into the pan. They sizzled and spat onto his hand, but he paid it little mind. He was lost in thought. He quickly glanced over and saw that Clara hadn't moved from the window. She was spying something that might or might not be there. He looked out across the street and saw his neighbor. Victor sat on the steps with a full bottle of liquor in his hands. It wasn't open, and the man glared at it with suspicion, as if it were something alien. A glimmer of shame in his squinted eyes. Almost a mixture of disgust and desire. The neighbor licked his lips and rubbed his chin. There was a wetness to him. His shirt was dark with sweat despite the cool. Ronnie flipped the bacon with a fork and continued to watch the toper. The caramel colored liquor gleamed in the sunshine.

After admiring it, Victor twisted off the top and drank. Ronnie sadly shook his head. But for the grace, he thought, and turned his attention back to breakfast.

While Mary was in her bedroom getting dressed, Ronnie spoke to Clara softly. He tried to discuss going to an NA meeting and completing her GED. She looked at him without knowing. A blank stare that was haunting. Clara's hair was crazed and her eyes were glassy and hollow. He exhaled. She didn't hear him. So, he stopped.

None of this was right.

She looked him in the eyes for the first time. Harsh and severe. A flash of something real crossed over hers. For a brief moment, she looked aged beyond her years. Even older than himself. A glimmer of concern that he didn't expect. Heartfelt apprehension that he'd end up hurt. Something warmed his cold heart. The real Clara was there hidden behind her drug crazed and glassy eyes. Her being bore an impending sense of dread. A distressed attitude that he might actually go and leave them. Her ink black pupils were dilated all the way and she sat motionless with a hand over her mouth.

The bedroom door opened. Mary was dressed for school and smiling. That cheerful look quickly faded. Her expression turned pensive as she took in the whole room at once. Ronnie could tell that Mary had noted the tension in the air. He watched as Mary took several steps towards her mother. Then she paused. Ronnie put his hand on Mary's shoulder. A light squeeze meant to express that everything was all right. Don't worry. Shadows of grief in the room that he hoped to dispel.

Clara didn't look up and Mary didn't turn away, so Ronnie pointed to the kitchen table. Mary finally went over and sat down for breakfast. Ronnie walked into the kitchen and prepared her school lunch. Ham and cheese sandwich with tomatoes and lots of mayonnaise. He placed it in a bag with yogurt, a moon pie, and potato chips. To break the strange sense of animosity, Ronnie hummed a tune, but none joined him. He closed his eyes tightly. This was all wrong. He wanted to scream that he wouldn't go. He wanted their lives to return to the way they were. Before it went haywire.

Yet, he knew that was stupid to entertain. You can't turn back time.

Clara wouldn't leave the trailer, so Ronnie and Mary walked to the school bus. They went hand-in-hand down the street. It was chilly outside and their coats were zipped all the way up. The soft colors and eerie sounds of the dreary winter day seemed heightened by the ill assurances that everything would be all right. Ronnie turned momentarily to glance at the profile of Mary, who skipped lightly down the bleak and craterous road. Ahead, he noticed that the main thoroughfare was alive with activity. A crowd was gathered ahead. The people mulled about in a circle and looked towards the ground. Children were wild eyed and whispering together. A woman stood with her hands on her head and mouth agape. Grown men were wandering in circles without understanding and an aged crone was sobbing uncontrollably. The elder was hollering words such as *accident* and *unintentional.* There was a rusty car parked along the edge of the road, smoking, and the smell of brakes permeated everything. Drops of oil pooled in the grass. The front of the rusty Buick was smashed and covered in matter. Streaks of blood and a shoe were among the skid marks.

Ronnie and Mary approached cautiously. She screamed when they neared the solitary shoe. It held the dismembered foot of its prior owner. The porcelain white bone snapped and jutted out from dark skin. Ronnie didn't need to see more. He held his hands over Mary's eyes and faced her away. He knew who the foot belonged to. Victor's body lay in ruin on the asphalt. A lifetime ago it seemed, he sat drinking whiskey in the sunshine. He was slack and disfigured. Limbs at horrible angles and his head turned wickedly at two-hundred and seventy degrees. The smashed whiskey bottle was by his side. A death's smile plastered across his face. Almost joyous in eternal reckoning.

A blood curdling scream signaled from behind. It sounded disembodied. The group of watchers drifted away to make room. Ronnie turned and saw the woman from across the street running with her child cradled in her arms. Her mouth was wide open and she was howling with heartache and rage. The boy looked unafraid, a semblance of unknowing across his face. The woman dumped her son by the body and screamed for Victor to get up, but the dead man didn't answer. The boy seemed confused and he held his father's lifeless hands. His eyes were open. She cradled his head to her breast and wailed. The upturned whites of the dead man's eyes shone and his wet tongue hung distended.

Her screams were of unarticulated grief over her husband's broken body. The day was bright and the sun glistened off her tear streamed face. She looked to the heavens and swore at God. The little boy tugged at his father's shoulder and begged him to rise. She pounded her chest and yelled, "My God, my God, why have you forsaken me?"

No one knew the answer. Perhaps not even the almighty himself. Many of the watchers moved away, as if even viewing this tragedy made them complicit. This breached the boundary of proper conduct. An ambulance siren roared in the distance and grew louder as it approached. Ronnie squeezed Mary's hand and led her onwards. He saw that she cut her eyes to watch the scene. He hurried her away.

Before she got on the bus, Ronnie held her close, sat back on his heels, and kissed her on the forehead. They were eye to eye. "You shouldn't have seen that. You need to block those bad things out of your mind."

"Why?"

"Because, it's very sad and terrible to see."

Mary took on an air of maturity that surprised him. "Ronnie, this world is full of bad things. I've seen and lived it. I can't hide from them. None of us should."

Something sank in his gut. He knew she was right. A young clairvoyant or soothsayer wise beyond her years. He hoped for some words of wisdom but found none. There was only one thing to say. "I love you, Mary."

"I love you too." She turned and climbed on the bus. Ronnie stood and watched it drive away. He waited until it drove out of sight. It faded to a yellow speck and, then, was gone. Even after it disappeared, he stayed a little longer. A breeze blew and he watched trash roll along in the whirlwind.

Chapter 21

Clara stood by the phone. She quaked with anxiety. Ronnie's work number burned in her consciousness like a thing afire. All she had to do was call.

She looked over at the small kitchen table. It was filled with books for the GED. That was a dream and goal that she'd since given up. She tried to remember the function of American government and the elements of the periodic table, but those things flittered away. Presidential procedures and mathematical algorithms were irrelevant in the face of white powder and oblivion. The books seemed to taunt her with the allure of betterment. Heaven forbid she do anything to raise herself in the world.

Subconsciously, Clara was morphing back into what she used to be. She was once again forgetting how to live. Returning to that place where she didn't care about anyone or anything. The path so delicately planned to help her escape ignorance, addiction, and prostitution was thrown aside and quickly forgotten.

Clara pushed the books onto the floor and sat down with her head in her hands. It seemed awfully fitting. She needed to toss away any feeling at all that might change her course. Push them out, but for anger and desire. There was a part that desperately begged for salvation. Yet, a bigger one that trudged slowly towards damnation.

With the bag open, Clara sprinkled the last of her meth onto the table and crushed it with one of Ronnie's lighters. The light flowed through the trailer window and ebbed across the room. She snorted until the dope was completely gone. Licking the table just in case. A vision of Mary as a baby flashed though her mind. It blinded her to the point of physical sting. Her body contorted and she felt dislocated. Then, she rested and waited for the inevitable. It wasn't long. Her pupils expanded. The drip left a puckered and bitter taste in her mouth. Swallow that with all her feelings. Shovel dirt over everything else. The world became clearer and a little more certain. A stream of bubbly saliva dribbled out of the corner of her mouth. The numbness took over and she felt nothing. Any molecule of regret had vanished and she was completely hollow of emotion. It enveloped her like a blanket and all was right in the world.

Finally, she picked up the phone and dialed the number.

Chapter 22

He was carefully putting a lawnmower's engine back together when the phone rang. Ronnie rushed over and picked it up on the third ring.

"Donahue's Hardware and Repair, how can I help you?"

"Hey, Ronnie," Clara said.

"Hiya, Clara." He spoke with a sort of worried benevolence. He had to dance the fine line between concern and frustration. He'd learned while sitting with Clara in the Narcotics Anonymous meetings that if you pushed too hard, you could drive the person away from recovery. He knew that she had the ability to get sober again, if only he was patient and kind.

Yet, he couldn't enable her. That part was paramount for saving her life. She had to hit rock bottom. A loving friend can kill the addict even with the greatest intentions to see them get clean. He struggled with this balancing act every single day.

Ronnie swallowed hard. "What's up?"

"I've got something important to tell you," she said. "I was studying for my GED when your ex-wife called up to the trailer. Said her name was Sandra. I didn't believe it was her at first. But, who else could it have been?"

Ronnie started to tremble. A picture of his ex-wife burned into his mind. The vibration seemed to come up from the ground like the onset of an earthquake. It made its way slowly up until he nearly lost his grip on the phone. His mouth went dry and he tried to speak, but nothing came out.

Ronnie felt light headed. He wanted to form words, but his lips were taut and pinched tight.

"She wants you to come for dinner tonight," Clara said. "Introduce you to your daughter. The woman sounded real serious, but, I guess, in a good way."

He finally choked out, "Where?"

There was a pause, then she said, "Same place you saw her before. When you and Mary were together."

"The night trick-or-treating?" he asked.

"Oh, yes, yes that's it," she said.

"Okay, will you be all right by yourself tonight?"

Ronnie asked the question with genuine earnestness. That was the only thing which might keep him from finally meeting his daughter. If going meant that Clara might continue her spiral and leave Mary alone, he'd turn down his ex-wife's invitation. He waited for any response on the other end of the line. Soft music was playing over a speaker in the workshop. The ballad of a sea captain forsaking a girl at harbor, because his true love was the ocean. A song he knew well and felt closely akin to.

He felt unseasonably hot and smelled of a dank muskiness that was his sweat. Beads tracked down his chest and dampened his work shirt. His jaws were flexed so tightly that his cheek muscles began to hurt. All of this was involuntary. Nervous anticipation of joyous news. There was an incessant rolling and writhing in his stomach that hinted at something good. Much different from what he'd felt earlier in the morning, while rubber-necking a dead man. He stared straight ahead at a calendar on the wall that showed a puppy playing in the grass. Ronnie swallowed hard and waited for a sound to come from the other end of the line.

"Yes, I'll be in with Mary. I need to keep studying."

Chapter 23

Clara's mouth trembled as the meth boosted her heart rate. She stuck her tongue between her teeth to keep them from grinding. There was a stinging sensation and she felt warm blood enter her mouth. She'd lost control and couldn't stop tapping her feet. It got faster and faster until she shook all over. The telephone jangling against her ear. Her nerves seemed almost completely ruined. A wave of confusion rippled over her and Clara forgot why she'd called Ronnie. There was a visible tension in her body that kept her rigid.

"Okay, if you promise. I'll go. What time?" he asked.

"Seven o'clock," she said.

"I'll see you after work," he said. "Do you need anything?"

"No, thank you," she said.

She did want something but couldn't bring herself to mention it. She needed all the help in the world but was too afraid to ask.

They said their goodbyes.

Clara sat back and held her head in her hands. Tears sprang to her eyes and she tried to stop the flood. She'd done lots of bad things in her life, yet this seemed like the worst. She set the telephone back in the cradle and lounged back in the chair. Her body temperature soared and she felt ripples of heat under her skin. She raked at them and broke open old sores. Everything was silent but for her shallow breathing.

After what seemed like a long time, she picked the phone back up and made another call.

Chapter 24

The day waned and grew cold. After school, a stiff gulf wind rose and drove Ronnie and Mary inside. They played guitar and chatted about life. The strange twists and turns. Incidents beyond comprehension and the possible hand of God in all things. No discussion of church or dogmatic interpretation. Just an exchange of ideas between friends in search of answers. Even in tragedy one could hear that still small voice. Just listen or go and see.

When Clara got home from work, she looked dazed and strung out. Her eyes were sunken in the back of her head, almost like cavernous tunnels devoid of habitation. She seemed to crouch inside the trailer, like someone unaccustomed to the light. The tang of her was rank. Almost like a dusty musk. It permeated everything when she walked through the door. It wasn't from want of bathing. The meth seeped through her pores. A stench radiating from the inside.

Ronnie questioned leaving Mary. The little girl prodded him along, and he left despite his better judgment. He wanted to be angry with Clara, but all he saw in his mind was her smiling face looking at him, like her sobriety was set in stone and none of the bad had happened yet.

Before leaving, he pulled Clara aside. He beseeched her not to leave Mary. Wait until he got home and she could go where she pleased. She crossed her heart in promise, and he tentatively left.

Ronnie was so worried about Mary that he'd hardly had any time to fear the venture to come. He felt like he was at a point in his life where everything changed, but, perhaps, not for the better. Ronnie drove down the street and looked at the weathered trailers as he passed them. He saw the place where his neighbor met with death. Police tape surrounded the spot, but the car and body were gone.

It was twilight when he pulled out onto the coastal highway. The landscape looked haunted and impoverished. The lights of Pensacola grew large in the distance. Tortured scenery leading in. Or, perhaps that was only in Ronnie's heart. He took out his pack of cigarettes and lit one with the window cracked. The wind was cool and had the faint smell of salt and ice. He felt something in his bones, but it wasn't the weather. It was the floating memory of the unexplained. He exhaled smoke and pondered the sagacity of this. He often fretted over missteps and he wondered what sort of insane recriminations he would conjure from tonight.

He drove on.

After some time, he arrived at his daughter's house. The outside lights weren't turned on, but inside the house was lit up like a great beacon. He sat in his truck and lit a cigarette. The car was running and the radio played country music through the old speakers. Deep down inside, a courage brewed softly that he tried to pull from the depths of his soul. He was absolutely terrified. A swirling of emotions wracked his brain. For so long while locked up, he imagined this reunion. Ronnie was fidgeting slightly. He was unsure what to do with his hands. A pang of regret overcame him. The scene about was familiar from trick-or-treating. He thought about his ex-wife, Sandra, and it made him nervous. Ronnie took out a cigarette and sat smoking.

He was thrust back to the long ago. He remembered what Sandra had said to him after one of their fights. She'd told him he was inexperienced with the real world. That enraged him. He'd killed men in Vietnam. He knew the hard truth. Yet, she stopped him with the slight shaking of her head. *No*, she'd told him, *you think that the world ought to exist based off your consent—as if you must give everything a kind of dispensation to continue. If you feel like it doesn't, you become resentful and angry. Even then, just because you have it doesn't mean it's yours. That's not how life works, Ronald. It's full of hardship and disappointments. The sooner you learn to accept it, the better off you will be.*

It took him a long time to appreciate how right she was.

He tossed the cigarette out the window and walked up the long driveway. He moved woodenly and seemed to have picked up a limp somewhere along his travels. Perhaps it was psychosomatic, yet he'd never really known what that meant. At the brick steps, he heard a whippoorwill call out and for some unexplained reason it made him afraid. He knocked on the door and waited. Every single muscle in his body was tight. He heard the sound of steps along a wooden floor. The doorknob turned, and his daughter stood wearing a huge grin. A mixture of confusion and welcome at the same time.

She carried a toddler on her hip. His granddaughter laughed and smiled at him. A baby wave with both hands. He looked down at his feet and fought the urge to vomit. His nerves were a jumbled mess.

Finally, she spoke. "Hello, sir, what can I do for you?"

The question caught him off guard. "I'm here for the dinner."

"I'm sorry?"

"Sandra—excuse me, your mother—called. Said we were eating."

"Momma's not here, and sorry, but I don't know what you are talking about."

"Really?" His brain was jumbled.

"I'm sorry, but you are mistaken."

It finally occurred to him that Clara made this whole thing up. Ronnie turned and fled down the walkway. His vision swayed and he felt like he was swimming. The world about spiraled for a moment and he fought against the urge to collapse. He closed one eye that seemed to right his warped world and he walked on. This stumbling and unsteady cyclops reached out for anything and fell hard onto the pavement. He crawled for several feet and sat panting. Ronnie fumbled in his pockets for the cigarettes. He placed one in his mouth and tried to flick his lighter, but his hands weren't cooperating. After several unsuccessful essays, he lit the cigarette. He exhaled the smoke and his hands were trembling. Long, deep drags accompanied enormous wafts of emission that dissipated into the night sky.

He dared not turn around. Ronnie feared his daughter's disappearance and appearance with the same amount of dismay. He looked ahead. The cigarette burned a long line of ash between his fore and middle finger. All about the night was so dark that it looked purple. Thunder rolled off in the distance and a slight breeze set the leaves to shake lightly. Lightning flashed across the sky that seemed to harken a pale horse of biblical reckoning. Then, the lights of the house went off and he was left in darkness. A door closed.

There was a crisp and calm finality to this.

Ronnie stood and walked away. His mind began to form coherent thought and he remembered his girls back home. Clara's possible motives.

He thought about Mary. Then, he started to run.

He jumped into his truck and sped off down the street. The moon shone through gaps in the clouds and it draped the street with shadow and faint reflection of light. The wind shook the palm trees about which created a ghost silhouette that danced before him.

Ronnie shouldn't have even considered meeting his family. He hated himself for thinking that. He thought how his life was like a puzzle. He tried to make it whole, but just when he thought he found the piece, it didn't fit. Over and Over, he kept moving things around with no success. Some of the parts were missing and gone forever. Now, he had some great incomplete picture. This would have to do, he thought. There was nothing else.

He sped home down the coastal highway.

Darkness enveloped him. Ronnie put the windows down despite the cold and let the breeze clear his scrambled mind. He often hoped that he'd find answers to his queries and those yet asked. Yet, he was incapable of deciphering the visions or configurations set in the ether. This burdened his soul and he often felt shackled by great irons. Now he held the key to his release.

He kept asking himself why Clara did this, yet, deep down, he knew. She needed him out of the trailer for some reason. Perhaps bringing a drug dealer or old friend over so she could get high. He just prayed that Mary was safe.

Ronnie pulled into the Palms and drove down the main thoroughfare. Several bouquets of flowers rested on the spot where Victor had died. A nice gesture by the people of the trailer park. These residents viewed as benighted rabble by the outside. Poor trash of varying hues brought together by their perceived ignorance, violence, and depravity.

But, that wasn't so.

Ronnie's trailer was brightly lit. He took his cigarettes from the dashboard and quickly exited the truck. He felt better by just being home. Clara had a great deal to answer for.

Then, terror gripped him because something was odd about the scene.

What he noticed first was that the television volume was blaring. It made the windows shake. He shook his head and thought about Mary's bedtime. He went up the porch two steps at a time. When he turned the knob, Ronnie found that it was locked. He knocked, but no one answered. He banged his open palm against the doorframe and hollered for Clara. Nothing and no movement from inside. Only the pulsing sound of a commercial.

He fished out his keys and unlocked the door. Ronnie stepped inside and looked around. No one was about. Then, clarity hit him like a bat to the face. He ran to Mary's room and flung open the door. He kept screaming her name. He used such force that the knob bashed a hole in the wall. She wasn't inside. Ronnie raced down the hall and saw that one of the kitchen chairs was propped up under the door handle to his bedroom. He heard Mary shrieking and crying for help. She screamed his name over and again. Ronnie tossed the chair aside, threw open the door, and fell to his knees.

He thought he'd seen sadness. Sworn he knew despair. But, looking into Mary's eyes, it was clear that he had not.

She jumped up and hugged his neck tightly. Mary was practically choking him. She shook terribly and her tear streamed face soaked through his shirt.

"She left me," she sobbed. "She left me all alone. I was so scared."

"I know, sweetie. I'm here now." He carried her into the living room and sat her down on the sofa. When he went to turn off the television, she held onto him and wouldn't let go. So, they walked hand-in-hand to turn down the volume. Then, they went into the kitchen to get Mary a glass of milk. She'd calmed down except for the occasional sniffle. Ronnie held Mary until her eyes grew heavy. She'd cried herself into a fitful exhaustion. After a time, she went to sleep. He rose to retrieve a blanket. At this slight movement, Mary woke with a start and whimpered like puppy. Pleading eyes and arms outstretched.

He gathered Mary and carried her into the bedroom. He laid her on the bed and pulled the covers up around her neck. Then, he softly walked around to the other side and laid down next to her. He listened to her breathe. Ronnie almost felt her heart beating through the mattress. A rhythmic and repetitive thumping that let him know she was alive. He watched the ceiling fan turn slowly and tried not to think about Clara. Where she was and what she was doing. Ronnie didn't know, but he had a good idea. He'd completely forgotten about the dinner fiasco.

Outside, the heating unit droned on. Every so often, it clanked noisily and it sounded like a furtive beast holding court in the outer dark. Lightning from far away sparked at infrequent intervals. It flooded the bedroom with flashes of light until it too was gone. Ronnie cautiously rose from the bed and went out.

He walked out onto the porch with his pack of cigarettes. He lit one and sat down on the porch swing. Ronnie pushed back and forth and listened to the faint squeak in all that quiet. The cigarette hung loosely affixed to his bottom lip. He looked up at the sky and saw it clear. The clouds swiftly moved inland and the black sky was replaced by a heavenly host of stars. The winds blew and dead leaves rushed across the street. The new light of the moon made the world seem eerie and outlandish.

The night scene was something wholly alien to the light. As if it morphed into something foreign only to be set right again by the bringing of day. Like twilight turned the familiar landscape into another dimension where monsters live. He listened closely for any sound of Mary waking, but nothing moved from within. The cigarette tasted rough but soothed his weary soul. Still, his nerves were grated, but the black comforted him like a horrible shroud.

Ronnie wondered where Clara was. He spoke to the almighty in faint whispers. He listened. He'd found that you hear far more in silence than you could ever possibly imagine. The ways of the world were strange for things like that.

Then, Ronnie continued and prayed that she was unharmed. Discretion will protect you, and understanding will guard you. He pleaded with God to bring her safely home. Keep her from the hands of the wicked. Protect her from the violent.

Amen.

Chapter 25

Clara hustled along the street and tried to ignore the voices in her head. The chatter was faint and grew like a waving Doppler effect. The voices were familiar yet slightly distorted. Walking down the desolate street in the winter dark only heightened her trepidation. The voices crooned words of vile threats and oaths. Soft and sweetly sounding warnings and diabolical omens. The evil serenade spoke with such earnestness. Clara nearly wept at the misfortunes they promised. She prayed they were just the ramblings of a bitter soul.

Yet, there was no such thing as accident of circumstance.

It was misting slightly. The moon's light hovered, shrouded behind clouds. It hung above the trailers in the east and it seemed awkward and out of place. She looked down the street with circumspection at a burn barrel posse. They looked innocent from this distance. She kept on. Clara was failing. Her reserves were exhausted but the thought of crystal conjured up a thin recollection of strength. The men around the fire looked at her with toothy grins and lustful eyes.

"Damn, girl," one said. "Ye gonna catch your death. Come over here and let me warm ye up." The men guffawed and passed a bottle. "Have ye a drink."

Clara took the bottle and placed it to her lips. She let it linger just long enough to imitate a seductive tease. She swallowed and handed the bottle back. The barrel popped and ancient looking smoke rose in the air. A mixture of sparks followed.

She opened her jacket playfully to show what she wore underneath. The tiny top that hid absolutely nothing. Some of the men fidgeted and the others were slack-jawed. One sputtered and slapped his knee like an imbecile. Clara cocked her hip and showed the full length of her leg. About a mile of flesh that drew their attention. She watched as their gaze traveled from her calf up to her crotch. These men were like putty in her hands. The golden light from the barrel reflected her pale and naked skin. The warmth of it glistened beads of sweat off her chest that almost sparkled.

"Whose red car is that?" Clara asked, pointing to a ratty-looking Buick. "I sure could use a ride into town."

"That's mine, darlin'," said a tall asthmatic. He spoke through his nose and looked vaguely like a half-wit. A demeanor of desiring cruelties flashed across his face. "I might could give ya a ride." He looked at his buddies and adjusted his belt. "What'll ya give?"

"I've got something in mind," Clara said, licking her lips. She swallowed several times quickly to keep from vomiting. "You know. Help you drive into town."

"Ye got yerself a deal," he said. His nostrils were whistling. "After ye, darlin'."

The man took a swig from the passing bottle and motioned to the car. Clara slid into the passenger seat, and the man got behind the wheel.

The men around the barrel looked on with jealousy in their hearts as the man cranked the engine. It sputtered twice and shut off. A few of the men laughed. Finally the the car kicked to life and slowly pulled away.

The driver didn't last long. Clara sat up and swallowed. She turned and opened her mouth to satisfy her chauffeur that it was gone. He motioned her hand to the wheel and he zipped up his pants. He took control and sat back, beaming.

Clara looked out across the blacktop and studied the rhythm of the road. She felt jostling, but was unsure if it was the motion under her feet or her body recoiling.

The driver rolled down the window and let in the cool breeze. Clara couldn't feel it, but it seemed to rejuvenate him. She looked out the window towards the darkness and strained to remember specter trees or houses they passed. A tortured and deserted landscape shrouded in pure black. Their headlights bobbed atop the blacktop as they sped along. The traffic was sparse and the few passing cars created flitterings of uncertain light in the cab. A truck passed at speed and it made her nervous. In an instant, she saw Ronnie's face flash momentarily in the headlights and there was a sad malignancy to his expression that she couldn't place.

The lights of Pensacola burned brightly like a beacon. The driver slowed when they passed the welcome sign. "Whereabouts ye headed?"

"Discount Liquor. Off Pelican street."

He nodded. "Dick's old place. God rest his soul. Use to be where I went every day."

The Buick pulled up to the liquor store and stopped. The driver turned to Clara and squeezed her thigh tightly. "Anytime ye need a ride, just holler at yer daddy. Ye hear?"

Clara leaned forward and pecked him on the cheek. She whispered "okay" in his ear and watched him shudder involuntarily. She touched his thigh and gave him a tight squeeze.

She asked for his number and he sputtered it out. Clara flipped open her phone and saved it. She momentarily slid her hand gently over his crotch. "If I get stuck here, could you come and get me? I promise we'll do whatever you want." She gave him a sloe-eyed look of lustful promise.

"Ye betcha," he said. He looked around cautiously. "Just be careful when you call. You know. Just in case me missus picks up."

"No problem. Thanks, baby." She blew him a kiss and exited the car. Now it was her turn to shiver. The man smelled like moldy cheese, dried piss, and fresh diarrhea. Yet, he had served his purpose. Clara's need to get high outweighed any sort of self-respect.

A single faint streetlamp lit up the small parking lot. It was all but empty. The few cars parked were none that she recognized. Here she planned to meet with Angie, an aged whore who was once part of Joe's stable but swore to Clara she had quit him. Doubtful as this seemed, Clara was a beggar.

The larger consequences were pushed to the side.

Standing on the corner, Clara saw Angie move out from the shadows. She was silent as a cat and her suddenness frightened Clara. Angie's body jerked unnaturally like a marionette in the hands of a novice puppeteer. The wind had blown her hair into a crazy bouffant and she looked half-mad, hobbling along. She wore very little, but streams of sweat ran down her face. Angie smiled, waved, and hopped towards Clara. It was wooden and painful. With her face done up, she seemed like a minstrel taking the stage.

Or, perhaps, this was all in Clara's head.

Angie struggled forward with her purse swinging. A car passed blaring music and she eyed it with a mixture of suspicion and unassailable want. "Hey, sugar," Angie blurted. Her voice was hoarse and deep like a chain smoker or coal miner.

"Hi, Ang," Clara said. She stood uncertainly and looked around. Searching for something portentous in the shadowed night. Anyone lurking from whence she came.

"I got whatcha need right here, honey." Angie reached into her bra and palmed a small baggie. "Your medicine," she said, smiling. Her rosy cheeks and candy apple lipstick reminded Clara of a movie she'd seen in her youth. An evil clown who led children into the sewers like a nightmare pied piper from storybook reckoning. Clara took the bag and hugged Angie in thanks.

"I got more, but you'd have to pay," Angie said. "Friend prices, of course."

Clara nodded. "Yeah, no problem." Her whole body was alight. She needed her fix.

"Go on into the store's bathroom. Aasim don't mind."

"Okay, thanks," Clara said. "I'll be right back."

She marched off towards the entrance with an almost gleeful step. The windows were barred all along the outside and the sidewalk was encrusted with ancient filth. Broken glass and bottlecaps were scattered about. A pool of piss was beside the door and archaic and hardened mucus dangled from the handle. Clara was unperturbed and entered the shop cheerfully.

An enormous buzzer sounded as she opened the door. The interior was brightly lit and the place smelled strongly of bleach. The cashier behind the counter was encased in glass. He didn't look up. He was nonplussed by the outlander and was reading a newspaper intensely. Eastern music blared from a small handheld radio. The middle of the store was stocked with cheap wine and the walls were covered in shelves holding liquor bottles of various types and sizes. She walked past enormous refrigerator units that held beers and malt liquors. In the back were the restrooms. She entered and turned on the light.

The inside of it stank. Dried bits of filthy shit were caked around the bowl. The last person hadn't flushed and the water looked like a terrible milieu of brown and buttery soup. A lone floater bobbed unperturbed. The insubstantial faint light of the small lavatory made it deceptively cleaner than the ruined wasteland that it was.

Clara set her purse down on the sink and took out the baggie and eyed it. The crystals glittered a yellowish glow. She put the toilet lid down and tried to imagine something less horrible. She dumped out the contents and took an old motel key card and crushed the meth into a fine powder. Next, Clara took out a dollar bill and rolled it tightly into a straw. Her mouth was watering in anticipation. The cells in her body were practically screaming for relief. She bent down towards the weltering stench and took the massive line in one go. Nothing was left. Clara turned her head up and closed her nostrils. She was breathing out of her mouth and felt the slow metallic and creosote tasting drugs drip down the back of her throat. She swallowed several times and relished in the sick taste. Satisfied, she turned off the light and left the grimy restroom.

Back in the shop, she wandered down the aisle and picked up a small bottle of orange flavored Mad Dog. The meth was taking hold and she felt good again. Her heart rate spiked and her drug addled mind focused on nothing and everything simultaneously. Clara walked to the counter and slid the bottle through a window. The cashier looked up from the paper and smiled.

"Hello," he said. "Will this be all?"

"Yes."

The man scanned the bottle and absently said, "Four thirty-seven."

Clara picked out her wallet and handed him a five under the protective glass. The man doled out the change and placed the little bottle in a small paper bag. He smiled at her and rubbed his nose. Clara was confused. The man raised his eyebrows and rubbed again under his right nostril. Then, the realization hit her. She daubed the fine powder with her pinky and sniffled audibly. Her cheeks burned. The cashier smiled and nodded. He pushed the bottle and money under the glass.

Outside, the wind blew but she didn't feel it. The meth warmed her despite the revealing clothes she wore. She twisted the cap off the Mad Dog and took two large swallows. It washed away the taste of paint thinner. The bitter residue of the barrel man. She wiped her mouth with the back of her hand. Clara turned the bottle up again and drank deeply. She felt good. A third time and she finished the bottle.

She tossed the flask into a trashcan. It fell into the receptacle and clanked against a host of others. Clara swallowed several times as she made her way back to the parking lot. The cheap wine sloshed in her empty gut and a wave of nausea washed over her. She'd not eaten in several days. Any feign of weakness subsided as the meth shocked her system back to life.

Back in the empty parking lot, Clara spotted Angie over near the lone street lamp, talking on the phone. She spoke hurriedly and in whispers. Clara quickened her pace to hear the conversation. The scene was strange. Yet, Ang saw her coming and quickly hung up the phone.

"Hey, doll," Angie said. "Feeling better?"

"Much."

"You ready to work?"

"Yes, I need the money."

"Okay, sugar." Ang looked around. "This area is dead. Let's go out towards Piedmont. We can work together. Maybe meet a twofer. We'll get out amongst 'em and make good a deal of money."

Clara nodded and followed Angie out of the parking lot. Like a little girl following a harlequin to certain doom. Or, conspirators marching into trouble. Her high heels clicked loudly on the cement. She should've noticed that Angie wore tennis shoes. A subtle thing, no doubt. Easily overlooked by outsiders or novices of the profession. But, that type of footwear was a necessity in their line of work.

At the corner of Piedmont, they stood like sentinels. Clara wore her ridiculous garb meant to attract a good time. She watched all but didn't understand. Angie took prominence under the weak spotlight and touched her shoulder three times. As if on cue, a jet-black Cadillac cruised slowly down the street. It pulled up and stopped in front of the two women. Angie didn't make towards the vehicle. Instead she took a step back and held her hand out.

"Sugar, you take this first one."

Clara walked up to the car and the window rolled down. Inside was a nice looking young man with close cropped hair. Neat and tidy. One hand lay over the wheel while the other sat in his lap. There was a coolness to him that Clara found strange. Most men were nervous and fidgety, but he seemed like a man completely untroubled. Her reticence was momentary. A vision of money and drugs flashed through her mind and caution evaporated. She leaned down to show off her cleavage.

"Hey," Clara said. "You looking to party?"

"You bet. Slide on in here." He motioned towards the door.

Clara opened it and entered. It smelled fresh and new. The man rolled up the window and Clara waved to Angie. Her compatriot was on her cellphone and gave a halfhearted smile. The man smelled rich with cheap cologne. A lightweight gold watch dangled from his wrist and a tan line shone pale and naked in place of a wedding ring. Music played softly through the speakers and the man hadn't taken his eyes off her. It wasn't a look of lustful want. More, a twinkle of curiosity. As if, she was something to study.

"How much?"

"One hundred for one time," she said. "Do you have a place?"

"I'm in a motel down the road. Not far."

He put the car in gear and pulled off down the road. Slow and tentative he traveled. The john tapped the steering wheel with his thumb. It was to a song in his head because it didn't match the music. They kept driving in silence. Clara rubbed her palms together and looked out the window. Ahead was a sign for the motel.

"What'll you do for the money?"

"Anything but anal."

"Sounds good."

He pulled the car into the motel lot and Clara's heart hit the floor. She was struck with a wave of nausea and dread. An overwhelming sickness retched the contents in her gut. A police cruiser was parked out front. A huge smile crossed the man's face and he cackled sinisterly. The cop car's lights turned on as the driver drove into the lot. He pulled up beside the officer's vehicle and stopped. The policeman got out and Clara immediately recognized him. It was Officer Brooks, Joe's crooked cop friend. The man who'd used her many times before. He walked around to her side of the car.

She calmly slipped out of her high heels.

Then, she abruptly pushed open the door, slamming it into the officer's knee. He yelped in pain and swore. The man in the vehicle tried to grab her arm, but, instead, took hold of her jacket sleeve. Clara slid out of it and started to flee. She got a few feet before her head whipped back. Officer Brooks had closed the gap and snatched a fistful of hair. Clara's legs flew out from under her and she dropped to the pavement. Officer Brooks yanked her up. She heard something tear in her head and felt a clump of hair rip free. He tried to cuff her hands while she flailed.

The driver was coming around the other side of the car. He bent down to grab her feet. Clara did the only thing that she could think of. She leapt up and kicked him barefooted in the throat. She struck with force. A sickeningly loud snapping sound emitted from the man's windpipe. The smug man dropped to his knees and held his neck. He was gasping and struggling for breath.

Meanwhile, Officer Brooks was wrenching Clara's arm halfway up her back. She screamed and arched her shoulders. He was trying to take her other wrist. She walked on her tip toes in a bizarre dance and ended up beside the driver. In a fit of blind rage, Clara reared back and kicked the kneeling man in the jaw with all her might. The loud thud was followed by the man pitching sideways onto the blacktop. He breathed slowly and stared blankly into the heavens.

Satisfied, Clara quit struggling. Officer Brooks took her other hand. He brought out the cuffs and manacled her hands behind her back. Then, he lifted her up.

He pulled Clara back to her feet by the cuffs. Her arms were wrenched at an ungodly angle. The pain was unbearable. Her scream reverberated throughout the night. Then he slammed her against the car and cussed her soul. He shoved his elbow into her neck. The force of it knocked her head and she bit through her tongue. Warm blood pooled in her mouth that she spat away. She watched it run slowly down the car's window.

"You stupid fucking bitch," he screamed. He roughly snatched her from the side of the car and bundled her towards his cruiser. "You have no fucking idea how much trouble you're in," he screamed. "Dumb fucking junkie hooker. I can't wait to see how Joe fucks you up." He kneed her in the back of the leg as they marched. This caused her to stumble forward. The cop still held onto her cuffs and she heard something snap. Searing red hot agony raced down her spine. Her vision flashed white and then she passed out momentarily. Only his forceful pull brought her back around. They kept going until he slammed her against his car. Next, he opened the door and shoved her inside.

Clara tried to sit up, but he kicked her with his massive boot. "How do you like it, you stupid bitch?" The thud cleared her halfway to the other side and he slammed the door shut.

Clara was tentative to move. She lay on her side spread across the backseat. She didn't know what was wrong with her, except that everything hurt. Painfully, she sat up. Her mind was in chaos.

Then, she saw him propped against a pine tree, smiling.

There was an enormous shit eating grin spread across his evil face. He found this terribly amusing. Their eyes locked and Joe waved with his fingertips. He wore a terrible doll's expression. Something even more sinister in that. Finally, it clicked. A vision of terrible. The call from Angie. How she touched her shoulder to signal the detective. The location and now Joe. This was all planned from the beginning. She had walked right into the trap.

Shouts and orders echoed, but she couldn't make out what they said. She sensed a nameless feeling long past dread that etched itself in her mind. Clara sat forward and rested her head against the plexiglass that separated the front and back of the patrol car. It felt cool against her brow. She thought of nothing and everything at once. In a bizarre moment of clarity, she focused her anger inward. This wasn't Joe's fault. He was only a catalyst. This was part and parcel to her addiction. Clara had run with open arms into the life she'd turned from. She wasn't dragged or forced back into it. All her addiction needed was just a little push. No one else was to blame.

The door opened and it shocked Clara out of her trance. Officer Brooks stood by the door, and Joe was next to him.

"You have a minute or two before I take her downtown," Brooks said.

"Thank you, my friend." Joe shook the officer's hand. "When she's back with me, I'll let you fuck her all you want. On the house."

The officer smiled.

"Well, well," Joe said. "Someone's in trouble." He laughed in a manner that chilled her to the bone. He looked strung out and menacing. A look of self-satisfied stupidity was etched across his face.

Perhaps it was just the light.

"Fuck you, asshole."

"That's no way to talk to someone who can help you."

"I don't need your help."

"I beg to differ. See, if you want out of jail, you come back and work for me."

"Never," Clara hissed.

"That's a strong word. I figured you'd say something like that. Seems that I'm holding all the cards. Or will, here in a couple of hours."

"Don't you fucking dare," Clara felt sick. "You can't. She's with Ronnie and he'll never let you take her."

"True, he won't. But, when I show up with my cop friend here, he'll have to. I don't think he'll know the difference. Bring along some bullshit paperwork." He laughed. "First thing in the morning, I'm going to take back my sweet little girl from the ex-con. The murderer." He was smiling. Clara struggled against the restraints. They bit through her skin down to the bone. She'd have killed him if she could.

"Please don't. Joe, I'll work for you again. I swear."

"See," he said. "I don't trust you. I think I'll bail you out and you'll skip on back to the killer. Or, he could bail you out and I'm back at square one." He looked her dead square in the eyes. A deep blue glazed look of pure evil. "I'm going to take little Mary as collateral. You use your one phone call and talk to me tomorrow night and we'll see what we can work out." Joe stepped back. "Have a good night, Clara. I'll be hearing from you real soon." Then, he closed the door.

Clara was screaming his name. Pleading for him to come back. Yelling for him to talk to her. Just for a second. Tears streamed down her face. Beseeching a God that wasn't listening. A celestial being that didn't care. Instead of turning back, he walked over and shook hands with the officer.

A large wad of money was exchanged, and Joe wandered off and disappeared like a ghost into the cold dark night.

Chapter 26

Mary woke to the sound of arguing. She held her breath and listened. Ronnie was yelling and she figured it was a fight with her mother. Rightfully so, she thought. Yet, something chilled her. There was a voice, but it wasn't her mom's. Another voice yelled back, but it, also, wasn't one she recognized. She heard Ronnie swear loudly and harsh threats met his oath. A door slammed shut. Mary was holding her breath. The floor creaked as someone approached her bedroom. The knob twisted and she expected to see Ronnie beaming warmly and promising that everything was all right. Instead, a stranger stood shaded from the light of the hallway. The room turned perceptively colder.

"Hello, sweetheart," a strange male voice said. "How are you this morning?" Mary was terrified and tried to speak, but her tongue seemed to quit working. "I'm with the police and here to return you to your caretaker Joseph Billings."

Her blood ran cold at the name. "Where's my mom?" A phantasm of terrible visions of events flashed through her mind. "Is she okay?"

The man entered her room. She noticed an enormous bruise on the side of his face. It was swollen and garish. The man sat down on the bed and smiled painfully. Trying to evoke some warmth that rang false. A purveyor of an altered world that only made the situation worse. No comfort from those eyes.

"Yes," the man said. There was a pause. Too long. Like someone gauging words that even a child recognized as wrong. "She's spending time away. You'll see her real soon. But, until then, you are going to stay with Mr. Billings." The man tried to reach towards Mary's arm, but the child recoiled at this cheap excuse for comfort. "Will you get dressed for me?"

Mary didn't move.

"I need you to get dressed. Let me help you." Any sort of smile disappeared. The injured man walked over to the small dresser and selected some clothes at random. Perhaps hoping for order among these things, but finding none. A man whose knowledge of children extended to little more than nothing at all. Mary watched as the man turned back with a hodgepodge selection of clothes. He placed them on the bed, but Mary didn't even look at them. Like doing so would force this nightmare into a reality. The man noted this and his expression changed. Perhaps benevolence to annoyance in the matter of a seconds. "Do you need my help? Or can you do this on your own?"

These were posed as questions, but were clearly meant as an order.

Mary exited the bed and stood slowly. The man gave her a fake and obviously painful smile of thanks. Mary selected her clothes a piece at a time and expected the man to turn away, but he didn't. Instead, he watched her with suspicious eyes. Mary faced the wall and took off her clothes. She felt the man's eyes burning into the back of her. She dressed with feelings of shame and fear.

Yet, something else welled within Mary. It was anger. She'd not felt it with this intensity since she tossed her fruit punch at the bully.

"Do you have a bag to put some clothes in?" the man asked.

Mary's eyes darted towards her new backpack. The man picked it up and starting stuffing clothes inside. The fake ghoulish grin bathed across his battered and ugly face.

"Time to go," the man said and held out his hand. Mary didn't touch it. The man smirked and whispered, "Fine, you little stupid cunt," under his breath.

They stepped out of the trailer into a world brightly lit. The sun was up and Mary saw Ronnie in a corner on the porch with a Police officer. Ronnie's face was red and anger seethed from every pore. Mary tried to run towards him, but she was stopped by her escort. He clenched her arm painfully. She started to scream and cry. The man picked her up and carried her down the porch steps. Mary kicked and fought as best she could. She looked over and saw that Ronnie was doing the same. The cop was holding him back and threatening him. She saw that parked in the driveway was a new black car. It shone and had silver wheels that reflected the sun. A dealer's price sticker was attached to the window. Standing out front of the car was Joe. As they approached, he sat back on his heels. The man plopped Mary down in front of the man she'd grown to hate.

"Hiya, princess. I'm here to keep you safe until Mommy comes home," Joe said.

Mary slapped him as hard as she could. Simultaneously, she tried to flee, but Joe clutched her tightly.

"Come now, princess," he said. "I know you're scared. But, let's get you back where you belong."

"You cock sucking mother fucker," Ronnie screamed. "Don't you fucking touch her."

Mary looked at the porch and saw Ronnie scuffling with the officer.

"For fucks sake. That mother fucker is high. Drug test them. All of them." Ronnie was pushing harder. "What is your name?"

"Name is Brooks, Mr. Wells," the officer said. "This paper shows that he's her rightful guardian. There's nothing you can do." He spoke with ferocity. As if, the cop was trying to perpetuate a falsehood.

The officer held Ronnie against the wall of the trailer. He was glaring at them. "Search their fucking car. I guaran-god-damn-tee that they have weapons or drugs."

"We can't," said the officer. "You might contest this at the courthouse on Monday. But, I wouldn't recommend it. Until then, there is nothing you can do."

Mary was hauled forth by Joe and he carried her towards the car. She was flailing her limbs wildly. Then, she saw that behind the wheel sat a mean man who visited when they lived next door. Brought bags of bad things. The realization terrified her.

As if, this were all a dream and none of this had happened yet.

She'd wake and eat pancakes with Ronnie and forget all about it as the day went on. Too bad, it wasn't. Mary scratched Joe across the face and tried to break free. He pinched her on the back of the arm hard and Mary screamed. He whispered harshly that he'd beat her bloody if she didn't stop. She ceased fighting. The driver exited the vehicle and stood leaning against the hood. Violence both old and new became him. He raised his eyebrows twice in a diabolical movement that made her shudder.

She was in deep trouble and knew it.

Joe opened up the back door and shoved her inside. She hit her knee on the frame and yelped in pain. She looked back towards the trailer. None of this was right. She didn't belong with them. She belonged here. Ronnie was loose from the wall and standing by the railing. He seemed momentarily defeated. Yet, there was an intensity to his expression that gave Mary hope for deliverance. The cop blocked his way down the porch steps. He was seething mad. She hadn't seen him like that since Ronnie beat Joe before.

"Don't worry, sweetheart. I'm coming. We'll be together shortly. I love you."

The driver screamed, "I doubt it, old man." He was laughing nervously. Like someone pretending.

"Believe it, you mother fucker," Ronnie screamed. "This isn't over, you fucks. You could bring her right back and it wouldn't matter. You're already done and you don't even fucking know it."

Joe and the driver glanced at each other. There was a moment of hesitation. Then, they responded with the false bravado of men truly scared. "Yeah right."

"That's right. I'll be seeing ya'll real soon." Ronnie's eyes burned with conviction.

Joe shoved Mary across the seat and sat down beside her. He tapped the headrest and the driver-supplier put the car in reverse and pulled away. Mary turned her head and watched Ronnie fade from sight. He waved and blew her a kiss. Then, the car turned down the main thoroughfare of the trailer park and he was gone. Something hard hit her back and made a loud smack. She turned around and held her side.

"Sit the fuck down," Joe said. Then, he slapped her again. "That's for scratching me, you little bitch." He looked towards the front. "I can't believe that dumbass fell for it."

Mary crouched as far away as she could get. She practically hugged the door. The driver switched on music and blared it loudly. The noise was oppressive. The speaker system in the back shook the car. Mary noted that Joe never took his eyes off her. There were droplets of blood on his face and she felt his skin under her finger nails. She tried to imagine herself anywhere but here. This wasn't happening. She clinched her eyes shut in hopes that this was all a terrible dream. Yet, this was her troubled reality and a place without escape. She struggled for this to make sense. Most of all, she wondered what had happened to her mother.

The expensive new vehicle pulled out onto the coastal highway and headed towards Pensacola. The vast ocean rolled gracefully upon the surf. The driver lit a small cigarette that smelled funny. He passed it back to Joe. It made Mary light headed. She tried to roll down the window, but it was locked. The glass was tinted so dark that the sunlit outer world seemed perpetually in twilight. The smoke fogged the interior and burned her throat. She coughed and her eyes welled up with tears. She struggled to think straight. She wanted to spit the strange taste out of her mouth, but thought better of it. Outside the electric poles passed rapidly and Mary counted them to keep from being sick. The wires waved like the ocean's surf and it lulled her weary mind. When her captors finished smoking, they tossed the stub into an ash tray.

She hoped they'd roll down the windows but that didn't happen. Instead, they drove on with the car in complete fog. Mary felt funny and relaxed. The world she witnessed seemed alien and outlandish. She sat up and rested her head against the cool glass. Ahead was the sign for Pensacola. The dunes swept from sight and town came into view. She'd lived here her whole life, yet this new visage was like looking through stained panes. Everything the same and, simultaneously, different.

Mary's mind wandered somewhere else. She escaped the car and thought of playing her guitar. Singing and playing up on a stage. Ronnie and her mom sitting in the front. Her eyes were closed and it was real. As if, it was right in front of her. Mary almost forgot where she was and who she was with.

The car slowed to a stop. The men were arguing and their shouts brought her back. Gone was the stage and lights. This daydream was broken by oaths and anger.

"...I don't give a fuck where you go. But, she's staying." The driver spoke with absolute certainty. "Take it or leave it."

"You don't need the girl, Andre" said Joe. "Come on." He seemed agitated. Fearful and upset. Like he was betrayed but this mistake was irreversible.

Mary looked out the window and saw that they were in an abandoned parking lot. The cop car was pulled up next to them. The man with the bruise who gathered her belongings from the trailer got out of the passenger seat and walked over to the car. He stood next to the rolled down driver's side window. The cop car pulled away.

Mary saw that the area served a ruined and empty shopping mall. Desolation all about. A world unmapped and blustery. She tried to open the door, but it was still locked. The manual button was broken off. Mary wanted to make a run for it, but she didn't know where she was. Where could she go?

Obnoxious graffiti was spray painted throughout and all the windows not boarded up were shattered. Enormous weeds grew through the cracked pavement. Trash was littered everywhere and a dead opossum lay rotting in the sunshine. Legs rigid and pointing towards the heavens. A final plea for clemency beyond the comprehension of mankind.

She was very confused. Yet, she felt like laughing. Mary was still lightheaded. None of it made sense. Why wasn't she going with Joe? How would she get home? When would she see her mom? Whatever was in the smoke had clouded her mind. She didn't understand the sort of trouble she was in.

"Look stupid mother fucker," said the man outside. "You need to get gone before I hurt you."

"Please don't do this," Joe pleaded.

Andre turned around. "Look you junkie. You have two options." He reached into his console and took out a wad of bills wrapped in a rubber band. "I give you three grand. Consider it a finders and a shut the fuck up fee. You owe me three grand already that I'm willing to let slide." He held the money out but Joe didn't take it.

Something stopped him. His hands trembled.

"Or," Andre continued. "I have my man outside break your fucking neck." He motioned the bills towards Joe. "No matter what, she don't leave the car."

"What are you going to do with her?"

Andre laughed. "Do you really want to know?"

"Yes," Joe croaked.

"I got this doctor from Tampa. Hooks me up with pharmaceuticals in bulk. Well, he likes kids. Said he'd pay big bucks for one. Imma sell him this one. I dunno what he's gonna do. Fuck'er, kill'er, eat'er. I don't give a fuck. Told him he could have the girl. He's a nasty fucker, so use your imagination. Worst thing you could think of and multiply that." He laughed. "While you were playing hero in the trailer, I called him. He's bringing thirty grand and a load of OxyContin. Be here tonight."

Despite the haze that hung in her mind, Mary knew that this was bad news. She thought perhaps she should pray but she was at a loss for words. God might've forgotten her. A frayed understanding of the almighty's workings. Confused by the tenuous realm she inhabited. Mary studied Joe critically.

Joe reached out and took the sheaf of bills. There was something almost biblical to the transaction. He turned and looked at Mary. There was real regret etched across his face. Perhaps a hint of sadness. "I'm sorry." He cast his gaze downward and shook his head.

"Good boy," said Andre.

"What are you going to do about him?" Joe asked. He pointed vaguely towards the world at large. Mary knew that he meant Ronnie.

The only man who she believed might save her.

"That's easy," said Andre. "Imma have my man here go and visit him."

"He doesn't have a very long life expectancy," the man outside chuckled.

Joe nodded. There was real fear that he'd gotten in over his head. Mary noticed this without comprehension. No turning back now. He'd set this in motion. It was his own damn fault. The bruised man opened the door and Joe got out. The smoke streamed and for a moment it clouded the men's view. This was her chance. Even in her youth and inexperience, Mary knew that if she didn't break for freedom she'd never get another.

Mary pushed with all her might against the seat and bent running towards the open door. There were screams from all sides and the loudest came from her. She saw in a flash that Joe was pushing the man out of the way. He formed a small barrier for her escape. He yelled for her to run and she didn't need any encouragement. When her feet hit the pavement, her legs were already pumping as fast as she could go.

Mary headed towards the abandoned strip mall. It held her only chance to hide. She looked back momentarily and saw that Joe was hopelessly grappling with the bruised man. The supplier was already out of the car and gaining ground. Almost cat-like, Mary juked to the left and ran towards the street. She prayed for a passing motorist to come along and provide salvation. She glanced back again and saw that Andre was right behind her. Mary surged forward. Already, her lungs burned.

Mary was no more than twenty feet from the empty street, when he snatched her around the waist and lifted her in the air. Her feet kept pumping at a dead run. She screamed with all her might, but there was no one to hear. She stared at the road as he carried her back. A car wasn't coming. There was never going to be a car.

Andre forced her head around. There in full view was the man standing over Joe whose back was against the tire. His face was covered in blood. Left eye already swelling shut. The man kept punching him repeatedly with his right hand. Horrible thuds echoed until she heard a snap. He crumpled over and lay face down in a growing pool of gore. He looked distorted with his eye hanging crazily where his cheek should've been. Joe loosely held the money that was red and slick. The man snatched it out of his limp hands and kicked him for good measure.

Mary stopped fighting. She feared similar treatment from her captors. Yet, she didn't realize her value.

Andre carried her over to the car and the man opened the trunk. Mary quit fighting and seemed to accept her fate. Her only chance up and vanished. Mary watched Joe as she passed his broken body and something akin to sadness overcame her. Despite it all, he tried to save her. In the end, it was too little and too late.

With a jolt, they tossed her into the empty trunk and slammed the lid home. It was pitch black. She lifted her hand but it was lost in the darkness. She heard the captors talking outside and it sounded muffled. Then, doors opened and the car depressed as they entered. The engine cranked and rumbled to life. The car lurched forward and Mary slammed into the door. Pain seared across her shoulders and she cried out. Yet, she couldn't hear herself. The noise of the road drowned out all else. Luckily, they'd turned off the radio. She tried to remember the direction of the car based on the turns, but lost count. She rolled around the trunk as the vehicle made a host of changes. Finally, Mary gave up and curled into a ball.

After a time, the sound of the road changed and the vehicle continued at speed in a straight line. A small thin ray of light shone through a crack and she pushed hard against it. The door didn't budge. She fiddled with the mechanical lock, but it only made her fingers bleed. She shifted around and found some metal tools in a bag. They were hidden in a small compartment. Inside was a metal rod that she clutched for dear life. Finally, she sat back and felt the highway underneath.

While locked in the trunk, Mary tried to calculate how far they'd gone, yet time seemed endless. She was shaking uncontrollably with fear. The car slowed and turned off the pavement. She was bouncing around and it scrambled her already confused brain. Rocks ricocheted off the wheel well like the sound of gunfire in movies. Soon, she felt the car slow and then it came to a stop.

The engine was running, but she couldn't tell what was happening. She clutched the improvised weapon tightly to her chest. Mary already decided that she'd attack whoever opened the door. She concentrated intensely on the sound of the car. Something great shifted in the vehicle, but the engine remained on. Just when she thought that they'd forgotten her, the lid flipped open. Both men looked down on her. She wasn't prepared and half-heartedly swung the tool at the driver who stepped back and laughed. Mary waved it again but he caught the tire iron and yanked it out of her hands. He reached towards her and she kicked his hand. His smile went away. The bruised man took hold of her by the hair and dragged her screaming childish remonstrations from the trunk.

She noted her surroundings to forget the pain. There was a large new-looking home that seemed out of place. They were clearly inland from the beach and the ground seemed eternally wet. The driveway leading to the house was gravel and far from any sign of civilization. It curved sharply and Mary saw no way to escape. The timber surrounding the property looked dark and menacing. Almost black despite the day. Everything shrouded in shadow.

This filled her with dread. Even worse, her arms were held out in front and the man from her room slipped on plastic ties that locked her hands. They sounded like zippers and were tight around her wrists. Already cutting off blood supply to her hands. He shoved her forward and she tripped on the loose gravel. Mary fell with no way to stop herself and slammed hard onto the rocks. There was laughter and the supplier pulled Mary to her feet. Blood trickled down her scared knees.

"All right," Andre said. "You, go handle that old mother fucker. You know what to do." He motioned to the Cadillac. "Use the blade, but take the gun just in case."

"With pleasure," the man said. He walked over to the running car and got behind the wheel. He cranked up the music and backed down the driveway.

Mary and Andre were alone in the yard. "Come on," he said and shoved her forward. He followed behind Mary with his hands at the small of her back.

She stayed on her feet and walked towards the house. It was an enormous single-story home. The interior was brightly lit and Mary feared what fresh horrors awaited her. She didn't understand what was happening. Despite this, she found an inner resiliency that she'd never known. Something told her that she'd be alright. That she'd be okay. Deliverance was soon at hand. The plan the men discussed earlier hadn't formed a coherent narrative in her mind. You can't just sell a person.

Mostly, she worried about Ronnie. Trouble was on the way.

At their approach, the front door opened and a man stood with a rifle by his side. Light beamed through and shaded his visage. "Hidy, boss."

Andre didn't respond. They walked up a high set of steps to the porch. "Lock her in the back room. Make her appealing too." There was a matter-of-factness that put Mary on edge. Like she was nothing more than a misbehaved dog. He reached in his pocket and took out a bottle of pills. "Give her one of these."

"Yes, sir." The man grabbed the pill bottle and pulled Mary into the house.

Inside was a strange mixture of clean and awful. It stank of kerosene, cleaning solution, and cigarette smoke. The furniture looked brand new and an enormous television was attached to the wall. A football game played without sound and rap music blared from a set of speakers that almost reached the ceiling. Men were lounging in various conditions of slovenliness, but sat up straight when the supplier entered. Each goon carried weapons of various sizes and styles. Beer cans and liquor bottles covered every available surface. A mound of white powder sat square in the middle of a coffee table. A young man rose and started picking up trash.

Mary was led farther inside and she saw three women who sat naked at a dining table before a humongous pile of glass. They were smashing it into small shards and placing the crystal on scales. None of them paid her any mind. The supplier went over to the mound of powder, dipped his thumb, and shoved it in his nose. He snorted noisily and sat down in a large comfy looking chair. He turned his attention towards the football game.

The man with the rifle led her across the room and to a dark hallway. She hesitated momentarily and he gave her a shove. Halfway down the corridor a door opened and out stepped a man wearing a strange suit. He looked like a spaceman. The door was left open and the inside looked like a small factory of some kind. Stainless steel equipment was everywhere.

The man lifted the mask. "Tell Andre that the next batch will be ready here in a little."

"You tell him."

"Fuck off."

Mary's warder laughed and pushed her forward. They kept walking down the hall. At the very end was a large heavy door. It looked reinforced and had a huge lock on the outside. The man fiddled with the combination and undid it by spinning left, right, and left again. It was too dark for Mary to see the numbers. The man unlatched the cell and it made an enormous metal clank. A mechanism built to last a thousand years. Perhaps, more beyond that.

He pushed her inside.

The room was freezing cold. There was a small window in the corner that shone a thin speck of light through. It was barred from the outside. She could make out small limbs of trees and other greenery. In the middle of the room was a small bare mattress. Nothing else.

"Turn around," the man said.

She turned to face him. He was holding a knife and motioned for Mary to stick out her hands. She did and he cut away the plastic cuffs and placed them in his pocket. Then, he took out the bottle of pills and dumped out two in his palm. He pushed them towards her. She was too scared to move.

"Take them," he said. His expression changed. "If you don't take them, I'll shove them down your fucking throat. And, trust me, you don't want that."

With the added threat, she reached and took the pills. "I don't have anything to take them with. Can I have some water?"

"No! Chew them up."

Mary placed them in her mouth and chewed. It tasted awful and she wanted to spit them out. Bitter and chalky to taste. He watched her closely and there was nothing she could do. After she swallowed, he opened his mouth and stuck out his tongue. Mary copied him and showed that the pill and all traces of it were gone. He smiled.

"Good girl. Now strip outta them clothes."

"What?"

"Did I stutter?"

Her cell was already cold. Yet, she didn't protest. She took off her shirt and handed it to the man. Then, she slid off her bottoms and passed them over as well. He didn't leave nor turn away. She started shivering. Her teeth chattered. The floor was freezing. The chill raced up her tiny legs. She stood on one foot and then the other.

The man pointed to her underwear and Mary's heart sank. He glared with a look of impatience. All modest emotions were out the window. She stepped out of them. He snatched them from her clutches and left the room. The heavy door slammed shut and locked. It sounded enormous in that small room. It was darker yet and Mary's eyes took a long time to adjust. She walked over and stood on the mattress to help brace against the icy concrete. She wanted to see out, but the window was too high upon the wall. A strange feeling overcame her.

The pills were affecting her. She felt queasy and light headed. As if, someone was slowly covering her vision with a thick shroud. Mary's mind couldn't concentrate. Nausea swept over her in waves. Everything blurred and she felt devolved of her body. Like she was drifting away. Her eyes grew heavy. After a time, the coldness disappeared. Mary lay down on the soiled mattress. Despite the horrors of the situation, she experienced a calmness.

She knew Ronnie and her mother would save her. That kept the fear at bay. It wasn't long before Mary went to sleep.

Chapter 27

The cell's lights blazed and she slipped in and out of consciousness. Her hair was damp with congealed blood. A vision of Mary sleeping on her bed flashed through her mind and she pleaded for it to go away. There was a threadbare blanket on the floor that she wrapped around herself. It didn't keep out the cold, but it was comforting nonetheless. At some point in the night, she felt someone else in the cell. Be it death, she'd welcome it with open arms. Embrace the end like a long-lost friend.

Clara looked around and saw that she was alone. It was a world of concrete. She trembled with meth withdrawal and ached from where the police roughed her. Wrapped in a tight ball on the cold ground, she used her arm as a pillow and strained to block out the light. She tried to sleep, but it was a long time coming. When it finally came, she dreamt of terrors.

She was being taken to a place she didn't want to go. Carried by strangers traversing the wilderness only by torchlight. She tried to reason with her captors but they kept on. She screamed and shouted, but the carriers ignored her. The posse marched for miles in this timeless world. Nothing to coax them and the group sallied forth like a procession of an execution. It was cold and there was naught to brace against the elements.

Finally, there was a small peck of light in the distance that looked like a candle. As they approached, the light grew and turned into an enormous bonfire. The heat was immense and the flames flashed yellow, red, and blue. One of the captors dragged Clara kicking and screaming towards the conflagration. She feared she was going to be cast into the burning inferno, but she was not. She was forced to watch the fire dance and see the stories they told. Molestation, abuse, and rape. All the things that haunted her.

After witnessing the visions, she wished they'd thrown her onto the pyre instead. For they were scenes from her past. Monsters of the future. The truth laid bare. She begged for conjecture but it wasn't so. Clara pled for partial reality. Anything to stop the memories.

In the jail cell, Clara kicked and whimpered like a dog. She shivered like in a seizure. The blanket fell from around her. In Clara's dreamscape, she heard a familiar voice scream her child's name. She opened her eyes without understanding. A world of light and shadow.

"You need to help her. They stole her," yelled the voice. "They're going to sell her." It was muffled slightly through the metal door, but she understood it nonetheless.

She ascertained another speaker. "Shut up, junkie. Quit hollering bullshit and lies. No cop has kidnapped a girl. You're just geeked. I'll put a fucking muzzle on ye. Quiet down."

Clara stood uneasily and wandered over to a small window set deep within the door. She hurt all over, but pushed through the pain. Through the glass was the booking lobby. Joe was seated and cuffed to a metal bench. His face was practically deconstructed. A huge bandage hung crazily over part of his head. Blood seeped through the white gauze, but he seemed unaffected. He beseeched for someone to listen to him. He was crying and spittle ran down his chin. Panic set in and Clara banged on the window with the heel of her fist.

Joe turned. "Clara! Clara! They have Mary. Andre and them have Mary at his place! I tried to stop it. Oh God, they are going to sell her." He turned to the officers behind the desk. "They won't fucking listen to me!"

A huge warder stood and strode purposefully over to Joe. He unlocked him from the bench and dragged Joe away. Clara couldn't see him anymore, but she could hear him screaming about Mary. She laid her head against the door and tried to puzzle out the great narrative of this tragedy.

A million possibilities bounded through her head. Yet, the most important was contacting Ronnie. He'd help Mary. No matter the sins of the mother. She pushed a button by the handle-less door. After a second or two, a voice came out of the speaker.

"Yes?"

"I need to use the phone. I haven't used my one phone call."

"All right."

A buzzer sounded and the door unlocked. The jailer escorted her out. She heard Joe's muffled wailing down the corridor. She looked at the desk and the corrections officer pointed to an ancient looking phone attached to a wall. Clara walked over and read the plaque full of different bail bondsmen numbers. She didn't need that. There was only one person to call. She punched in the numbers and listened to the ringing.

"Please pick up, Ronnie. Please."

Chapter 28

Ronnie was pacing back and forth. He was chain smoking and mumbling harshly to himself. Foul oaths and other swears against the police, Clara, Joe, and the world at large. He called the Sheriff's office right after Mary left and they gave him the bad news. Clara was arrested for a host of offenses. Prostitution, drugs, and assaulting a police officer. She was held on twenty thousand dollars' bail. He called a bondsman whose rate was ten percent non-refundable. The news hit him in the gut and he tried to keep a semblance of composure. Ronnie needed two thousand cash, which he didn't have. His truck wouldn't bring near enough. He felt sick to his stomach. He knew where to get the money. He was entrusted with the combination. He even had a key. Can you do it, old man? Are you prepared to throw it all away for that little girl? He already knew the answer.

You're goddamn right.

Then, Ronnie abruptly paused and held his breath.

In prison, he'd grown accustomed to the slight sounds that wrought peril. The slicing of his truck tires gave away danger's approach and Ronnie went out the window.

Ronnie crept along the side of his trailer. He moved and stalked like a cat despite his advanced age. He hugged the vinyl cladding and stared ahead with intense eyes. There was ferocity in his heart. He saw flashes of the Vietnamese jungle and the Vietcong. The limitless numbers that he mowed down in droves. Only for more to plunge out of the forest and charge into the hellish wasteland. See Ronnie at eighteen laughing with a crazed bloodlust. Joyous in murder. Waiting for the smoke to clear so he and his comrades might wander among the fresh dead and gather the ears for trophies. Stringing them on lanyards. Wear the gory pendants with pride. He was never fully alive unless facing trouble. Vietnam was heaven. He lived on the edge of life and death and it suited him just fine.

These were the scenes that crossed Ronnie's mind. Memories of something he'd left behind in a faraway country. It all flooded back. A calm rage burned within him. Viciousness ran through his veins like molten lava. He felt the intense burn and loved every second of it. He embraced the thirst for violence like a long-lost friend. The only promise in life is death and he loved to dance with the reaper. Make friends and listen to its sweet words. Sing along as they swayed to-and-fro. Oh death. Oh death.

His truck leaned and sat on flat tires. Ronnie snuck up the porch soundlessly. He moved with precision. His shadow burned elongated in front and he feared it might give away his approach. Too late to worry about that now.

He crouched over to the doorframe and peeked inside with his back against the wall. Just slightly. Ronnie saw the bruised police officer staring out the open window and trying to decide what to do next. Perhaps looking for an aged figure running away. Not on your life, he thought. He slipped off his shoes and tiptoed into the trailer. The man with the bruise on his face held a knife in his right hand. It was small, but deadly. Ronnie hadn't carried a weapon with him. Ronnie's foot creaked a single board and he turned. Maybe recognizing the danger.

More likely not.

The man was half turned when Ronnie punched him hard behind the right ear. He hit him again in the blackened and swollen portion of his jaw, and the man fell over onto the couch. The man bounced back up in an agile motion with the blade in hand. He slashed at Ronnie. The knife glinted and disappeared into Ronnie's shirt. It was gone and then reappeared with red blood across the edge. He backed away when the knife slit into his arm. Not quick enough. Ronnie didn't feel any pain, but knew it was deep. He kept stepping in a circular motion until his hip hit the kitchen counter. Nowhere to go.

The man wore an evil smile on his face. He never spoke a word.

Ronnie felt along the counter for a weapon, but there was nothing to take hold. He felt momentarily pissed at himself for keeping such a clean house.

The man lunged forward and stabbed him in the left shoulder. He was aiming for the heart, but Ronnie ducked at the last second. Unlike the first cut, this one he felt. Every inch of the knife going in. It burned like fire and he grit his teeth in rage. He nearly lost his breath. There was a scratching noise of steel on bone. The blade was inserted to the hilt. The man kept trying to extract the knife, but it was slick and slipped from his grasp. Ronnie punched him in the face with all his might. A snap followed and blood gushed from a huge gash over his eye. The man only smiled and reached behind his back.

The gun was pointed directly at Ronnie's gut. Not a foot away. Without thinking, Ronnie reached and grabbed the top of the pistol. The hammer was decompressing and he caught it just in time. A millisecond later and he'd have a hole in his stomach and Mary lost forever.

They struggled with the gun ready to explode. Ronnie's grip never slacked and he yanked the gun away. He tossed it behind him and it fired. The pistol clattered to the front of the trailer.

The man tried to take Ronnie in a headlock, but he was too quick. Ronnie extricated the knife from his shoulder and in a flash dropped to one knee, leaving him grasping at open air. Ronnie took the blade and sliced the man's Achilles tendon. It went through the flesh and cartilage like a hot knife through butter. The assassin tried to step forward to tackle the old man, but his foot remained flat on the floor. A ripping sound followed as the great weight of him tore the skin. The man cried out in agony and fell forward. As he did so, Ronnie passed the blade lengthwise across his waistline and left a huge cesarean smile. The man rolled over on his back. He was crying. He looked at Ronnie in wonder as to how this happened.

Ronnie stood with his back against the counter. He was breathing heavy and blood dripped down both arms to the floor. The man's arms were flailing wildly as if trying to take hold of something, anything, for help. Ronnie laid the knife down and opened a kitchen drawer. Inside was a roll of duct tape. He brought it out and peeled back the end with his teeth. He stepped forward and kicked the man in the head. This failed assassin brought his hands to his face. Ronnie anticipated this and lashed them tight as quick as a rodeo cowboy. He saw a pool of blood growing around the man's waist.

"Did you know," Ronnie said, breathing heavily, "that on average we have twenty-five feet of intestines. Both large and small of course."

No recognition from the man, but he watched Ronnie intensely.

"No? Well, it's true." Ronnie walked slowly over to the gun and picked it up. He switched the safety on and secured it behind his back. "This trailer is ninety feet in total. Lengthwise, that is. So, I bet from where you are to the front is about forty feet, give or take." Ronnie stepped towards the prone man and spoke clearly. "You're kind of a tall fella. I bet yours is longer than twenty-five… Now, if you don't tell me where Mary is, I'm going to start taking yours out and testing my hypothesis. I'll string it around the trailer like decorations. It will look like a bloody fucking Christmas. How does that sound?" Ronnie bent down over the man. "Be a good boy. Tell me, where is she?"

The dying man spat blood and weakly said, "Fuck you."

Ronnie shook his head. "I'm not going to lie to you, Officer. This is going to hurt like fuck." He reached down into the open wound and dug around in the man's belly. He screamed. Ronnie squeezed some internal organ and extracted his bloody hand. "That was just a taste." The man was crying and making a strange moaning sound. "I'm going to ask you again. Where is Mary?"

"Fuck you," the man said with burning eyes.

"Okay, here we go." Ronnie was reaching back towards the man's stomach when the phone rang. He paused for a moment and thought about what he should do. He was half crazed with blood lust and wanted to let it go to voicemail. But, thought better of it. Ronnie undid a portion of tape and placed it over the man's mouth. He stood, calmly walked over, and picked up the phone.

"Hello?" Ronnie said.

"Ronnie, Oh, thank God." Clara said. She was breathing heavily into the phone. "They've got Mary."

"I know. I'm working on finding her as we speak."

"I know where she is." Ronnie was silent. "Joe doesn't have her. This big drug dealer has her. He's going to try and sell her or something. I don't know… We need to get her. We can't wait." There was a pause on the line. "We can't go to the police. They won't believe me and we don't have time. Each second we wait, the more lost she becomes."

Ronnie clinched the phone tightly and swore under his breath. "Yeah, I've got a situation here with one of their own…I think…Damnit…Okay, call Marcus Bail Bondsmen. Tell them that I'll be at the jail in thirty minutes with the cash."

"Thank you…I love you." Clara said.

Ronnie placed the phone on the cradle. He'd nearly forgotten about the dying police officer on his floor until he saw that the phone was sticky with blood. If, he even was a real cop. Didn't matter, Ronnie was an ex-con who killed someone. The police would spend hours of wasted time trying to figure it out. By then, Mary would be dead or worse.

Ronnie was full of adrenaline and tasted something metallic on his vibrating teeth. Ronnie turned and noticed that the man was trying to roll over. Bits of his guts were dangling out from his stomach. Slick organs that looked blue in the sunlight.

"Well, Officer, it seems that you aren't needed anymore." Ronnie collected the roll of duct tape and walked over to him. The man's terrified eyes followed him. Ronnie crouched and cradled his head. He whispered something in his ear that purveys the stuff of nightmares. An anti-prayer. Ronnie then took the tape and began wrapping it around the man's mouth. He circled the head four times. Then, he shifted the tape over the condemned man's nose and wrapped that as well. Ronnie rose. He went and leaned against the counter and watched the scene that followed.

The man lifted his hands towards his face and tried to pry away the tape. It was too tight and he didn't have any strength. His fingers couldn't slip under the bindings. His back bowed and he thrashed his good leg about. There were muffled screams and exultations. Breece's face turned bright red and it was grotesquely swollen. Ronnie watched this unfold with growing satisfaction. He took great pleasure in watching the life drain slowly from his eyes.

After the man was long past dead, Ronnie took off his shirt. It was plastered to his skin and slick and sticky with blood. It took him a while to peel it off. The pain kicked in from the knife wounds and it was torturous moving his left shoulder. With his shirt removed, he studied the wounds and watched the blood run down his arms. He picked up the duct tape and studied it for a moment. Then, he stepped over the body and walked down the hall to the bathroom.

He turned on the faucet and stood before the mirror. He looked all right besides the wounds. When the water steamed, he wet a washrag and cautiously wiped away the blood. Before long, it was soaked through and dark red. He left it in the sink and took a towel from the cupboard underneath. He tore it in half and folded each half into squares. The blood kept running down his arm as he worked. He took one and placed it over the stab wound. With the tape, he secured it down. He repeated the exercise with his sliced arm. He stepped back and studied his reflection. The white towel was splotchy, but it looked okay. Ronnie shut off the light and left the bathroom.

He went back into the kitchen and collected a large black trash bag. Ronnie moved like a man on a mission.

He entered Mary's bedroom and stuffed all her clothes and blankets into the bag. Then, he went into his room. He went to the dresser and slid his and Clara's clothes on top of Mary's. Ronnie walked to the closet and pulled off the hanging clothes and placed them in the trash bag. He left a black sweatshirt out that he put on. He stood before the mirror and turned back-and-forth. He touched the pistol that rested in his waistband. It seemed okay. The towels weren't noticeable unless you knew what you were looking for. He glanced at his watch and saw that he was running out of time. Quickly searched the room for anything important he'd forgotten. Nothing that really mattered. Everything could be replaced. He picked up the bag and left the bedroom.

Ronnie walked down the hall to the door and gave a last look around. You aren't coming back, old man, he thought. It's gone forever once you walk out that door.

His eyes scanned the room and fell on the guitar. He went over and collected it by the neck. On his way back to the door, he looked out the window and saw his leaning truck. He put the guitar and bag down and stepped over to the dead man. He rifled through his pockets and came up with a set of car keys. These he pocketed. As well, he collected the dead man's wallet. He took out the cash and threw the billfold away. "Thanks, cocksucker." Then, Ronnie gathered his few possessions and walked out onto the front porch. The last mourner to leave. The sun was beautiful and shining brightly. There wasn't a single cloud in the sky. He looked down the street and saw the black Cadillac parked in Clara's old driveway. He adjusted the bags in his hand and set off down the steps and across the yard.

He unlocked the car and opened the back door. Ronnie placed the trash bag and guitar in the backseat. He got behind the wheel and cranked the engine. It was a nice vehicle. The leather shiny and it smelled brand new. The car sounded faint but he felt a powerful rumble. He slid it into reverse and backed out of the driveway. Through the rearview mirror, Ronnie looked at his trailer. His truck leaning on its rims. The rubber squished against the gravel. His whole world outside the penitentiary was on that small plot of land. He was leaving forever with only a few shirts and his and Mary's guitars.

Yet, he wasn't sad. Perhaps a little nostalgic, but that was all. Now, it was home to a bloated and decomposing corpse.

Something strangely prosaic about that.

Ronnie set off down the road in the dead man's car. He turned onto the main thoroughfare. He looked at the cracked cement and the ruined road. He saw a group of kids who watched the fancy car with soft expressions. Farther on, he passed the barrel bunch who lounged in different stages of drunkenness and smiled at Ronnie's fancy windfall. He studied the scene about one last time. Trailers in various states of decay and the inhabitants fairly better.

But, that was only skin deep. The blight and poverty weren't at the real heart of this benighted community. They were the salt of the earth. The cleaners and cooks. Garbage collectors and convenience store clerks. Individuals segregated to localities like the Palms by the better sort. People who take for granted the significant role that poor people play in their lives. Rich folks who are an ill-advised investment, a traffic accident, or a surprised sickness away from the Palms or worse.

Ronnie turned right onto the coastal highway and headed towards his, now, old place of work. There were a host of bad things nestled on the horizon. He was undoubtedly going to have to kill more people. That much was certain. The fact that he was about to steal from a magnanimous friend hurt his heart. Yet, there was no way around it. Perhaps Tim might understand. The money wasn't selfishly procured. It was for something far greater. Later, he'd write to him with the amount enclosed. Set the record straight.

That didn't make it right, but he'd long known the world wasn't black and white. This was deeply set in the realm of gray.

His shoulder ached and he kept moving it to relieve the pain. Little shocks that felt good as they passed. The sliced arm was bleeding again and it weighed heavy his makeshift bandage. As the car glided down the highway, Ronnie took a bit of comfort in that. He pressed the accelerator and the Cadillac sped onward. It didn't seem to touch the road. The car surged with very little effort and Ronnie was already late.

Chapter 29

Mary woke disoriented and shivering in the freezing tomb. She almost saw her breath. It looked like smoke euchred out of the darkness. Her mind was in a fog and she was confused. Waves of exhaustion hit her like the swells of the sea. Mary was curled up in a ball and hugged her knees tightly. She'd never felt so cold. Only a faint light from the barred window teased shapes out of the blackness. Something moved in the room that caught her attention. She wasn't alone. Mary sat up. She looked around and saw a strange shape by the door. Her teeth chattered and she tried to speak, but nothing came out. As if, her very words were frozen inside. Her body was covered in goosebumps. She shook uncontrollably now and Mary didn't know if it was because of the temperature or fear. Probably both, she thought. Someone was watching her. The eyes burning onto her flesh. She felt dirty and ashamed. Mary covered herself as best she could.

Finally, a man stepped forward with an enormous and evil grin.

One of her kidnapper's henchmen was barely visible through the light. He reeked of bad news and worse beyond her childish reckoning. She was absolutely terrified. He held something in his hand that was indiscernible. He brought it out and Mary was momentarily blinded. It was a flashlight that he kept trained on her face. Nothing of her life seemed ordinary but even this surprised her. When her eyes adjusted, she saw that he held his hand out. She clasped it without thinking and he hauled Mary to her feet.

"Let's go," he said matter-of-factly. "Boss needs to see you."

Mary felt strangely torn. She wanted to leave this cold prison, but feared the questionable world beyond.

In the end, she went. It wasn't exactly a question and she didn't have a choice in the matter.

She walked naked and shuddering down the little hallway. Mary covered herself as best she could. Her skin tingled with the precipitous rise in temperature. Like basking in the shock of the burning sun's rays. The music grew louder as they approached the living room. It was filled with smoke and the men were braced throughout the room in attitudes of relaxation. The nude women were still seated at the table and measuring out quantities of meth for distribution. Mary slunk into the light and tried to conceal her modesty. Some of the men watched her lustfully, while others turned away. She strode into the middle of the room and stood next to her handler.

"Here, boss."

The kidnapper turned and looked her over. His eyes were glassy and he smelled like alcohol. A half empty bottle set nestled between his legs.

"Hello, little girl," he said with a huge grin. "Sit over there on the sofa." He turned and shooed the men away. They rose and stood in the corner.

Mary cautiously crept over and sat down. Her legs were crossed and she tightly hugged herself.

"Lucinda, get your ass over here," he hollered.

One of the women rose from the table and walked over. Her drooping breasts swung like wayward bowls as she approached. She looked old and badly used up. There was a hint of past beauty from another life. A gorgeous woman a lifetime and million bad decisions ago.

"Yes?" she said.

"Get next to her and look sexy. I'm gonna send a picture to doctor man."

He took out a cell phone and held it up. The woman did as she was told. She sat next to Mary and put her arm around her. She shivered at the icy touch of Mary's skin. The woman spread her legs and proffered something that might've been a smile. Mary remained locked in her own embrace and the supplier frowned. He dropped the phone in his lap and placed his hands together as if in prayer. Then, he spread his fingertips. Mary's heart sank because she knew exactly what he wanted.

She shut her eyes tightly and copied the woman seated next to her.

"Good girl," he said.

Mary covered herself again and opened her eyes. The supplier was pushing buttons on the phone and quit paying attention. The woman stood and walked back to the table nonchalantly. Like this was nothing out of the ordinary. Just another day on the job.

The supplier spoke without looking up. "Take her back." His henchman stepped forward and pointed towards the hallway.

Mary stood slowly. She was almost too afraid to speak, but found some inner resolve. "Can I have my clothes?" She followed that with a fake and nervous smile.

His eyes didn't move from the phone's screen. There was a long moment of silence. As if he were weighing this simple question very gravely. A flash of fierce malice crossed his face. Finally, he nodded. "Sure," he said and shooed her away with a gesture of his hand. She turned and followed her warder back down the hall.

Chapter 30

Clara felt half crazed with anxiety. Ronnie said thirty minutes but it was long past that. She'd even started counting but forgot her place after somewhere after six-hundred. Her mind seemed directionless and lost in a thick fog. It wasn't for lack of drugs. Oddly, that physical craving disappeared. She sat huddled by the door with the little woolen blanket wrapped around her. She listened closely for the metal mechanism in the lock to turn and presage her release. The whore's uniform she wore invited cold, but stress burned a warmth within her.

Scenes of her daughter raced through her mind. Mary's first words and distrustful steps. Cradling her when she was sick. Laughing along as they played silly games. Her first day at school and the hundreds of days in-between. Dread passed over Clara as she wondered what was happening to her sweet child. Innocent beyond any reckoning. Delivered into the horror show by Clara's own maternal failings. It mustn't happen again.

Then, the door sounded and a voice hollered her name from without. She dropped the blanket on the floor and stepped outside. The guard was motioning her towards the desk that separated the convicts and staff. An enormous fat guard stood and beckoned her with the nonchalant wave of a hand. Clara strode forward and rested her arms on the counter. The man's expression changed and she quickly stood up. He placed her high heels on the counter. He handed her a manila envelope that had her name stamped upon the front. Inside where her meager possessions. The man handed her a stack of papers. They were warm and freshly printed.

"You made bail. Imma need you to sign these." He handed her a ball point pen. "They aren't an admission of guilt. Just stating that you know the charges against you. Also, that you understand when you need to show up to court. Attached is a list of your release restrictions. We can revoke your bail at any time. Do you understand?"

"Yes, sir."

"Good. Now, just sign where it says signature." He held another stack of papers. "These are copies for your records. You won't need to sign these. It's just the same info."

"Okay." Clara began signing the documents. She didn't look them over. Just glanced at the charges. Prostitution, drug possession, resisting arrest, assault, and a few others that they'd added for good measure. It didn't matter now. She rushed through and scratched her autograph on each page. When she was done, she pushed the stack back.

"All right," he said, pointing towards a door on the far side of the room. "Head over there and wait for me to let you out. And, don't forget these papers."

Clara collected the stack of recriminations and her folder. She strode across the room with a strange gleefulness that seemed inappropriate. A voice stopped Clara in her tracks. The jailer hollered again and she turned around. He was shaking her heels aloft. Clara quickly returned and gathered them under her arm. She rushed back to the metal door and went through. There was a long hallway and she walked down with her bare feet slapping against the tiled floor. There was a small kiosk at the end. She stopped and looked through. A benevolent looking old woman smiled.

"Do ye have ye property?"

"Yes, ma'am."

"Okie dokie."

The woman pushed a little button on the desk and the door to a lobby swung open. She saw Ronnie seated with a stranger at the far end. Both rose as she entered. Clara ran to Ronnie and threw her arms around his neck. He rocked her back and forth slightly. She started to cry and he quietly shushed her. Her sobs were muffled into his sweater. She rubbed his arm and touched something turbulent underneath and he twitched in shock. She felt an overpowering urge to hold on forever. Almost like she feared he wasn't real and all this was a dream. Ronnie massaged her back. He crooned words of love that soothed her weary soul. The unimaginable sadness diminished like a plume of smoke. Everything disappeared like the wakening of a fevered nightmare. The turbulent future wound back to her mind and she let go. She clasped his hand tightly and turned to the bail bondsmen.

"Greetings, Clara. I need you to sign some forms and you are free to go." He held out a clipboard and a stapled stack of papers. "I'll walk you through them. I've already given copies to Mr. Wells." She nodded and sat with pen in hand. He pointed to the bottom of the page. "This signifies that you know your court date. You have to be there. If not, you will be in contempt and get in more trouble." She signed the bottom. She turned the page. "These are the rules for your bond. You must check in weekly via phone or in person to our office. If not, bail is revoked. No alcohol or drugs. Again, revoked. If you are arrested for another crime, your bail is revoked. If you leave the city, you must notify us." Clara scribbled her name. "Basically, if you do anything that we deem problematic, we will revoke the bond and send you back to jail. At that point, you won't get out again. Do you understand?"

"Yes, sir."

"Okay, good."

She signed the rest of the papers and handed the clipboard back.

"You understand that Mr. Wells is accountable for your actions. As your cosigner, he is financially responsible. If you don't show up, that's on him for twenty thousand dollars."

"I'll show up. I swear."

"Excellent. Well, Ms. Bennett, I'll see you and don't forget to check in. It's very important."

Clara stood and shook his hand. Ronnie did also. All three left the lobby together. Clara scanned the parking lot for Ronnie's truck, but it wasn't there. He clasped Clara's hand and led her towards a shiny black Cadillac with a dealer's tag. The same car she got in the night before. Ronnie handed her the keys and motioned for her to drive. She went around the car and entered. The stoicism he wore before disappeared and the look of searing pain shot grimaces across his face. Clara watched him from behind the wheel. He returned her gaze.

His breathing was labored and bands of sweat ran down his face. Ronnie reached into the backseat and rifled through a plastic bag in the back and brought out a shirt and sweat pants. He handed them to her. She quickly changed clothes in the car and Ronnie handed her a pair of tennis shoes. She felt better getting out of her whore's garb. Stripping away the fabric of filth that carried her to this place. Ronnie looked out the window and was seemingly lost in deep concentration. Clara wished she might read his thoughts.

He seemed different. Almost menacing. She'd have felt afraid were it anyone else.

"Crank her up and let's roll."

Clara started the car and backed out of the parking space. She exited the lot and headed north away from the coast. "I know where he lives. The man who's got her."

"Is that where you think he'd take her?"

"I don't know, but that's the best place to look."

Ronnie was tapping his fingers on his knees. "How long will it take us to get there?"

"About thirty minutes."

"Okay."

They rode in silence. The city rushed past but she paid it no mind. Things swept across the landscape as a blur. The scenery about was inconsequential. All that mattered was finding her daughter.

The world rotates without our consent. Life acts in the same way. It continues its source-less passage and sometimes we are left behind. The choices we make dictate our course. Yet, that's as far as we control.

She glanced over at Ronnie. His eyes were burning and he stared straight ahead. She noted that he radiated violence, which was at all other times restrained. An indolent mask covered it, but, now, it was open for all to see. There was a plan forming in his mind. She almost saw it clearly as him. Something that grew from consideration. Like a picture forming slowly in a photographer's darkroom. Clara sensed she was about to break the seal of proper conduct. As if, it might unleash some sort of hidden anger directed at her. It didn't matter. She asked anyway.

"Where did you get the bail money?"

"I borrowed it and a good bit more without asking... It's all right. I'll pay them back... Eventually. The real unlucky bastard is the bondsman."

"Why?"

"Because we are splitting this town after we find Mary. We've got a dead body at the trailer. Some officer tried to kill me but I got the better of him. That bastard is stone dead and I don't feel the least bit sorry about it. He messed me up with a knife. Cut and stabbed me in the shoulder and arm. I'll need you to dress it later. I hope you know your way around a needle and thread." He chuckled and took out his pack of cigarettes. "But, good news is that he's no longer part of the equation." He lit a cigarette and exhaled rich blue smoke. "I don't know who else I've got to kill today. No matter what, we've got to skip town. Just get away from Florida and start over. The three of us making a new life for ourselves. I've got us enough money to make it for a while. I say California."

Clara reached her hand over and clasped his. "That sounds perfect. A fresh start."

He squeezed hers. "I ain't mad at you."

Tears sprang to her eyes and the road turned blurry. She was on the edge of breaking down. The wretchedness of the last twelve hours flooded back. Her heart ached to the point of pain. Clara's insides were twisted in agony that wouldn't abate. Psychologically she was drained and only intense fear kept her going.

She winded the car through town almost mechanically. Like it was on autopilot and she solely pushed pedals. The sky about was cross cut by broken and dark clouds. The sun was waning in the distance. The clock on the dashboard read six-thirty and she prayed that they weren't too late.

They left town and descended into a scene far different from the coast. The homes formed a unique menagerie of styles. They had a sort of strange rhythmic nonconformity. The sandy soil made way for rich amber clay. Only a few miles north, the landscape fluctuated from beach flora to evergreen timber. They passed homes far from the road that looked cloaked by spidery and naked laurel. They stood cantered at odd angles as if either sinking into the earth or blown away by an enormous wind. The car was the only place without shadow. It all seemed dimensionless and strangely familiar. A mile ahead was a hidden drive with a sign cautioning against trespassers. No heeding the warning. This was exactly where they needed to go.

She slowed the car and turned into the gravel driveway.

Chapter 31

Mary was shaking on the filthy mattress. She pictured someplace warm, but it only made her colder. Everything was silent, but the beating of her own heart. Mary had no idea how long she'd been in the cell. Hours or minutes since they'd made her pose. The looks on the men's faces made her afraid in a way that she didn't understand. She clenched her eyes tightly and imagined her mother and Ronnie sitting on the porch swing. Envisioning riding her bike back-and-forth along the street. Warmth bubbled up like a wellspring.

Mary held on to that scene.

It took her so far away from this place that she didn't hear the door unlock. When it opened, Mary was thrust back to this horrible place. She heard what sounded like the door closing. She looked towards the noise and saw nothing at first. Just the darkness. Then, a small man walked into the light. A devilish grin etched across his face.

Mary sat up and scooted back against the cell wall.

The man followed her with soundless steps.

"Don't be alarmed, little girl," the man said. "I'm a doctor."

She saw him lick his lips.

"I'm here to help you. I'll take you far away from here. You will live with me."

He took another step. Mary was pressing so tightly against the cement wall that hot pain raced down her spine.

"Before we go, though, I need to make an examination."

Mary watched absolutely petrified as the man slowly undid his belt.

The disturbing scene that followed was so atrocious that it's hopefully beyond the realm of your imagination.

Chapter 32

Clara stopped the car at the foot of the driveway and they discussed their plan. Ronnie spoke coolly and instructed how they'd approach the situation. She told him the layout as best as she could remember and he calculated his plan of attack. His shoulder was dealing him misery but the adrenaline pushed the pain aside. Clara put the car in reverse and backed down the driveway and Ronnie hid in the front seat. He gathered one of his heavy shirts from the plastic bag and wrapped it around the gun. Twilight shrouded everything in shadow and he bet on it to fool the captors into thinking that the petite driver was an enormous man. He held the pistol at his chest and breathed slowly. Ronnie rolled down the window and watched the side mirror as the house came into view.

The house was depthless and black in the failing light. It held no recognizable pattern he could glean from the swirling chaos about. The guard was standing on the porch and smoking a cigarette. Clara told Ronnie that he was waving them on. He whispered to Clara to keep going and stop right at the stairs. She was sweating and nervous. He saw her hands shaking as she cautiously navigated the huge Cadillac. Ronnie watched the mirror and saw that they were not fifteen feet away. An expensive sports car was parked to the right. Through the open window, he smelled a putrid dankness that he guessed was a river. Or, perhaps something else. The decomposing stench of bitter recriminations. He knew it well and faced it stoically. The moon was bright and created an environment that looked blue. Up close, the steps were clearly visible in the haunted light. He calmly told her to stop. Any closer might give them away and raise an alarm. They'd give up the element of surprise.

"Pop the trunk," he whispered.

Clara pushed the button and the lid sprang up. It blocked any view of the cab. Next, Ronnie signaled for her to kill the engine. When it quieted, he held his breath and listened intensely. The wooden porch creaked with the sound of someone walking down the steps.

"Hey, do you need help?"

The sound of gravel crunching underfoot grew louder. Ronnie softly pulled the door handle and opened it just enough to slide out. The dome light turned on, but the man was too close to the trunk lid to see inside.

Ronnie held the wrapped pistol in his left hand and slunk towards the rear. He was crouching and peeked over the side. The supplier's crony was looking in the trunk with a puzzled expression. Ronnie stood and leveled the pistol at the man's head. He was partially turned when Ronnie fired, its sound muffled.

The bullet entered the man's forehead just above the right eye. The back of his skull was blown away and part of his brain was left exposed. He was graveyard dead before he hit the ground. There was no cry or death rattle. Only a stifled pop and a thud. The shirt caught fire and Ronnie unwrapped it from the gun and tossed it to the side. He reached down and collected the machine pistol from the recently departed. He slung it around his shoulder and walked to the driver's window.

"Watch me through the mirror. When I signal, I want you to lay on the horn. Don't stop until they open the door. Okay?"

"Okay," she whispered.

Ronnie crept up the steps silently. He concentrated on any sound outside his own breathing. It reminded him of the jungles of Vietnam. The intense thrill of life and death. A horrible manifestation of the reaper flashed through his mind. Not yet, he thought. I have promises to keep.

There was a heady stench from fried vegetation and it looked like gray green parchment paper strung on poles. All about reeked of sulfurous gun smoke and burnt cotton. He wiped the sweat out of his eyes with his forearm. He felt no wind despite the slight noise of it. Perhaps he was in a geographical oddity and beyond the realm of climate. The air was oppressive and almost too thick to breathe. He thought about Mary and it calmed him. Her laugh the incubator of peaceful waters. The image of her smile steadied his pistol bearing hand. His anxiety shook the boards beneath his feet. He prayed that the horn would bring them all to the door at once. Then, he thought how dangerous that would be.

You're already in the shit, old man, he thought. You just need to breathe through your mouth and wade in. It's almost over. Just find your sweet girl.

He flattened himself against the wall just to the right of the door and held the cocked pistol by his ear. He hoped they'd rush out to see what was wrong and he'd shoot them last to first. Ronnie looked down and saw that the dead man was clearly visible from the doorway.

"Shit," he whispered. Now, he counted on their eyes adjusting to give him that split second of time. That's all it takes. I've got the element of surprise.

Ronnie mouthed a little prayer. He wasn't certain what he'd meet at the threshold, but he knew the kind. He'd known them all his life. They were of him and he of them. Men indentured into an enigmatically dark covenant. This would turn out one of two ways and both were shaded with violence. Ronnie was mad beyond all reckoning, yet strangely calm. It's now or never, he thought.

Then, Ronnie waved his hand in the mirror's line of sight. He waited and nothing occurred. Only, a solitary whippoorwill called out. It grew faint and drifted away like a transparent and drifting fog. Just when he thought Clara hadn't seen the signal, the horn blared enormously. She laid down on it for a while, then started rapidly pressing the steering column. Ronnie's ear was pressed flat against the side of the house and he heard the music shut off and confused voices from within. Sweat poured down his face as he tried to gauge the number of men he'd have to kill. An authoritative shout rang out and floorboards creaked. Ronnie watched the knob turn and the door open. He saw a thin line of interior light spread across the porch.

A squat fat man appeared and was followed by a lanky giant. Almost like two cartoon characters wandering into the night. Both held guns at the ready. The largest walked to the edge of the porch and looked at the scene without comprehension. Ronnie watched the doorway and saw that those were the only two coming. He stepped forward out of the shadow and placed the muzzle of the pistol behind the lanky man's ear. The shot was unmistakably loud and the crony pitched over onto the fat man. He hung suspended in the air and then fell straight forward into his fellow. A rhythmic shuddering spasm of the fresh dead. For a brief moment, it looked like the tall man was hugging his comrade in a final death throe. The squat crony turned and stared into Ronnie's eyes.

There was understanding. Perhaps, almost acceptance.

The barrel of a pistol was the last thing he'd ever see. Not his family or loved ones. Just a flash and, then, nothing. He didn't even try to raise his gun. Ronnie pulled the trigger and shot the man in the face. He quickly double tapped the man's chest on the way down just to make sure.

Ronnie swiveled to face the house. He burned with justifiable murder.

The opened door was now closed. Fuck, Ronnie thought. If they've locked it, I'm in some more deep shit.

He held the gun at the ready and reached with his left hand for the door knob. As it turned, a loud shot rocketed from within and the door exploded. Ronnie looked down and instantaneously saw a softball sized hole in the paneling. A massive force struck him that slung Ronnie around into the porch railing. He felt nothing and, then, everything. He was praying and swearing alternatively. Indefinable pain raced up and down his body. It was concentrated outward from his pelvis. He reached down and felt huge splinters sticking out from his hip. He couldn't move his right leg. It felt dead. Blood poured from the wound and he almost fainted. Mary's face flashed through his mind and he fought the urge to fall.

You won't get back up, old man, he thought.

He looked at the door. Light shone through where they'd blasted it with a shotgun. Ronnie limped towards the wall and swallowed back the nausea. He fought the urge to vomit. Ronnie's pistol was gone and his right hand was covered in blood. He worked his fingers and he felt the pellets scratch that were imbedded against the bone. He still had the machine pistol wrapped around his shoulder. Ronnie held it in his left hand and switched off the safety. His plan was fucked. Now, it was up to improvisation.

Luckily, the men inside were stupid enough to do him a favor.

A man pushed open the door with his foot and stepped onto the porch. He held an Uzi. Ronnie lifted the machine pistol and fired. Three quick shots tore the man's hand away. The gun disappeared into the darkness and the crony screamed in agony. Ronnie limped towards the associate and punched him in the face. The man brought his arms up to block another blow. One hand only. The other was a stub. Ronnie grabbed him by the throat and spun him around. He placed the gun to his head and whispered in his ear.

"Do what I say or I'll blow your fucking brains out." The handless man was nodding and sobbed. "Go through that door. You try anything and you're dead," Ronnie warned.

The wounded man stepped towards the light of the open door. Ronnie held his machine pistol at the base of the man's neck. Ronnie pressed the muzzle forcefully into his spine and they went into the house. The leader held up his hands in surrender. Ronnie stayed very small behind his human shield. The pain in his hip was excruciating and he knew it was very bad. Blood squirted every time he limped along. Ronnie tried to see into the room but it looked empty.

Then, another explosive blast sounded from the shotgun.

The human shield rocketed back into Ronnie and dropped dead to the floor. The supplier shot his own man to pave the way for the real target. It happened in a flash. Quicker than he'd ever imagined.

Each pulled the trigger.

The shotgun blast and three-round burst occurred simultaneously. The supplier was knocked off balance so the shotgun hit to the left of its mark.

Yet, both struck the other. The pellets entered the side of Ronnie's face, neck, and chest. He flew back from the force of it and blacked out. Ronnie's machine pistol bullets struck the supplier in a running upwards motion from his sternum to his neck.

Everything turned black. Ronnie felt nothing and thought he was dead. That was until the cries of fleeing naked women affirmed his continued existence.

You are going to die, he thought, but not yet.

Ronnie tried to open his eyes, but only the right one produced a cloudy vision. A pellet was lodged into the cornea of his left and it was unmistakably gone. His breathing was labored and blood pooled in his mouth. He spat it out down the side of his face only for more to return. He couldn't sit up properly, so he rolled painfully to his side. It was too much.

A white flash of pain and he blacked out again.

She visited him.

Mary formed out of the utter blackness and smiled. She clasped and squeezed his hands.

"Hi, Ronnie!"

"Hello, sweetheart."

"Will you do me a big favor?"

"Of course, darling. Anything."

"Will you get up?"

He opened his one eye and saw the supplier sitting propped up against the couch. Almost patiently waiting for death. Ronnie sat up on his elbows and watched the man. The supplier held his neck and looked around wildly. Every so often, a spout of blood rocketed between his fingers. Bubbles and strange froth formed from the wounds in the man's chest. Each time he breathed, they popped and were replaced by others. Finally, the supplier pitched over onto the floor. He lay unblinking with his mouth open. The depths of the dead man's eyes were void and black. Then, the supplier's hand fell away and blood poured.

Ronnie shifted slightly and vomited bloody bile into his lap. It was stringy and lay like ropes down his chin. He hurt in ways he didn't know possible. Ronnie was half-senseless and the world about seemed illusionary. Not enough oxygen reached his brain and he was solely moved on by his baser instincts. He was dimly conscious of his own existence. Then, Mary's voice echoed in his mind.

Get up. Get up.

He pushed himself to one knee.

Get up.

Ronnie righted himself and screamed in agony. It was filled with a barbarous rage. He was momentarily disoriented and forgot where he was. The mortally wounded cyclops scanned the room. He saw the shotgun lying on the couch. Ronnie limped over and picked it up. He emptied the spent shell from the barrel and slid a live round into the chamber. Something caught his solitary eye. There was a partially open black bag on the glass coffee table filled with money. He hobbled to the satchel, zipped it shut, and slid it over his good shoulder. He moved like a drunken man with fragile legs. A wave of nausea hit him and he threw up in his mouth. The sick drained slowly down his neck. All he could do was moan in pain.

Yet, he kept on. This wasn't over.

The shotgun wore a pistol grip. He struggled down the hallway with it held out front. It bobbed unsteadily with his wounded body. The pathway was dark and he was temporarily blinded by blackness. He held his thick and bloody arm out to feel his way through the darkness. He blinked several times and various shapes took form. Ronnie hobbled on and used the wall to brace himself. It was harder and harder for him to catch his breath. Each was weaker than the last. Soon he'd run out of strength. Ronnie had to find Mary. His mind felt like it was teetering on the cusp of consciousness. All he wanted to do was sit down. A forbidden yearning. He'd sell his soul to the devil himself to just lie on the ground and go to sleep. But, Ronnie knew he couldn't do that.

You stop and you're dead, old man. And, so is she.

He passed a room that looked like a lab of some sort or a prison kitchen. He looked through the window and it was empty. She wasn't there.

Something told him to keep going.

Blood dripped continuously and created small echoes in the corridor. He kept stopping and was cloaked in the burning urge to sleep. Ronnie recovered and marched on.

There was a heavy looking door down the hall. He mumbled words that beseeched for death to wait. Just a few more minutes, please.

Ronnie trudged forward but the way seemed endless. A faint light shone through the cracks. He looked again and the light blinked. Or, he thought it did. Were they real lights or corpse candles that beckoned him onward?

He struggled to comprehend anything outside placing one foot in front of the other. Ronnie hobbled and winced forward. He stood before the last door on the left. What manner of mysterious beast resided inside?

He opened it slowly. It felt like it weighed a ton and took all his strength to crack it open. He kept pushing until there was enough space and Ronnie limped inside.

There was a single naked bulb that hung from the ceiling of the concrete cell. Yellow and brittle light shone through the aged globe. His vision was failing in a way that was Ronnie's last push for life. Nothing made any sense. A filthy blood-stained mattress sat in the middle of the room. An unglazed barred tiny window was built into the wall. It reminded him of the penitentiary. Ronnie's solitary eye scanned the room. Huddled in the corner was a blurry miniature figure.

Mary was crouched in the corner and crying. When she saw the disfigured being enter the cell, she let out a blood curdling scream. It reverberated an agonizing echo around the concrete walls. A hundred Marys from every conceivable direction were pleading in terror. For whom did they toll?

Something shifted to his right. He couldn't see it, but the mere presence was unmistakable. An unseen sepulcher was sensed from the bowels of the world. Ronnie turned painfully and saw a dwarfish man hiding in the corner. He was naked from the waist down and had a puddle of piss by his feet. A being wholly terror stricken. The man held his hands up in surrender and gibbered something that Ronnie didn't comprehend.

All a misunderstanding. Take the money. I'll give you more. I'm so sorry. We can work something out. Just, please, let me go.

These words meant nothing.

Ronnie tried to knit together some coherent narrative of the room. He forgot why he was here. Certain themes were tagged down, but it lacked a proper understanding. Evilness permeated everything in the cell. It clung to Ronnie like a rider. He ran his broken tongue and felt malevolence on his teeth. He saw stacked bodies in preparation for burial. Tombstones and the rich smell of freshly turned earth.

Mary crept forward into the light. He saw streaks of slick blood smeared between her legs. She was shaking and her face glistened with tears. A mixture of agony and fear. Something was broken in her soul. Irreconcilably altered and ruined in such a cruel manner that it couldn't ever be put right again. Her childish countenance was gone. Innocence lost. He pictured his little angel laughing and smiling as she rode her bike up and down the street. Her biting into a fried bologna and cheese sandwich. Giggling as Mary wiped away bits of mayonnaise with the back of her hand. Posing in her witch's costume and prancing around the trailer with her broom. Jumping with joy at the sight of her own guitar. Walking along the surf and staring out across that great expanse of ocean.

Now, he looked into Mary's eyes and saw a child forever scarred. Her world darkened and irreconcilably changed. The sweet innocent girl was no more.

There was only one thing for Ronnie to do.

He lifted the shotgun and fired point blank into the man's face.

The top portion of his head was blown away. It ceased to exist. Everything from the bridge of his nose to the crown was scattered in bits and pieces across the wall of the cell. Ronnie looked at the remnants of the pedophile. The perverted destroyer of children's worlds. Brain matter and bone meal dripped slowly down the concrete. Bits of all this pedophile would ever be was imbedded in the cold dark material. Something almost poetic in that. Ronnie dropped the shotgun and it clattered to the floor. He held out his hand to Mary.

Finally, he was finished.

Chapter 33

Clara watched it all through the little rearview mirror. Ronnie worked like a man possessed. It was almost like watching a movie. Like gun battles in westerns. Yet, this was real life and those men were unmistakably dead. She jumped with each gunshot. Since the two men exited the house, everything happened so quickly that in the twilight Clara lost sight of him.

Everything but the porch was brilliantly lit with moonlight. It was surreal and an unearthly blue. More gunshots and she turned around. The trunk blocked her view. She carefully stuck her head out the window. Her eyes just barely visible outside the car. Clara saw that the front door was open and two silhouettes entered the light. One held a gun to the other's head.

In panic, Clara exited the car. She closed the door with care. She crept around the side of the vehicle and watched the house for any movement. There was a dead man lying by the rear that stared crossed eyed into the heavens. A tiny trickle of blood poured from the entrance wound. Even in death, there was something sinister about him. Perhaps it was the insane smile carved on his lifeless face. Vague anger seared through her and Clara spat.

The dearly departed would've taken you with him. She tried to imagine what she'd do if something happened to

Ronnie. Would her daughter be lost? Could she get into the car and drive away?

No, absolutely not. She'd die first.

More gunfire sounded in the interior. The shots didn't sound the same. Clara left the safety of the car and approached the steps. She searched the ground for a gun, but it was too dark to parcel one from the shadows. At the base of the stairs were two bodies stacked together. The romantic moonlight turned them into mismatched couple in the act of love. Upon closer inspection, their expressions were of outrage that she knew well. Clara held her breath but was met with silence. Not even nature spoke of its presence. As if, it thought better of this place and fled for deeper timber.

Clara was halfway up the stairs when three naked women burst out of the open-door shrieking. None of them slowed or even looked her way. They bounded down the steps and sprinted across the gravel driveway to a badly treated Ford sedan. It cranked on the first try and raced away from the house. Bits of rocks and dirt sprayed with the fishtail and Clara watched the car disappear from sight. Clara continued into the doorway and nearly slipped in a huge puddle of gore. She scanned the living room. Neither body was Ronnie and that gave her heart. The supplier was among the new slain dead.

Walking towards the hallway, Clara heard a muffled shot and a child's scream. It was Mary. Clara was frozen in terror. Unsure if she wanted to follow the sound and possibly find her whole world dead in a growing pool of blood. Horrible visions raced through her mind. She imagined burying Ronnie and Mary side-by-side. Killing herself to join them. Clara shoved the palms of her hands into her eye sockets in protest. She was crying and dropped to her knees. Then, she heard Mary's voice.

"Mommy! Help me!" Clara opened her eyes and saw Mary trying to steady a badly injured Ronnie. Her heart nearly exploded with love and terror. Cords in Mary's neck stood out and the veins pumped visibly. Her eyes were sharp with intent. Each step by Ronnie was followed by a wincing cry and he was covered in blood. Upon entering the living room, he stopped and vomited a reddish bile mixture. It dripped down his chin and drooled onto his shirt. His eyes rolled into the back of his head and he nearly toppled over. Stubbornness hardened his resolve and he took another step.

Mary was crying and pleading. "Mommy, we have to get him to a hospital!"

Clara's heart sank because she knew they would never make it in time. She rushed over to them and braced herself under Ronnie's arm. A bloody hand lay across her shoulder. The warmth of it dripped down her shirt. He leaned all his weight on her and was trying to speak, but he was incapable of forming words. Almost like he'd forgotten how and was debased to communicating with grunts. His brain was hardly getting any oxygen. Clara's hands clamped around his waist. He kept trying to shove a black bag into Mary's arms but she wouldn't let go of his leg. Ronnie kept motioning for the bag. He was wheezing and gasping. It sounded like blood was filling his lungs. Soon, he'd drown on dry land.

Finally, Clara took the satchel and slid it over her head. She glanced in the opening and saw that it was full of money. It nearly took her breath.

Ronnie stumbled over his own feet and nearly carried the girls down with him. They kept going towards the outer dark. Clara led him around the dead obstacles. Ronnie shook violently and she feared he was descending into shock. Clara grit her teeth and clutched him tighter. She whispered to him in hopes of encouraging him forward. His throat was making a high-pitched whistle that wasn't a good sign.

Ahead, Mary was trying to tug the bodies out of the way and trying to make a path. Her baby girl was covered in their fresh and sticky gore. Mary ignored this house of horrors to help Ronnie. Facing head on the scenes of awful to help her friend. Perhaps she truly believed he'd make it. Just a few stitches and he'd be all right. Thankfully, the magnitude of the situation was lost to her.

Clara navigated the narrow passageway and exited the nightmare house. When they stepped out onto the front porch, the windblown branches made the scene about look alive. Before, she'd not noticed that they were so far into the woodlands. A chorus of crickets and tree frogs set up a melodious orchestra for their departure. Oddly acoustic quality to the noise. Ronnie's death rattle joined the fray and it was strangely beautiful. The evergreens danced amid the blue moonlight and characters formed out of the shadows. Mary stood and stared speculatively at the steps. She turned to help Ronnie. She stood with her hands out as if to brace him from a fall. Her little arms outheld to catch him. Ronnie managed the first step without trouble.

Yet, on the next, his legs gave out and he fell with the girls in tow. They lay together on the ground next to the dead couple for a moment. Mary stood and tried to get Ronnie to rise, but he would not. She was screaming and trying to tug at his arm. His dead weight was too much and he seemed to fight against it. He shook his head uncompromisingly. Clara sat back on her heels and felt tears stream down her face. He lay staring up into the heavens at the brilliant intensity of the phosphorescent moon. Blinking ever so often. Mary was hitting his arm softly and sobbing. She kept pleading with him to get up. Spittle formed and she buried her head in his chest. She swore into his shirt and damned him as only loved ones could. Merciless and immoveable last moments. He put his ruined arm around her and rubbed her back Mary was rocking back and forth crying. Completely inconsolable. Ronnie opened and closed his mouth repeatedly like he was trying to speak. Clara leaned close.

"California," he said softly.

She whispered, "Yes."

Ronnie nodded and formed words. He was repeating something over and over. She kissed him on the cheek and he smiled. The last he'd ever give. His murmured chanting grew louder and then faded off. He recited, "Father, into your hands, I commit my spirit. Into your hands, I commit my spirit. Into your hands, I commit my spirit." This went on until his mouth barely moved. Just a twitch of the lips.

Then, he exhaled heavily, shuddered painfully, and died.

Chapter 34

A soulless and unpromising dawn broke as they left Florida forever. The trove of constellations burned brightly before the advent of morning. They drove away from the principal of light that was birthed in the east. The pale flame rose slowly and washed away the blue-black world like an aubade. The stars petered out like the slow death of a thousand molten suns. Something eternal in knowing that they'd return. It made her think of Ronnie. Perhaps he was of their number now and burning for them.

Mother and daughter drove out of the panhandle into the unknown. The terrain morphed into high pine woodlands mixed with flat bottom land. The future gray western landscape was utterly exhilarating. Each mile marker felt weightless. There was sadness and potential rolled into one. The road was lonely, yet wonderful all the same. She seemed an interloper or trespasser in this picturesque world. The environs shifted as they drove and the sky remained a beautiful cobalt blue in the west. Sometime in the early morning hours, they crossed an enormous river that was dark brown like moving mud. They drove on through neutral terrain that held no claim or precedence. It was all alien and at oft junctures in their travels, both mother and daughter felt endowed with profound clarity of their journey. Clara didn't stop to rest until Midland, Texas.

Mary cried herself to sleep. Clara pulled exhausted into a motel on the outskirts of town. She checked in, carried Mary inside, and placed her on the bed. The room was exactly like her old work. Then, Clara lay down next to Mary and closed her eyes. Soon, she was fast asleep. She feared a visitation of some nightmarish figure, but there was none. Only a dreamland snapshot of Ronnie cooking breakfast and laughing heartily at something Mary said. He looked so happy. Clara woke with a smile on her face. There was peace in knowing such events were real and set in stone.

He'd never ever be forgotten.

While Mary showered, Clara turned on the news. His face on the screen took her breath. All she knew was that the news had it all wrong. The anchors called it the Pensacola Meth Lab Massacre. The reports were that convicted murderer Ronald E. Wells killed drug-associate Breece Grimsley at Wells' trailer in the Palms Paradise Villas. It was the residence where Wells lived with the now missing Clara G. Bennett and her daughter, Mary. After murdering Grimsley, Ronald drove to Donahue's Hardware and Repair where he worked. There he was spotted on camera stealing a large amount of cash from the safe. The owner, Timothy Donahue, is distraught by the theft and crimes committed. He stated that Ronald was quiet and a hard worker. Mr. Donahue believed he'd turned his life around.

Yet, clearly, the perpetrator had not.

After robbing the hardware store, he bailed out the missing Bennett who was arrested on unrelated charges. His movements between the jail and the murder house are unknown. It is believed that he collected the daughter before arriving at the Methamphetamine Laboratory. An all-points bulletin is currently in effect for mother and daughter. But, a police insider notified our reporter that the authorities do not have much hope in finding them alive. What we do know is that Mr. Wells arrived at the methamphetamine laboratory and a gunfight ensued. After an anonymous tip, the police found a total of six bodies. All died from gunshot wounds of various caliber. Among the dead was a well renowned pediatrician from Tampa. Respected in his field and among his patients. The police have yet to release the doctor's name until further information is gathered.

Clara shook her head. She saw her and Mary's picture flash in front of the screen. Just then, her daughter entered from the bathroom and was drying herself. Clara quickly changed the channel.

"Mommy, I'm hungry."

Clara spread her arms. Mary approached and she hugged her tightly. "Okay sweetie. Let me shower and we'll go get something to eat. Then, we need to stop at Walmart and get some personal things." She paused as if weighing an idea. "How would you like to color your hair?"

Mary smiled.

The two drove through terrain totally alien to either's understanding. These renegade outcasts fleeing all they'd ever known. About was a world so flat that the distance gestured at eternity. Watchful shadows strung out gaunt and thin for miles. In the night, source-less lightning grew out of the ground and shot towards the heavens. It seemed for a moment that the world was upside down. That was alright by Clara.

In the morning, they passed a field that was ablaze and growing. The flames mixed with the ruinous pandemonium of the cresting remorseless sun. In the rearview mirror, it looked almost like the tangential cities they fled were imbued in apocalyptic ruin. It was so deadly and beautiful that it brought them both to tears. They continued west through small and large towns that were hewn of strange and ancient architecture. Unlike any either had seen. Building models originating out of Spain that were hundreds of years old. No fauna about but misshapen and burnt looking naked trees. They drove on in silence and watched with huge and curious eyes. Curious pilgrims fleeing from darker portents like refugees. Racing from ominous cities like places under siege.

They stopped next in Quartzite, Arizona. Almost to California. She'd heard of open country before, but this was something new. The miles of endless highway formed metallic and shapeless pools of water that disappeared and migrated with each passing rotation. Countless fence posts and mile markers came and went. Iridescent mirages that beckoned them further westward. Hundreds of dust devils crossing the cooking asphalt. The beautiful desert drive was magnetic. The barren sand and sky swam together in the endless distance. The faultless void without feature seemed to go on forever. Farther on, the remote mountains sat shimmering against the western sun. They glistened blue above the ground like islands. They seemed to kiss the very heavens above. A kestrel flew before the car, circled, and dropped out of sight. The freedom of it warmed something in her as it was something she'd long been without. The unbroken vastness warmed something within mother and child. They spoke of Ronnie and happier times.

Twilight found them still on the road. They saw dry heat lightning flash in the distance. The scenes about vanished slowly in a brilliant miasma of color. A tapestry of striking and smoky hues formed as the heavens darkened incrementally until it merged dimensionless into ink black. Night multiplied into utter nothingness. Yet, they felt safe and secure together behind the car lights. Again, they stayed in a similar and familiar cheap motel. Both now wearing homespun haircuts and blond highlights. Wretched-looking with fatigue. After Mary fell asleep, Clara turned on the news for any sign of Ronnie. She found it.

The anchor interviewed his ex-wife. She was happy and relieved that he was dead. A vile human who was a waste of good and free American oxygen. A living nightmare finally over with. She was outraged and was going to sue the state. The parole board was at fault for ever freeing him. The murders were on their head, his ex-wife claimed. The news anchor reported that all further discharges from prison were halted for the time being. Florida corrections were investigating the matter and tightening up the protocols for release.

The anchors reported that his body was cremated and his ashes were claimed by the family of the Michael Murphy. The reporter noted that Michael was the young man Wells murdered all those years ago. When asked for comment, his twin brother, Matthew, stated that there was a small family service and that Ronald's remains were scattered in the Gulf of Mexico.

Mr. Murphy said that, despite killing his brother, "everyone deserves forgiveness. You cannot live your life with hate. Resentment will destroy you and those you care about. Forgiveness will set you free. Anger consumed my life for a long time. It kept me from being a better husband and father. No matter what Ronald did, he was a child of God."

The news anchor reported that the service was held on the beach and presided over by Pastor Frederick Long of Second Pensacola Methodist. Those in attendance were Mr. Murphy, his wife, their twin boys, and a Sue Ellen Paisley. It was reported that there were tears in Matthew's eyes as the ashes disappeared into the sea. As he watched the remains vanish amid the green salt water landscape, he finally felt at peace. He hugged his sons and told them he loved them.

Of the Bennett's, still no sign. The police were combing the swamps, but it was highly unlikely that their bodies would ever be found.

Ronnie's words floated through her head. Life wasn't a problem or machine that you could forcibly make right. The noumenal comes at you in fits and starts. Bits added later that won't work. It's a free-flowing thing with no real set of instructions. All you have are vague ideas of what you want and how you wish it to go. We all have a deceptive vision of how things are. Those are phantasms and delusions. You must see it's all wrong. The world you long for is counterfeit.

You know, he once told her. *It don't make no difference what anybody thinks.*

She shook her head in disgust and turned off the television.

With bitter sadness, she thought how he was right about everything.

Clara stood up and walked over to the window. She looked out the opening in the blinds at the blueish world. With each passing moment, the environs had the faint look of diminishing trouble. She saw the pale gray moon hanging in the sky and watched it black out now and again by the running clouds. The stars looked like muted light. Pale Joshua trees practically shone bright like white bones. The shadows they created bobbed slowly in the faint wind. Then, it started to rain. A soft mizzle that clung to the glass and blurred out the world.

Chapter 35 - Epilogue

Fresno, California 2027

For the past eleven years, Clara and Mary lived under new identities. The satchel full of money helped them start life anew. Thirty-thousand dollars purchased near perfect birth certificates and social security numbers. Despite still being classified as missing persons, the two lived in splendid anonymity in the eyes of the law.

Sara Rodgers drove south with her husband from Stockton, California on interstate ninety-nine to Fresno. Brandy was in her second year at Fresno State studying music education. Her dream was to teach young people the joys of music. She attended on scholarship for both the university's orchestra and marching band. There, Brandy played the cello and trombone, but her passion was for the guitar.

In truth, almost any instrument Brandy picked up, she quickly mastered.

To supplement her income, she played live music at Lamberts Steakhouse and Bar, which was where her mother and stepfather were headed.

Nine years before, Sara married a man named Jason Rodgers in a simple ceremony. He was a drug counselor at a rehab and they ran a halfway house together. It was a happy marriage and he was a good man. He legally adopted Brandy soon after and treated her like his own. He knew everything of their past life in Florida, but didn't care.

Sara loved him even more for that.

They pulled into the packed parking lot thirty minutes before Brandy's gig. The sign out front said: Live Music by Brandy Rodgers. Sara took a picture of it with her phone.

Inside, they sat near the little stage and ordered waters and two steaks. Brandy was talking to her large group of friends at another table. She was beautiful in every sense of the word. She radiated goodness and everyone loved her. They were students from band, orchestra, and a handsome young man who was an accounting major from her math class. He liked her and she liked him, but neither had, as of yet, notified the other. Jason reached into his pocket and took out a one-hundred-dollar bill. He walked over to Brandy's tip jar and placed it inside. She caught sight of him and jumped out of her chair. Brandy raced over and gave him a huge. They walked over to the table and Brandy embraced her mother.

"Hi guys," she said. "Thanks so much for coming."

"We wouldn't miss it," Jason said. "Are you nervous?"

"Sorta."

"Why sweetheart?" Sara asked.

She skirted her eyes towards her friends' table. The lingering look of young love. "I dunno. I just am," Brandy said.

Smiles of understanding. "You'll do great," her mother said.

"Thanks!" She checked her watch. "It's time."

She kissed them both on the cheek and approached the little wooden stage. She tuned Ronnie's guitar. It was ancient, scratched, and a little worse for wear, but still played like a dream. As fine as the first day Ronnie let her hold it and strum a few chords. The guitar was her most prized possession. Brandy wouldn't trade it for all the money in the world. That wasn't an overstatement. The guitar was priceless. It was more than just an instrument. When she touched it, the guitar felt like an extension of her old friend. Almost like an electrical charge of remembrance. His interaction with them seemed like a lifetime ago, yet, through the guitar, he was made flesh.

It was memory so sweet Brandy could taste it.

She took the stage and sat on a stool before the microphone. The spotlight radiating her beauty. "Good evening everyone. I'm Brandy Rodgers and I'll be your entertainment for the night. If you have any requests, just holler them out. I'm going to begin tonight with my favorite song. It was the first I ever learned and was taught to me by one of the greatest men I've ever known." She looked over at her mother who smiled with wet eyes. She dabbed the corners with a napkin. Of Ronnie, their bond in grief was strong. Yet, their memory of love was stronger. "It's by an Irish band. The song is *Mary*." She strummed the chords a few times and began to play.

She closed her eyes and sang into the microphone. There was a smile on her face. Brandy smelled fried bologna and felt the salty gulf wind in her hair. A pleasing reminder of the little moments that transcended time. She recalled shared events so sweet they brought tears that slowly tracked down her face.

All those years and her love for him had not changed. The very fabric of her existence had transformed, but never that.

Never her heart.

About the Author

Clay Anderson is an Adjunct Professor of History at Reinhardt University in Waleska, Georgia. He received his BA in History from Kennesaw State University and MA from Mississippi State University. He has six diverse publications, fiction and non-fiction. These publications include two non-fiction book reviews in *Texas Books in Review* and *East Texas Historical Journal,* one non-fiction article in the *Journal of Big Bend Studies,* and three fiction shorts in the F*ourth World Journal, Adelaide Literary Award Anthology*, and *The Bangalore Review.* He is currently an MFA student in Creative Writing at Reinhardt University. *The Palms* is his first novel. He lives in the mountains of North Georgia with his two dogs.

Made in the USA
Columbia, SC
21 April 2022

59181754R00178